A
LETHAL LISTING

Diana Rittenhouse Mystery 1/5

Kate Merrill

A Lethal Listing

Cover art: Kate Merrill

Merlin-Janus Studio, Inc.
Davidson, NC

Publishing History
First Edition 2013
Second Edition 2022
Print ISBN 9780615846552

Published in the United States of America

For

SUSAN

ONE

A new life...

Dennis Crawford pulled up a chair, pinning Diana behind her desk. "You can do it. You're poised and classy, the old coot will love you."

She met his cool confidence with an icy blue stare.

She'd worked for difficult brokers before back in Pennsylvania, but at least they'd earned the right to be obnoxious. Not Dennis. Without his football talent, he would have flunked out of The University of North Carolina. When a knee injury ended his short career in the NFL, he ran home to Davidson, where his daddy gave him Crawford Realty as a consolation prize. Lucky kid, but it wasn't enough. His glory days behind him, he still behaved like a pouting quarterback, benched against his will.

"Liz agrees, don't you, doll?" He turned his charm on the pretty redhead who shared her office. "Diana has a feel for historic properties, she should handle this one."   Liz looked up from her laptop, winked at Diana. "From what I hear, the old Porter place isn't *historic,* it's a *dump*. Get real, Dennis. If it's such a hot listing, how come you're not grabbing it?"

He massaged his bad knee, a habit that always preceded a sneaky maneuver.

"Hey, I would, but Jed Porter's dead set against selling. His land is pure gold, but he doesn't give a shit. When they created Lake Norman, the prettiest coves just happened to fill up the valleys of old Jed's farm, and now he owns miles of prime shoreline."

"He's a farmer?" Diana got the picture. It was the same story everywhere down here. Sleepy towns, family farms, acres of unspoiled wilderness—all being converted to booming prosperity. All because Duke Power had the foresight to dam up the Catawba River and make a lake. Now everyone was getting rich, like it or not.

"Yeah, Jed *was* a farmer," Dennis said. "But, hell, he's eighty years old. Hasn't been on a tractor in two decades. Land's no use to him anymore."

"Maybe he doesn't care about money?" Liz shrugged. "If he won't sell, he won't sell. Why send Diana on a fool's errand?"

She was wondering the same thing herself as she doodled little drawings of backhoes raping virgin forests. When she finished with the pencil, she switched to a red pen and made the earth dripping from the backhoe's jaws the color of blood, the color of Carolina mud.

"Pay attention, Diana," Dennis snapped. "It's for Jed's own good. Even his daughter agrees it's not safe for him to live alone. You have an elderly mama, right? You can relate, can't you?"

Suddenly he had her attention. "His daughter wants him to sell?"

He averted his eyes, got busy picking at his fingernails. "Amy called about a week ago. Said her daddy had a heart condition. He could drop dead out there, and they wouldn't find him for days. Plus, the old guy's losing it. Doesn't have the sense to eat right, and when he lights the stove, he forgets and leaves the burners on. He's an accident waiting to happen, know what I mean?"

Diana knew all too well. This was Dennis' hook, but how did he know? She'd never told them about her own mother, Vivian Whitaker. How one fine day the old gal burned down their family home in Chester County. Thankfully, Mama wasn't hurt in the fire, but Diana was sick with guilt. Out of love and respect, she'd looked the other way as Mama became more and more forgetful. After all, Vivian was proud, independent, and determined to do for herself. Even when her past went up in flames, she refused to live with Diana.

"That's right," Liz said. "You brought your mom along when you moved to North Carolina, didn't you, Diana?"

"Actually, Mom was born here. She's living at Shady Oaks Retirement Community now."

After the fire, Mama had insisted she wanted to return to her childhood home: *If you're planning to put me out to pasture, it better be a familiar pasture.* She'd tried to convince Mama that after living up North so long, she'd become a Yankee through and through. But Mama disagreed. In fact, she decided it was time for Diana to start a new life, too. Never mind that Diana had just turned forty-five, with a perfectly good routine in Pennsylvania.

But Mama said, *Listen to me, child...your ex-husband's found himself a new wife, your kids are grown and out of the nest, your career's a dead loss...what are you waiting for?*

Mama had a knack for cutting right to the bone, so they had made a new start together.

Diana sighed and faced Dennis. "Tell me the truth. What's the real problem with Jedidiah Porter?"

7

He stopped picking his fingernails, got busy brushing lint from the knee of his trousers. "Nothing much. He's just a little eccentric."

"C'mon, Dennis," Liz piped up. "If you want Diana to fight your battles, at least give her live ammunition. What's the real deal with Jed?"

"All I know is what Brantley Craven told me..." He stood, walked to the cooler and poured a paper cupful of water.

Suddenly Liz's fair face flushed bright red. "God, are you still hanging with that snake Brantley? I wouldn't trust that fucker to wipe his own butt."

Dennis' left eye twitched. "Ignore her, Diana. Brantley's a respected developer in these parts. He's been trying to buy the Porter property for years, but Jed hasn't been receptive to his offers."

"Wonder why?" Liz scoffed. "Brantley's famous for his low-ball bids, Diana. He always wants something for nothing."

"Not true." Dennis poured more water, gulped it down. "He made six offers, each one more generous than the one before."

"What happened the seventh time?" Liz asked. "Did Jed go after Brantley with a shotgun?"

Diana was astonished when her young boss coughed up his last swallow of water. Once he got it together, he wiped his mouth on his sleeve and cleared his throat.

"According to Brantley, the old geezer shot both headlights clean off his car. Brantley hasn't been back since."

* * *

The sunset glazed the water blood red. Diana pulled over at the Perth Road Bridge to check her map and calm her shattered nerves. She'd been a Realtor longer than she cared to admit, so why on earth should a routine listing upset her so much? Clearly her new boss, young and cocky as a bantam rooster, hadn't bolstered her confidence. That morning at the office, his description of the reclusive Jed Porter shooting live bullets had scared the bejesus out of her.

As the sun slipped lower on the western horizon, and the pines and hardwoods on the far shore burned with light, she took a deep breath and concentrated on the job at hand. Maybe she was entitled to a few butterflies in the belly? The last thing she needed was a fatal encounter with the wrong end of a shotgun, but she reminded herself for the umpteenth time: *I am a professional.*

She consulted her map, and then cranked up the engine of her ancient Subaru station wagon. The car was a dinosaur, but God help her, she still loved Ruby. When she was new, the Outback was a show stopper, but now her burgundy coat was silvered with gray and her engine ignored all speeds above sixty. Fellow agents refused to ride in her.

Clients, who had no choice, made rude comments. But love was love, so she patted Ruby's dashboard and begged her not to stall as she pulled out into rush hour traffic.

This time of day, when shadows were long and light was golden, always filled her with sweet melancholy. The brush forests and ripening fields still coexisted with the crush of suburbia, and reminded Diana of her beloved Chester County.

This was the hour when she used to saddle Chessie and ride. They didn't practice for the show ring, just wandered leisurely, her faithful mare taking the lead. They ambled though favorite fields and secret copses, then returned to the stable by twilight. There, Chessie dined eagerly on grain and hay, while

Diana returned to her little cottage in Gladwyne for a solitary dinner of her own.

Damn! She hit the brakes. Daydreaming about the good old days, she'd missed the turnoff. She recalled crossing the water at Skipper's Marina, but then she must have sailed right past the sign for Porter Farm Road. What an idiot! She wasn't usually such an airhead, but the idea of confronting cranky old Jedidiah Porter had thrown her off balance.

Once turned around and driving in the right direction, her nerves settled and she realized what was really bothering her: she hated arriving unannounced, right at dinnertime. Everyone in real estate knew it was the best time to catch folks at home, just when they were sitting down to eat, but the whole concept rubbed her sensibilities raw.

She leaned forward, scanned the brushy woodlands, spotted the sign, and made a sharp turn onto Porter Farm Road. The so-called road was a gravel washboard designed to shake Ruby apart like a rusty tin can, and the drive leading up to the Porter homestead was more challenging still. The spring rains had turned the dirt passage to a sea of rutted red mud.

"Oh, no..." she groaned aloud. She should have taken Liz's advice. The young redhead had become her best friend during her six months at the agency, but Liz always criticized Diana's choice of footwear. She failed to appreciate that Diana preferred flip-flops or sandals to high heels, and Liz was always nagging her to purchase a pair of those clunky running shoes. *Just throw them in the back of your station wagon, in case of an emergency.*

Well, this was an emergency. She would have sacrificed her good riding boots, had they been handy. Now she'd ruin her stupid pumps, but did she care? No way. She'd hoped to impress

Mr. Porter by wearing a country print dress, rather than the khaki pants and sandals, which were her trademark. Common wisdom dictated that older gentlemen preferred women in dresses. Ruffles and lace were often more persuasive. So she prayed the feminine disguise would keep Jedidiah from shooting her.

At first the going was tough, but she finally got the rhythm of stepping and straddling the ruts. The forest seemed to close in as she moved down the lane, while the young leaves and branches blocked out most of the dying light. It was dark and utterly quiet, not even a mockingbird disturbed the uneasy silence. The road sloped downwards into a valley, and suddenly she heard the echo of footfalls, much like her own.

She stopped stock still, her heart pumping adrenalin. The echo stopped, too. So, she was being followed, or stalked. Dear God in Heaven! Her mind raced. Every instinct, every muscle, urged her to run. But her brain told her to stay put.

Seconds dragged like hours, until the footfalls began again. Not human. Pacing. Neither advancing nor retreating, the thing was hiding in the trees ten yards away. Had she been riding Chessie, with the comfort and weight of all that horsepower between her legs, she'd have fled at a gallop. But a panicked horse, like a running human, could incite some animals—wolves, mountain lions, or even bears—to chase and attack. Did any of those creatures live in the Carolina woods? With civilization encroaching on all sides?

Get a grip! She never thought of herself as a coward. She'd been in tough spots before. As a child, she once lost her seat during a foxhunt, broke her leg, and then lay in the woods for what seemed like hours before the rescue party found her. Never even cried. At least that's how she told the story now.

The idea was to stay calm and move slowly. It could be done. One foot before the other, she made her way forward. But the creature came too, keeping exact pace. It stopped when she stopped, moved when she moved, yet never once showed itself. In spite of the chill in the forest, she started to sweat and took long, measured breaths. At first she was terrified. After a while, she was merely unnerved, and then finally, her stalker seemed almost companionable. She listened for clues as to its weight and size. It was too heavy to be a small animal, but too light-footed to be a bear. She decided it was a deer, and hoped against hope it was not a wolf.

Just as her feet told her she'd begun to climb out of the valley, a shaft of light broke through the trees ahead, like a message of deliverance. She'd noticed this phenomenon before: just after twilight had fallen, the sun came around to glow with a strange orange light, like a last gasp of life before the death of another day. The creature saw the light too. It ran through the leaves and broke out of the forest into a clearing, or a field.

She, too, ran towards the light. Suddenly she stumbled and fell into golden grass—a meadow—and heard a blood-curdling howl. Blinded by the intense glare, all she could see was a huge black head with great white fangs. Two insane eyes, pale amber, stared deep into her fear. Her scream echoed through the valley, and the monster fled in a blur of long black legs. It cantered on air and vanished into an orchard of pecan trees that ran along the edge of a faraway ridge.

Jesus Christ! She angrily swiped at her foolish tears and cursed herself. She suffered a shooting pain in her knee and saw that her arms, legs, and silly dress were covered in red mud.

At the same time, an incessant howling began on the ridge. It was an excited, hiccupping sound, like the hounds used to make when they were hot on the fox's tail. This was no wolf, only a dog, and if anything, he was more terrified than she was.

She choked on laughter and gulped at air. She despised hysterical females, and here she was, a prime example. Taking stock, she realized that aside from the mud and a skinned knee, the only harm done was a badly hurt pride.

At last she was able to appreciate the view, which was stupendous. Lake Norman glittered like fire on three sides of the magnificent promontory, and on the crest of the western ridge, stood Jedidiah Porter's ancestral home. The paint had long since peeled off its sagging wooden walls. The structure boasted no white pillars, no gracious porch, it was only a humble bungalow. Generations of Porters had made haphazard alterations to the old place, so that any architectural integrity was long gone, but it radiated an eerie grandeur all the same.

Perhaps it was the haunting beauty of the moment, or the way the sun dropped directly behind the roof of the ramshackle building, but as she pulled herself to her feet, she was almost eager to confront the lion in his den.

TWO

The lion in his den...

The demon dog continued to howl as she knocked hard on the sagging old door, but the silence in Jedidiah Porter's house was profound as death. She'd come to confront the lion, but apparently he'd left his den.

Just as well. A flood of relief cooled her jangled nerves as she decided against knocking a second time. What was the point? Liz had called this a fool's errand, so it made perfect sense to leave before any real harm was done.

She was counting her blessings when the ancient door creaked open.

"What the hell?" The angry, rasping voice echoed from the shadows.

"Mr. Porter?" she gasped.

The door swung fully open, and a stooped figure stepped onto the porch. "This here's private property, and you're trespassing."

The man was frail, much smaller than she had imagined. In the dying light, she couldn't see his eyes behind his thick glasses, but at least he didn't have a shotgun in his hands.

"Sorry to bother you, sir, but can you spare me a moment of your time?"

His gaze traveled up and down the length of her body. "You had yourself an accident, or do you like wallowing out yonder in my red mud?"

"I left my car at the end of your road. It was impossible to drive up your driveway."

"If you had the sense of a mule, you'd a seen that mud and turned back to where you come from."

The old buzzard was playing with her, and his rude stare was exceedingly annoying.

He laughed, crossed his arms, and leaned against the wall. "Seems like they might could of sent a *man,* not a pretty lil' thing like you."

His eyes lingered on her breasts. His tone unnerved her. Jedidiah was old, to be sure, but he was a man all the same, and a stranger to boot.

"My name is Diana Rittenhouse..." She pulled a business card from her pocket and stood tall, taking comfort in the fact that she towered a good six inches above his bald head. "I'm here to discuss your property."

Jedidiah stiffened. A charged silence sparked between them. The eerie barking of the demon dog drifted down from the pecan grove, now shrouded in darkness. Finally, he grabbed the card, and without a second glance, stuffed it into the pocket of his suit coat. She couldn't take her eyes off his coat. It was blue, perfectly pressed, worn over a stained pajama top. Something about this gesture, his attempt to dress properly before opening the door, softened her fear.

"Last person who come round asking after my land got his head blowed off." Without ceremony, he turned his back and walked inside, but he left the door open.

She hesitated. The odor of burning hamburger grease drifted out from the room, and when Porter switched on a lamp, a golden glow issued from the small space.

His hoary eyebrows arched. "Well, woman? Ain't got all day. You comin' in, or not?"

She stepped inside. "You know what, Mr. Porter? I heard that story about the man and your shotgun. I heard he lost his *headlights*, not his *head.*"

His mouth gaped open in surprise, then spread into a grin. "That a fact? I thought I blowed his head off, but I was aiming at his balls."

Should she laugh, or cry? Somehow this disgusting old reprobate was growing on her. She cast around for a place to sit, but no surface looked promising.

He lifted the smoking burgers off an old cast iron stove. She watched to be sure he turned off the burners, but the man seemed to have his wits about him.

"Wasn't expectin' no company, ma'am." He pulled out a pressed oak chair, wiped it off with a dishrag, and gestured for her to sit. He eased down onto one just like it.

For long moments they said nothing at all. As her eyes adjusted to the gloom, she saw a clutter of dusty antique furniture piled high with magazines and boxes, the debris of a lifetime. Along with the cooking odors, the must, and the dampness, she noticed the scent of cinnamon.

"A wild dog chased me through the woods," she said.

He laughed and slapped his knee. "Lord, you're lucky to be alive. That bitch is a killer. She'd as soon bite your head off as look at you."

She stared at him, finally beginning to catch on. Jed had a flare for melodrama and a penchant for violent passages, especially ones having to do with heads being blown or bitten off. His fearsome approach seemed like a bluff, a charming style all his own. But when she eased the conversation around to how his daughter was worried about him, how she wanted him to sell his house, his anger was raw. He informed her that he had *two* children, hadn't seen them in years.

"Amy and Bobby. Damn 'em both to hell! I should a put them pups in a sack the minute they was born and sunk 'em in the river!"

Porter made it clear in no uncertain terms that he would never sell his farm. He was testy, abrasive, and not until she stood up to leave did his tone change.

"Now don't be in such a dad blame hurry. You reckon you'll be seein' my daughter, Amy?"

He opened a china cabinet and slowly lifted out all the cups and plates. He stacked them on the kitchen table. From the very back of the cabinet, he retrieved a square object wrapped in brown paper, with Amy's name written on it. He handed the package to Diana with great ceremony.

"Give this to my girl, you hear? Tell her not to open it till I'm dead and gone."

"What is it?"

A distant softness clouded his eyes. "Stupid old book called *The Yearling*. Amy's mama used to read from it every night, about some sorry little fawn. I'm of a mind to throw it out, but I reckon the girl would like it…"

As she staggered down Porter's pitch black driveway, tripping over roots and falling more than once, she wondered if she'd ever find her way home. She'd failed to get the listing, her name would be mud, like her ruined clothes. She'd suffered the

17

extremes of fear and anger, then finally an odd empathy for an old man who'd honored her by allowing her to bear his daughter's gift. In the end, she couldn't decide—was Jed a lonely old man grown crusty from years of solitude, or was he something more worrisome?

The night air was balmy, yet a chill shot up her spine as she recalled a fleeting moment when the lamp on his table had allowed her to see his eyes behind those thick lenses. And briefly, she had glimpsed the abyss and the essence of pure evil.

THREE

Love Liz first…

Dennis was behaving like a maniac, waving his arms and pounding his desk with one fist. Liz McCorkle watched the spectacle in disgust, feeling sorry for whoever was at the other end of the phone, and sorrier still she couldn't eavesdrop. He had slammed his door shut, so she couldn't hear, but clearly he was pissed.

She smiled and logged off her laptop. Liz enjoyed anything that pulled Dennis' chain, because lately he'd been the boss from hell. He was pushing all the agents to get more listings, close each sale, and to speed up their settlement dates. No excuse was good enough when a deal fell through, so that even the old pros fell victim to his anger.

"What?" He stormed from his office and bore down on her.

She batted her eyelashes.

"This is all your fault!" he sputtered. "I never should have trusted Diana with an important listing."

"That was *Diana* on the phone?"

"I'm afraid so. Her stupid car broke down, so she was calling from the middle of nowhere to tell me she'd blown the deal."

Her brain struggled up to speed. The Porter listing was no biggie, far as she was concerned, but if Diana's rusty old rattletrap broke down in redneck territory, she could be knee deep in shit. "Where exactly is she?"

Dennis shrugged. "I should've known she was too grand a lady to get down and dirty when it counts."

"This morning you wouldn't take no for an answer, Dennis. You begged her to get a contract from Porter. You said she was an expert on historic properties. Remember?"

He rolled his eyes and retreated towards his office. "So I made a mistake, okay? But she's your friend, so you better help her turn this mess around. Now I have to call Brantley Craven, and he'll have my ass!"

She shot mental arrows at his retreating backside, and then watched through the smoke glass window as he speed-dialed the snake. If Brantley was involved, she wanted no part of it. If she had a spoonful of courage, she'd quit right now and not get involved. Unfortunately, she needed the money.

Poor Diana! Her new friend was a consummate professional, but she didn't know the territory. The Porter farm was smack dab in the middle of hillbilly heaven, and Diana sure as hell didn't speak their language.

She was worried about Diana and furious with Dennis, so she decided not to take any work home. Termite inspections and well certs could jolly well wait until tomorrow. Right now, her number one goal was to get out before Dennis could confront her with yet another stupid project. She deserved a quiet evening alone with Chinese take-out, couple of beers, soft couch, and some mindless TV. She escaped before he could stop her.

The parking lot was dark as she crossed to where her awesome new Honda sparkled under the security lights. The car had just come back from the sign painter, with larger-than-life photos of herself on both sides. Her name: Liz *"Corkie"*

McCorkle, and her personal motto: *You're in good hands* were emblazoned under the photos. Naturally, Diana had been horrified: *You'll look like a moving billboard.* But what did she know?

"Hey, *Corkie,* put your *good hands* on *me!*" a familiar male voice hollered from the far side of the lot.

Liz groaned as she spotted Danny Capelli lounging against his white pickup truck. Obviously, he had been waiting to pounce. So much for a quiet evening.

"What do you want, Danny?" she demanded wearily. "It's really late, and I'm on my way home."

When he strolled up to her Honda and traced the contour of her photo with one long finger, she felt a blush crawling up her neck. The image she'd chosen for her car, a picture of her wearing a tight emerald green sweater, did little to conceal her bodacious boobs.

"Bet this will bring in lots of new business," he drawled. "Lots of *guys* calling you, Cork?"

She shoved him, but he grabbed her arms and spun her so they were face to face. By the twinkle in his laughing brown eyes, she figured she was blushing like a geranium, one of the drawbacks of being a redhead. Her skin was a traitorous barometer for every embarrassing emotion, and it got her into trouble more than once.

Get lost, Capelli!" She tugged loose from his strong grip. "I'm wiped. Piss off and let me go home."

He backed away in mock horror. "Lord, the *mouth* on you, girl! What you need is a gourmet dinner, washed down with a bottle of fine wine."

She glared at him, and he glared right back. It was one of their classic showdowns. Danny had been her childhood sweetheart. They grew up together in the same rough Charlotte neighborhood and had always delighted in using cuss words on one another. It was a contest—who gets grossed out first? She knew him better than she knew her own brothers, and she always won the stare-down routine.

Her green eyes were her best weapons, so she focused first on his curly brown hair, moved down his handsome face, then stopped to squint at his mouth. She stared at his lips until they began to twitch, and then transferred her gaze to his shirt. As usual, it was crusted with paint, so she puckered her lips in disgust and picked at the flecks with one long red fingernail.

Taking a deliberate step backwards, she crossed her arms beneath her ample bosom and stared at his crotch. Stared hard. She waited until he shifted nervously from foot to foot, until she was sure his eyes were glued to her chest. At just the crucial moment, with the hand tucked under her left breast, she shot out her middle finger and flipped him the bird.

The empty parking lot exploded with his laughter. He lost his balance and staggered backwards. "Have mercy, you win!" he sputtered. "Now, will you give me a break and let me buy you dinner?

Liz held her ground. Although she was high on her great victory, she loved to watch Danny squirm. "Why would I go out with you, dirt bag? Any decent restaurant would throw you out. You look like a grubby old house painter."

"I *am* a house painter."

She couldn't keep a straight face. Poor Danny was mortally wounded, on the defensive, and she giggled uncontrollably. It never failed. No matter how bad she felt, he always made her laugh.

"Does this mean yes?" he said.

"Only if we go to your place, and you do the cooking."

* * *

The red wine was warm and sweet. She sipped slowly and munched on the tortilla chips he'd set out on a paper plate. She was alone on his sagging back porch, her chair propped against the open screen door, so she could hear the comforting sound of pots banging in the kitchen and smell the rich aroma of spaghetti sauce simmering on his old stove.

The April night was unseasonably hot, and as she gazed into the dark of the shaggy backyard, she half expected a swarm of mosquitoes to dine on her bare legs.

"Smells yummy!" she called through the door.

"Wait till you catch a whiff of the garlic bread..." he called back. "Mama's own recipe."

Maybe it was the alcohol, but she felt all the tension from the office giving way to a strange sadness. She and Danny had grown apart, and that was that. They'd been childhood sweethearts and high school lovers, but then she'd moved on. First she got her real estate license, and then her job at Crawford Realty. Once the commissions started rolling in, she'd bought a little cottage in Charlotte's trendy Dilworth section. Since then, her new neighborhood had become thoroughly gentrified, and her little bungalow was now worth a small fortune.

In the meantime, Danny had been traveling a road to nowhere. Instead of moving forward, he carried on his Italian family's tradition of house painting, the same damn thing he'd been doing all his life. If she hadn't stepped in, he'd never have escaped the city. She'd convinced him to move up to Cornelius and take advantage of the booming lake economy. She'd even found him this ramshackle 1920's mill house, with sellers willing to do a lease-purchase.

She'd assumed that with all his remodeling skills, he'd fix the place up in no time. But now, two years later, nothing had changed. All the paint still peeled off his walls and all the sinks dripped.

"Hurry it up in there!" she called. "I'm starving!"

"Keep your pants on, Cork. You, of all people, should know that anything worth getting, is better when you get it slow."

She sighed and took a deep swallow of wine. Danny was a master at sweet, slow-handed love. He still attracted her with a force that left her weak with desire, but she would not allow it. He didn't meet the criteria of her *Love Liz First* rule, which was, simply stated: *never get involved unless he's rich, on the road to getting richer, and owns his own boat by the age of thirty.*

But it wasn't that simple. Liz had once married her definition of the perfect rich man and ended up divorced. At least they had no children. After that fiasco, who was there to pick up the pieces? Who proposed marriage for the hundredth time? Who else but Danny?

Once they were seated at a round table, complete with red and white checked cloth, he expertly twisted a strand of spaghetti and homemade sauce into his spoon. "You haven't said a word all evening, Cork. Are you sick, or what?"

She pushed a slice of tomato around on her plate.

"C'mon, what's wrong? Usually I can't get a word in edgewise." He put down his spoon and watched her. "I bet you're dating some rich new jerk, and you're afraid to tell me about it. Let me guess… you're sleeping with some old fart who got you pregnant, robbed a bank, and then ran off to Mexico. Am I right?"

"Jeez, Capelli, how'd you guess?" She laughed, but wasn't willing to confess how she'd been watching his hands, remembering how well they knew every secret part of her body.

"Oh, do tell me everything!" He vamped. "Was the old fart good in the sack?"

In spite of his clowning, she sensed a jealous edge in his tone, and for both their sakes, she decided to steer clear of dangerous waters. "Look, I've had a rough day at the office. Can we drop it?"

"Is Dennis still making you sit in that damned trailer?"

She blinked in surprise. She was flattered, amazed really, that he even remembered. Almost a year ago, Dennis had stationed her in a singlewide parked at the abandoned cotton mill. Her job was to lease space to tenants who, if they had eyes in their heads, should have seen the project would never fly. Somehow Dennis had borrowed the money to buy the derelict mill, probably through his father's good connections at the bank, and had planned to convert the old structure to a trendy mall, complete with boutiques and a restaurant.

"That project's dead in the water," she muttered.

"I thought that mill was gonna be the hot new thing at the lake. I saw slick ads in all the papers. What happened?"

"Dennis happened. What can I say...?" In fact, she'd heard rumors that toxic materials had been found under the site. They'd have to be cleaned up before the Planning Board would approve the project, and the clean-up costs would be astronomical. She suspected Dennis ran out of cash, or failed to bribe the commissioners.

"He made me sit in that freezing trailer for weeks." She frowned. "I convinced dozens of suckers to sign on the bottom line, but when months went by and construction never started, they demanded refunds. Guess who they blamed for the whole frigging mess?"

"What happened?"

"I quit. I told Dennis to take his cotton mill and shove it. Lucky for him, he came to his senses and begged me to come back."

"Good for you, Corkie."

"Yeah, good for me." The topic did nothing to improve her mood, and she started wondering all over again if Diana had made it home safely. "Danny, did you ever meet the new woman at the office, the one from Pennsylvania?"

"Yeah, Diana Rittenhouse." He wolf-whistled. "How could I forget? What a babe!"

She was astonished. "Whoa, Capelli, are we talking about the same person?"

"Mrs. Rittenhouse, right? Tall blonde with great blue eyes? Legs that go on for days? Man, imagine how those long legs could wrap around a guy!"

Was this a sick joke? She adored Diana. She was a classy lady, with a certain refinement Liz could never hope to achieve— but a sex symbol? No way.

"You're warped, Capelli. Diana's old enough to be your mother."

"You're wrong, Cork, but if she were my mama, I'd never leave home. Hell, I'd never give up breast feeding."

She tossed a dirty napkin at him and pushed away from the table. If this was another gross-out contest, he took the prize.

"Jealous, are we?" he pressed. "I confess I fell in love with Diana the moment I laid eyes on her. What's her story, Cork?"

She stomped out to the porch, with Danny close on her heels. *Jealous my ass!* How could he have a thing for Diana? She was *Liz's* friend. He had no right. It was too radical to be believed, lusting after someone like Diana. But what did Liz know about the male libido? Only that it was big trouble.

"Let's call a truce…" He shoved a steaming cup of cappuccino into her hands. "This is a peace offering. Now tell me about Diana. Like, is she married?"

"She *was* married," Liz snapped. "To some high-powered Philadelphia lawyer. They were together for years, and I don't know for sure what happened, but I bet he left her for a *younger* woman."

"Any kids?"

"Two children. Her teenage daughter lives down in Florida. The son was groomed to be a lawyer and follow in the family tradition, but he wants to be a school teacher."

Danny gazed into the night. "Too bad. Sounds like she's had a rough life. I feel like someone should be watching her back, know what I mean?"

"Someone like *you*, I suppose?" But she was no longer angry or jealous. Danny meant no disrespect. On the contrary, she understood exactly how he felt, because she too wanted to protect Diana. There was something vulnerable about the woman and her courageous efforts to start a new life in an alien land.

On the other hand, Diana was very determined. She had a *fist of iron beneath a silken glove.* Wasn't that how the saying went? In business, she was shrewd and unyielding, yet all her clients worshiped her. Clothed in genteel diplomacy, she could convince a buyer to bid higher or wheedle an extra concession from a stubborn seller, and everyone thanked her for it. Go figure? Liz couldn't accomplish those goals no matter how hard she tried.

Still, everyone yearned to shelter Diana, and Liz was no exception. Like tonight, where the hell was she? Dennis said she'd phoned in from the middle of nowhere. Was she still stumbling through the night with a truckload of boozed up yahoos close behind? Maybe she'd called an Uber and was home safe by now. Suddenly, Liz desperately wanted to phone her.

"Danny, I gotta go." She jumped to her feet and headed for the front door.

"Hey, what's the hurry?" He rushed after her. "There's a pie in the oven, damn it! Stay for one little piece?"

He snagged her around the waist just as she reached the threshold. His powerful hands pulled her backwards against his chest.

"Let go, Danny. I need to make a call."

"Slow down, baby…" He nuzzled against her ear. "You can phone from here."

"But it's private!" Worried as she was about Diana, she felt her resolve slipping as he pulled her closer. When he buried his lips in her hair and stroked away the tension between her shoulder blades, a familiar ache began considerably lower in her anatomy.

"Please, Cork…" he pleaded. "It's been a long time. Stay with me tonight…?"

FOUR

The devil himself...

"You look pale, Diana. Are you sick?"

Mama's extreme concern usually made her bristle, but tonight it felt good, like a hot toddy and an extra blanket.

"Knee hurts a bit. No biggie." The down home cooking at Shady Oaks was a comfort, too. The roast chicken slid off the bone, between her lips, settled in her stomach and made itself at home.

She hadn't felt this relaxed since the fiasco at Porter's farm last night. The incident had shaken her more than she cared to admit, especially the flat tire she found waiting at the end of Jed's lane. She'd called in sick that morning, partly because she was furious with Dennis. He'd behaved like a jerk when she told him she'd lost the listing, and he didn't give a rat's ass that she was stranded in the wilderness. Then, just when she was calling for an Uber, a pickup truck came along. The slightly inebriated twin brothers riding in the bed offered to help. They put on her spare and had Ruby up on all fours in no time.

Turned out Liz had also called in sick. *I spent the night with Danny!* She'd giggled. *Dennis is pissed about the Porter mess, but he'll cool off by tomorrow.* Good old Liz, ever the optimist.

Mama loved hearing about Diana's misadventure. She adored any and all conflicts, the juicier the better. Her blue eyes twinkled when she heard about the shotgun and how Jedidiah had once aimed to shoot an intruder's balls off.

"God, Diana! He really said that?" Her forkful of mashed potatoes froze in mid-air.

"Absolutely. It was bizarre, like a surreal dream, and all the time that awful creature kept baying from the ridge."

"You shouldn't have set foot in that place. Mr. Porter could have been a rapist, for all you knew. What were you thinking?"

In retrospect, she now believed old Jed was more lonesome than dangerous, but she didn't tell Mama. It made for a better story, more shock value, to describe how he hated his estranged children. "*I should have put them pups in a sack the minute they was born and sunk them in the river...* Yes, he actually said that!"

Mama snorted. "Fact is, half the people here at Shady Oaks feel the same way about their kids. Maybe your old geezer isn't so different from the gentlemen right here in this room."

She followed her mother's sweeping gesture. The elderly men in the dining room appeared to be mild souls, quietly enjoying their dinners. They did not remotely resemble Jedidiah.

"Nope, he'd never fit in here, and that's the problem," Diana said. "Amy Porter wants him to move into a retirement community. He has a heart condition, and living alone out there could be dangerous for someone who's getting a little forgetful."

Mama lifted her eyebrows, and Diana shut her mouth.

"You mean *absent-minded,* like me?" Mama winked. "Don't bother to mince words, dear. We both know I'd forget my own head if it weren't screwed on tight, but not every geriatric is dotty enough to burn down his house. Maybe Mr. Porter's just fine living alone. Maybe his children are greedy and ungrateful. After all, he did give you that gift to take to his daughter."

So Mama had been listening, after all. The old gal was a tease. She called her lapses *senior moments*, and loved it when Diana couldn't tell if she was cogent, or off somewhere in *la-la land*.

"You're right about the gift, Mama. I didn't expect him to do such a thing."

"See there? He's not a monster, after all."

As Mama reveled in her conclusion, Diana was suddenly bumped from behind. The impact jumped the coffee right out of her cup.

"Oh, dear, I am *so* sorry!" Clara Gable, Mama's best pal at The Oaks, rolled up beside them in her new electric wheelchair. "I ain't got the hang of the controls just yet…"

"No problem, Mrs. Gable." Diana mopped the spilled coffee from her saucer before Clara noticed. She didn't want to embarrass this jolly old woman, who added spice to Mama's bland routine.

"Sorry to butt in, but I couldn't help but overhear…" Clara said loudly. "Hate to be contrary, Vivian, but Jedidiah Porter is no ordinary monster, he's the Devil himself!"

The passionate outburst shocked not only Diana and her mother, but all the other residents seated nearby.

"Pipe down, Clara," Mama warned. "You were eavesdropping, so shame on you. If your hearing aid is turned up that high, then you better turn your voice down."

Clara nodded. She poked her head between them and modified her volume. "If you want to know the truth about Jedidiah, we best not talk about it here. Let's go to your room, Vivian…"

Diana was intrigued as she followed the two conspirators to her mother's suite. Mama was a taller, heavier version of Diana. She loped along with her cane and an oddly strident limp. Clara, wide as she was tall, huddled in her wheelchair like an intent brown mouse on electric wheels. What a pair! A million years ago, they'd both attended a little country school nearby. After that, Mama had moved north to marry the dashing Yankee, Will Whitaker, Diana's father. Clara had wed a local boy and lived out her days on his family's farm.

After Diana's father's death, Mama felt like an outsider in Pennsylvania and went into seclusion, but since their move to North Carolina, she'd crawled out of her sad cocoon and emerged a social butterfly. She and Clara had picked up where they left off all those years ago and never skipped a beat.

Once settled in Mama's room, among select pieces of massive furniture recalled from Diana's childhood, the older women unwrapped napkins filled with desserts stolen from the table. They shoved their ill-gotten gains in her direction.

"Take this, child," Clara urged. "You eat like a bird, you're wastin' away."

Mama agreed. "All those silly salads you eat won't put meat on those bones. No man wants a skinny woman."

Diana refused to go there. Once Mama got on the subject of men, more specifically, Diana's inability to attract them, she often spoiled a perfectly good evening. Yet the superb traditional cooking at Shady Oaks inspired her to endure the abuse. Her Friday night visits were regular as clockwork, and the food was a big incentive. She accepted Clara's apple pie.

Mama turned down the lights. "Now tell us about Jedidiah Porter..."

Clara's eyes glazed over as she began to speak:

"Jed and Ida Porter were our neighbors. My husband, Charles, farmed the acres next door for nigh on to forty years, so there was nothin' we did not share with the Porters. In drought or flood, we shared the crops. In good years, we shared the bounty. My Charlie once said if the Porter children caught a cold, our kids would share that too. So you best believe it when I say I *know* the man, and I'll say it again—Jed Porter is the Devil."

Clara pulled a lace hankie from her sleeve and held it in her lap. "I used to sit with Ida Porter of an evening, but only if Jed was still in the fields. Ida told me her troubles, and I told her mine.

"Ida was a simple mountain girl. She thought that Jed, from little ole Troutman, was a man of the world, come to save her from dirt-poor poverty. Truth be told, he was a low-down, white trash, son-a-bitch. Fits of wild rage, and then cryin' spells. One minute he'd be hacking the house apart with his ax, breakin' all the dishes and kickin' the cat—next minute he'd be layin' on the kitchen floor, sobbin' like a baby."

Diana finished her pie, then reached for the cookies Mama had swiped. To hear Clara tell it, Jed was either a classic schizophrenic or a hopeless drunk. Either way, it was a disturbing story, and she tried to match it with the old man she'd met last night.

"The Porter's first born was a daughter," Clara continued. "Amy was a fragile little angel with big, saucer blue eyes and hair of spun gold. That girl was smarter than the rest of the family put together, but she was scared to say a single word unless her daddy was gone far away.

"The son, Bobby, was a pathetic thing, the spittin' image of Jed. He was scrawny, but strong. Wild as a young coon. One fine night when Jed got into the whiskey and started beatin' on

Ida, Bobby clamped his teeth into Jed's leg. Jed drug him around the yard, but couldn't shake him off. He got a shovel and hit the boy upside the head, and Bobby's been slow ever since.

"Then Jed got religion." Clara sighed. "He got born again down at the Baptist Church, but it seemed like them *Bible beatings* was even worse than them old beatings. After he got saved, he turned mean and crazy. He quit the whiskey, but when he got steamed up, he claimed it was God Himself working through His humble servant."

Clara's tale was beyond depressing. Somehow Amy had survived and become a teenager, but as soon as she was able, she'd hitched a ride with a young trucker from Highpoint and never looked back.

"Amy ended up marrying that cocky bastard," Clara said. "And back at home, with Amy gone away, Ida's heart just broke. She died of pneumonia the very next winter, and once the women were gone, Jed took all his anger out on little Bobby. Many's the night that child come to us all bruised and silent. Too shy to come inside the house, so he took to sleepin' in our barn. Then, like his sister before him, Bobby run off too."

Clara's story seemed like a melodrama from the previous century. Was it gross exaggeration, embellished over the years and all jumbled up in an old woman's brain? Again Diana tried to square Clara's Jed with the frail little man from last night, but she couldn't bring the two into sync. Even monsters grew old and mellow, she reasoned, and yet....

FIVE

It might be murder...

Everyone clammed up when Diana entered the office. She called out her habitual cheery hello, but the gang just mumbled and refused to look at her.

"What? Is my slip showing?" Since she always wore slacks, she figured her joke was a decent icebreaker, but no one laughed.

Wonderful. That kind of behavior always preceded a scolding by the boss, or an outright firing, and no one wanted to be collateral damage. She braced herself for the worst, but got angrier with each step. So what if she'd flubbed the Porter thing? Dennis knew all along it was mission impossible. And yes, she had called in sick, but it wasn't like he paid her by the hour. She braced for a fight.

But as she rounded the corner, she saw Dennis holed up in his office, hiding behind his desk. Like everyone else, he refused to look at her, so evidently she wasn't being fired—yet. Something was definitely up, though, and clearly it involved her. Worrying about it, she nearly toppled Liz, who was emerging from the restroom.

"What's going on?" She snagged Liz's arm. "Everyone's avoiding me. Do I have the plague, or what?"

Her redheaded friend quickly pulled her aside. "Don't look now, Diana, but you have company waiting at your desk."

35

"So what?"

"Take a look..."

Liz and she shared a cubicle, and sure enough, a strange man was seated in their private space. He stood as they approached.

"Hey there, ladies. Which one is Diana Rittenhouse?"

Diana was rarely rendered speechless, but being confronted by the Iredell County Sheriff, towering in a crisply pressed uniform and toting a big ugly gun, was unusual indeed.

"*She*'s Diana!*" Liz quickly pushed her forward. "I knew she had a few parking tickets, but isn't this over-kill?" Liz laughed nervously, but when the officer didn't, she shrank into the background.

"You have unpaid parking tickets?" He smiled. "We'll discuss those another day." He turned to Liz. "If you don't mind, ma'am, I need to speak to Mrs. Rittenhouse alone."

She shot Liz her best *thanks a hell of a lot* look, but it only connected with her retreating back. After a silly little wave, Liz almost stumbled in her haste to disappear, leaving her alone with the sheriff. They stood in silence, appraising one another.

She was shocked to find a cop on her personal turf, but she was also intrigued. The man was handsome in a dark, swarthy way, with the long, sinewy body of a runner. His high cheekbones and wide set eyes were set beneath close-clipped, jet-black hair.

"Sorry to intrude, ma'am..." He extended a strong, brown hand. "My name is Wayne Bearfoot. I'm the Iredell County Sheriff."

"*Barefoot?*" She suppressed a giggle.

He lifted one highly polished boot and pointed at his foot. "Not *barefoot,* you understand, but *Bearfoot,* like the animal."

"Cherokee?" It would explained his exotic features, and his grin was downright disarming.

"I'm impressed, Mrs. Rittenhouse. Most folks don't know one Native American tribe from the others, and you aren't even from here, right? I'm full-blooded on my daddy's side. Mind if we sit down?"

"Be my guest…" She was impressed when he stepped aside and allowed her to sit behind her own desk, taking the smaller chair for himself. "Want a cup of coffee?"

"No coffee, no doughnuts. This isn't a social call, Mrs. Rittenhouse." The smile suddenly left his dark eyes, and the sheriff was all business.

He hadn't come to discuss parking tickets. "How can I help?" she asked.

"My questions won't take long. I want you to look at something for me…" He fished into his pocket and brought out a small, clear plastic bag and set it on the table between them. "Do you recognize it?"

A cold dread nagged at her as she fingered the object. It was a little rectangle of stained white paper with printed words, but the words were badly smeared, like someone had run the thing through a washing machine.

"Pick it up and take a closer look," he urged.

This time she saw color: a logo in faded red and white. "It's a Crawford Realty business card!"

"To be precise, it is *your* business card, Mrs. Rittenhouse."

"Where did you find it?"

"I took it off a dead man."

The absurd words hung between them. "You've made a mistake," she gasped.

"Sorry, ma'am," he continued more gently. "We found your card on the body of Jedidiah Porter. It was tucked neatly into his coat pocket. You knew he was dead, didn't you?"

She shook her head in disbelief. "Of course not! That's terrible news!" Suddenly her throat was constricted and she was edging towards tears.

"Near as we can figure, you were the last person to see him alive."

"That's impossible! How can he be dead?"

"How well did you know Jedidiah, Mrs. Rittenhouse?"

"Not at all. I only saw him once." *My God, did he consider her a suspect?*

"I've already spoken to Dennis Crawford. He confirms that you were at the Porter Farm Thursday night. Is that true?"

"Of course, it's true. Dennis sent me there. I'm sure he also told you I'd never met the man before"

"So he claims…" He took notes on a small black pad.

"This is horrible! How did he die? I understand he had a heart problem."

"So they say…"

The sheriff was beginning to annoy her. "So, did he die of a heart attack?"

Bearfoot glanced up. "No, ma'am, I'm afraid not. He drowned. We found him floating face down in the lake near his dock."

"He just fell in the lake and drowned? That's ridiculous." The vivid, terrifying image made her unaccountably sad.

"I agree, such an accident seems ridiculous. Can you help us?"

"When did it happen?"

"Near as we can tell, he died around sunset last night."

"Then how on earth can I help? I wasn't there last night."

His smile was condescending. Was this cocky lawman implying that she was connected to the death?

"Just relax, Mrs. Rittenhouse and tell me everything you know about Jedidiah. How did he look? What did he say? Was he worried, or tense? Anything out of the ordinary?"

Nothing about Porter was ordinary, but as far as she could tell, he'd behaved normally, which was quite abnormal by most civilized standards. She took a deep breath and recounted her evening with him. She included every detail, but failed to see how it would help.

Bearfoot shrugged. "Funny, I didn't see a dog around the Porter place."

"Do you suspect foul play, Sheriff?"

"*Foul play?*" he chuckled. "Let's just say we have questions."

"You think he was murdered?"

He did not respond.

"Look, if he didn't have a heart attack, if he simply drowned, what questions?"

"Mrs. Rittenhouse, did you call 911 when you found Jed's body?"

"I already told you, I wasn't there last night!"

"Well, someone called 911. Where were you last night?"

The hands in her lap curled into fists. His insinuations were absurd and offensive. "Last night around sunset I was eating dinner with my mother at Shady Oaks."

The sparkle returned to Wayne Bearfoot's eyes. "Aren't you a little young to be living at that place?"

Very funny. As far as she was concerned, the interview was over.

"C'mon, I'm just teasing." He smiled. "I know where you were. I already checked."

"Then why are you hassling me?"

"It's my job. I poke around, stick my nose in, make everyone and his cousin madder than hell. I apologize, Mrs. Rittenhouse. May I call you *Diana*?"

"You may call me *Mrs. Rittenhouse*, and if you'll excuse me, I have work to do..."

"Understood." He stood to his full, impressive height. "By the way, you weren't planning to take any vacations in the near future, were you, Mrs. Rittenhouse?"

She eyed her paperweight and considered heaving it at his smug face. "Unfortunately, I'm not taking any vacations. Are we done?"

"Sorry to inconvenience you," he answered sheepishly. "We'd prefer having you available, in case we have more questions. Who knows, maybe you'll think of something you forgot to tell me."

Highly unlikely. The nerve of the man! She walked towards the front door and the sheriff followed. She escorted him through the office, past the sea of curious stares, and right out to the parking lot.

"Again, thanks for everything, ma'am." He gave her a friendly little salute, and then began looking around, like he'd lost something.

"Misplace your pony, Sheriff?"

His eyes widened in surprise and he laughed. The sound was deep and contagious. "Matter of fact, seems like I did. Usually I gallop right up, toss my reins over the hitchin' post, and bust in guns blazin'. But I didn't want to panic the natives. A squad car parked out front is bad for business. Heap big trouble."

Okay, so the guy had a sense of humor. She laughed in spite of herself. "So you left it around back?"

"Yep." He blushed and changed course.

He waggled his fingers when his car pulled out from behind Crawford Realty, and as he drove out of sight, her mind was a disturbed jumble of unanswered questions.

SIX

The waters just kept on rising...

Ignoring the raised eyebrows, she stomped directly into Dennis' office. "Why didn't you warn me?"

For once the egotistical ex-jock was at a loss, both hands spread wide open. He was pale and jumpy. "What can I say, Diana?"

"For starters, did you know Mr. Porter was dead?"

"Where have you been? It was all over the morning papers, front-page news. When I heard they found your card on the body, I figured the sheriff would come snooping around."

"Surely that bit about my card was not in the front-page news?"

"Nope. Bearfoot told me when he got here. What the hell, Diana, it's a fucking mess!"

She almost felt sorry for him. He was green around the gills, like he was about to lose his breakfast. "What did you tell him about my visit to the Porter farm?"

"What's to tell? You went to sign a new client, but instead you lost one." He tugged at the tie around his neck and paced near the door. "I've lost clients before, but never to murder."

"The newspapers actually said it was *murder*?"

"Not in so many words. Jed drowned, all right, but they found a suspicious bump on his head, like somebody bashed him with a heavy object."

"Then left him to drown?" The implications were appalling. She too felt slightly ill as she watched her boss break out in a sweat. "Are you sick, Dennis?"

"I think I have a touch of the flu, or maybe it was that greasy fast food I ate last night."

"So the papers implied Jed was murdered?" She pressed.

Dennis' hand flew to his mouth and he made a dash for the men's room.

Whatever ailed him, she hoped it wasn't contagious. She picked up the Mooresville Tribune lying on the desk: *Local Farmer Found Dead in Lake Norman.* Much of the feature article was an obituary-style tribute to Jedidiah himself: *From one of the oldest families, prominent landowner, survived by two children,* etc. The word *homicide* was never mentioned. The story did say *Mr. Porter slipped, possibly hitting his head on the dock or a mooring post. Mr. Porter farmed the land long before the lake was made. They found him floating face-down...* The article reminded her of a particularly disturbing passage from old Clara's story:

The waters just kept on rising, fillin' all the valleys where the squirrels and rabbits lived. They all ran for higher ground. Charlie and me were ready to call it quits anyhow, so we took the buy-out money from the power company. But not Jed. Most of his acres were high ridge country, so he just sat still and watched the lake fill in all around him.

She'd asked Clara what had become of her land.

Well, child, if you stood at the end of Jed's dock and looked out across the water, you'd be lookin' at our front yard. Now the row of tall willow oaks, the pump and wishing well, and the big old wooden house are all gone.

43

The image had made her skin crawl. It reminded her of the movie *Deliverance*. "So all you owned is under the water off Porter's dock?"

Lord, no! It ain't quite like that. They chopped down the trees and tore down the house. They moved the graveyards, when they could, and they dragged it all away before the lake poured in. So they say. But the stumps are still there, our old foundation and the chimney, don't you know? It ain't natural, child...

She shuddered and watched as many of her fellow Realtors left for an early lunch. The idea of a world lost under water certainly was not natural. She imagined the frail body of the intense little man she'd met only two days ago, floating arms spread crucifixion-style, eyes wide open as he gazed down through the murky depths at the fields, fences, and farms of his former life—gone now for all eternity.

SEVEN

No one loves a cop...

The shiny new white Crown Victoria, with freshly painted black and red graphics, eased into the Sylvan Acres trailer park. Since it was early Monday morning, only a handful of residents were out in their tiny gardens enjoying the fresh spring day. Those who observed the Iredell County Sheriff's car quickly looked away.

Wayne Bearfoot breathed deeply of the new car smell, best aroma in the world, and decided not to let the hostile welcome get him down. After all, his weekend had been perfect. Knowing how a homicide investigation upsets him, his wife, Marianne, had prepared his favorite barbeque, kept the kids away, and surprised him with special favors in bed.

As he shifted on the seat, the muscles in his back and legs still ached from lovemaking. His crisply pressed light gray shirt and knife-pleated charcoal trousers had just been ironed by Marianne's hand, and were smooth against his skin. Fact was, murder both repelled and excited him. He always desired his wife more when the twin specters of danger and mortality were nipping at his heels.

He turned into a dirt road that led to the older, less respectable part of the park. A teenager, who was busy washing a rusty Dodge Challenger, threw down his hose, stomped into his doublewide, and loudly slammed the door. Same old story: no one loves a cop. On the highway, folks saw him in their rearview mirrors and slowed down even when they weren't speeding. Guilt was a fact of human nature. *Guilty* was something entirely different.

Wayne considered this case. Even the real estate lady, Diana Rittenhouse, got defensive when he questioned her. But she was a lovely woman. He'd pressed hard, shocking her with details of Porter's death, and yet she remained poised and relatively civil throughout the interrogation.

He'd known the moment he laid eyes on her that she'd never be involved in criminal activity, and yet he'd enjoyed wielding a little power. Normally he wasn't attracted to reserved, intellectual women, but Diana was different. As he listened to her low, cultivated voice and watched the fire spark in her amazing blue eyes, he fancied a man could drown in those eyes. How would it feel to sleep with such a woman? He sensed a bottomless well of passion just below her aloof surface, and he imagined plunging into those depths until her last pretense to dignity gave way and she begged for mercy.

Whoa, boy! Wayne loved his wife and had never been unfaithful. But death made a man want to sow seeds as a hedge against his own mortality. Putting that fantasy away, he took a deep breath and concentrated on the job at hand. He spotted the trailer belonging to Bobby Porter, the victim's son. If it wasn't the oldest mobile home in the park, it damn well looked it. The metal walls were streaked with rust and torn screens hung from the windows. The structure sagged on a rotten base that seemed to grow from the red earth, while chipped concrete blocks served as steps to the makeshift door.

He took out his Glock 40 semi and checked the clip. It was good to go, heavy and cold in his hand and smelling of oil. He carefully replaced it in his holster. Although stained shades were rolled down at all the windows and no one appeared to be home, he took nothing for granted. Last year one of their most promising young officers had responded to a routine drug tip right here in Sylvan Acres. The rookie knocked on the suspect's door and took a bullet through the heart before he even pulled his badge.

As he nervously tightened the knot of his tie and moved into the yard, something seemed off. A newly mulched bed of daffodils, tulips, and azaleas made no sense in this otherwise neglected setting. He knocked hard and identified himself, and while he waited for a response, he forced himself to watch the door, not the flowers. He knocked again and listened. Deep inside someone was running water, perhaps taking a shower? Blood pulsed through his veins and he rested his hand on his gun as footfalls creaked towards the door.

"Yeah? What do you want?" The woman who greeted him had thrown a towel over her nakedness. Her wet feet dripped on the floor.

"Sorry to bother you, ma'am, but I'm looking for Bobby Porter."

"Well, he's not here."

Wayne pressed one hand against the door closing in his face. "I hear you, but I'll take a look around anyway..."

"Give me a break, man," she whined. "I'm already late for work. Come back later, okay? I'm off all day tomorrow."

She was in her late twenties, short with big boobs. Her wet, raven black hair fell almost to her waist, and from her accent, he knew she was one of the many new citizens from south of the border.

"Sorry, but this won't wait," Wayne said. "I'll stand right here while you get dressed. *Comprende?*"

"S*i, senor*," she sarcastically replied, while staring pointedly at the front of his trousers. "You might as well come on in." She left the door open as she walked seductively to the rear of the trailer, allowing one corner of the towel to drift off her left buttocks.

He stood his ground. It was an old trap, an opportunity to accuse an officer of rape, and this little gal was just the type to plant the bait. On the other hand, he understood her bitterness. As a Native American, he'd experienced his share of prejudice.

Some of the men in his own department had been guilty of hassling the Mexicans. Clueless officers pulled them over as they drove to their construction jobs, sometimes gangs of ten or more in a truck, and searched them for work permits, drivers' licenses—you name it. The booming economy had attracted illegals in droves, and the community felt a fair amount of anger about the competition for local jobs. Yet Bearfoot had never tolerated such behavior in his ranks. Indeed, his practice of suspending those officers could well cost him his election next time around.

Soon the woman returned in shorts and an old Mickey Mouse T-shirt, rolling her eyes with obvious impatience. At least she seemed to have dropped the seduction routine.

"Your flowers are pretty. Did you plant them?" His opener was intended to put her at ease once they were seated at a sticky table in the breakfast nook.

"No way!" she scoffed. "That's Bobby's thing, playing in the dirt when he should be out making money."

The place smelled of cigarettes and stale beer. A box of half-eaten pizza lay near a sink full of dirty dishes.

Wayne studied her with interest. "Your English is very good. Have you been here long?"

"Too damn long. I learned my English when I lived in California."

She told him her name was Juanita Cruz. Apparently, she was Bobby's live-in girlfriend. "So, what's Bobby do for a living?"

"I've been with that loser two years, and he's screwed up at least six different jobs. He gets mad and quits. Or the boss gets mad and fires him. He gets drunk and doesn't show up for work—total fuckup."

"Okay, but what's he doing now?"

"He claims to be a *landscape artiste*. Bought himself an old white van and painted big stupid flowers all over it, like an old hippie. Somehow he convinced one of his drinking buddies to finance it, but then Bobby couldn't make the payments."

"So where's the van?"

"Where'd you think, man? The repo guy took it."

Bearfoot made notes in his little black book. A repossessed van with hand-painted flowers shouldn't be hard to find. It could lead directly to Bobby.

"What do you do for a living, Ms. Cruz?"

She ran fingers through her cascade of black hair. "I'm a stylist, you know? If someone's an *artiste*, it's me, not him. All the customers line up for me at the salon. I bring home *el dinero*, understand? Without my wages and tips, we'd have starved months ago."

Wayne believed her. He was sorry she seemed so uncomfortable with him. She was still damp from her shower and the T-shirt clung to her moist body, but he wasn't about to be distracted. She was holding something back, and he knew it.

"Where's Bobby?" he demanded.

"How should I know? We had a fight last Thursday, and he stormed off mad as a wet chicken. I haven't seen him since."

"What was the fight about?"

"Money, what else?" She spat out the words. "I told him over and over, if he fucked up one more time, I'd split."

But it was Bobby who left, he mused. He followed her into the living room. Her bare feet shuffled through the musty, orange shag carpet. She plopped onto a torn green vinyl couch and lit a cigarette. He brushed potato chip crumbs off a chair and sat across from her.

"Where'd he go?" he pressed.

"You deaf?" she snapped. "I know where I *told* him to go..."

Wayne could well imagine. "So, where do you *think* he went?"

"He has a rich daddy, would you believe?" She took a long drag. Her enormous brown eyes narrowed. "Says his old man is land rich, owns a zillion acres over on Lake Norman. The old fart keeps thousands rolled up in a coffee can hid away at the back of some closet."

"A coffee can?" He almost choked on his laughter. He'd heard it all, but this one was a classic. "And you believe this?"

A hurt look clouded her eyes, her full lips pouted. "It's true. Bobby told me so. He's always bragging on his rich daddy."

"Does he see a lot of his father?"

"You shittin' me? He hates the old asshole. Bobby was an abused child, you know...?" She lit a new cigarette off the old butt. "Bastard beat him, near killed him a couple times. Soon as he was big enough, Bobby ran away and never looked back."

Again, Wayne believed her, but what did old news have to do with Bobby's current disappearance? These people seemed desperate for money, and it wasn't a stretch to figure where they might get some fast. "Maybe Bobby paid his daddy a little visit?"

Juanita rubbed her cigarette out in an empty tuna can that doubled as an ashtray. "Yeah, maybe…" she said finally. "I told him to talk to his father. Blood is blood. The way I see it, the old man owes him big time, and I was sick of hearing about all that cash lying around doing nothing."

From out of nowhere, a cat jumped into Bearfoot's lap and started kneading his balls with its claws. With one swift swat, Juanita knocked the cat off into a corner. It yowled and scurried behind a curtain that concealed an evil-smelling litter box.

"You okay, Sheriff?" the woman giggled.

He composed himself, brushed the hair from his trousers, and took out his black book. "Let me get this right—Bobby went to his father's to get some cash?"

"I sure as hell hope so. He better not show his sorry ass unless he has the money."

There was another possible scenario, Wayne decided. Bobby took the money, but wasn't planning to share it with his girlfriend. He visited his daddy, but the old geezer wasn't willing to share, either.

"Thanks for all your help, Ms. Cruz. I'll get out of your way now, so you can go to work."

She trailed him to the door, and he handed her his card. "Please call me if Bobby turns up, okay?" He climbed down the steps and glanced back at her.

"Look, Sheriff, if this is such a big deal, why don't you ask old man Porter yourself? Maybe he knows where Bobby's at?"

Aw shit, she didn't know. He guessed she wasn't the type to read papers or watch news. "You haven't heard about Bobby's father…?"

Her face was blank.

Wayne shuffled uneasily foot to foot. Notifications were the pits. "I'm so sorry, Ms. Cruz, but Mr. Porter is dead. We think he was murdered."

"Jesus Christ, Mary and Joseph!" She crossed herself. "When?"

"Week ago last Thursday, the same evening your Bobby paid him a visit…"

He made a hasty retreat into his patrol car. This whole business was a damn shame. When he looked back, she was still standing there, looking sucker-punched.

All the living...

Rain slashed across Ruby's windshield, and the old Outback's wipers could barely keep up. Diana hunched over the steering wheel and strained to see beyond the gray sheet, while Liz, seated beside her, prayed to avoid a crash as they crawled forward on Interstate 77.

"How'd you talk me into this?" Liz moaned. "You owe me one, Diana."

"Thanks for coming. I couldn't have faced this alone."

"Pull over!" Liz suddenly exclaimed. "You can't even see the fucking road! We should've taken my Honda. At least its defogger works."

She had nixed using Liz's Honda, the *traveling billboard,* because it seemed inappropriate for this somber occasion. At the same time, she wanted to arrive safely, so she pushed on the flasher signals and steered off the highway onto the shoulder. The engine idled as they listened to the pelting rain.

"Why in God's name did I agree to come?" Liz wailed. "A graveside service during a storm? Not my idea of fun."

Nor was it Diana's "Maybe it'll stop by the time we get there."

"*If* we get there. Why did Dennis force you to attend this funeral? Jedidiah Porter wasn't even a client."

"Believe it or not, he still hopes to get a listing out of this tragedy. He knows Jed's daughter, Amy. Her son played football with Dennis all through school. He spent a lot of time at their house, and for some reason Amy trusts him. Since he's an old friend, he figures Crawford Realty deserves her business."

"So why doesn't he talk to Amy himself, and leave you the hell out of it?"

Diana longed to open the window. Liz's potent perfume was about to gag her. "He claims he's too close to the family to be effective, and he thinks Amy will relate to me. We're both mothers with grown children, and he says we'll *bond*, or some such nonsense."

"Dennis as Doctor Phil? Give me a break! All he cares about is his half-million dollar commission."

"That much?"

"Get real, Diana. The Porter place includes acres of waterfront and miles of potential commercial zoning on the road. Properly developed, it's worth millions. Big bucks are at stake."

Some quick mental arithmetic quickly confirmed that Diana's share of such a listing would pay off the mortgage on her condo at Lakeside and buy a new car—if she could bear to part with Ruby.

"Okay, I see how money would motivate Dennis to attend the service, but it's hardly the time or place to discuss business."

"That's why he enlisted you, Diana. Then he's free to act all mournful and ingratiate himself into Amy's good graces. But what I wanna know is, what's in it for me?"

"Drinks and dinner?"

Liz brightened. "I choose the restaurant?"

"You've got yourself a deal."

54

By the time they finished their negotiations, the rain had stopped and a ray of sunshine glowed from behind the steamy windshield.

"Life is good." Liz cheered. "It's gonna clear."

"Looks that way…" She pulled back into traffic, but stayed in the slow lane.

"I would've come to Mr. Porter's service anyway," Diana mused aloud.

"God, why would you?"

It was hard to explain, but she felt an odd connection to this family. She'd met Jedidiah, stood on his porch, entered his home, and looked into his eyes. She'd seen his loneliness and his anger, a kaleidoscope of emotions, and now he was dead. Gone. All memory, the daily actions and efforts of an entire lifetime vanished into nothingness. Maybe sharing his reality, if only for a moment, connected them.

Diana was no stranger to death. Having survived over four decades, she'd lost her father, numerous relatives, and even a few contemporaries. It never made sense, and it was never easy. And as far as funerals were concerned, she considered them somewhat barbaric. Lingering over corporeal remains had nothing to do with the vital soul now departed. She supposed it provided closure for some, but for her, death was deeply personal, and grief was not a communal affair. Her hope was that all the living could get beyond it and go on with their lives.

Liz plucked at her sleeve. "Did you hear me, Diana? Why would you want to go to this funeral? The whole thing gives me the creeps."

What could she say? "I've heard these southern funerals are a really big deal." Nonsense, but at least it was an answer.

55

"Yeah, right. Wailing mourner eat loads of food, and everyone gets to cry over the corpse. Is that what you heard?"

"I guess."

"Well, don't get too excited. Normally we do put on a good show, and the bereaved family feeds for weeks off the food folks bring. But I'm betting this guy Porter won't get a special send-off. From what I hear, he was not a popular favorite."

Liz was probably right. According to old Clara, Jedidiah's legacy was an entire family gone sour. Yet she felt a kinship to these people she'd never met, and truth be told, she was curious to meet Jed's children at the service.

Liz said, "It's especially creepy since he was *murdered*."

Diana swerved, nearly missing the exit to Troutman. "They've proved it was murder?"

Liz gripped her armrest as they sped down the ramp, then careened onto an unmarked country road. "Hey, watch it, or you'll murder us too!"

"Sorry." She started looking for signs to Old Mountain Road. "But seriously, how do you know it was murder?"

"They took Porter's body to the State Examiner in Chapel Hill. The autopsy proved he'd been hit from behind. His skull was crushed."

"Couldn't he have hit his head when he fell off the dock?"

"No way. An accidental fall couldn't have caused that kind of injury." Liz looked smug. "They even found the murder weapon. An oar was missing from his rowboat, but it washed up down the shore. Wiped clean of fingerprints, but they found traces of Jed's blood and skin on the shaft near the paddle. Radical, right? Someone bashed him with his own oar, then left him to drown."

Radical indeed. The thought of such brutal violence made her stomach churn. Though she'd never seen Jed's dock, the gruesome scene was now etched in Technicolor in her mind.

"How do you know all this, Liz? Surely they didn't print the lurid details in the newspapers."

"I have my sources…" She smiled mysteriously.

"Sure you do."

"No really. Danny told me." She blushed. "One of his buddies works in the sheriff's department. He said they're looking for Jed's son, Bobby, as a possible suspect. He's been missing since the old man died, and Wayne Bearfoot wants him for questioning."

The whole scenario was too sad to contemplate. She took a deep breath and made the last turn, from Old Mountain onto Wallace Springs Road. It seemed they were in the middle of nowhere, but if Dennis' directions were correct, they'd soon come to a small community cemetery in a field, just beyond a crooked tree at the edge of the woods.

NINE

A perfect stranger…

Liz was right. Only a handful of mourners were assembled at the tiny graveyard at the edge of an open, barren pasture. As they approached, stepping carefully to avoid the puddles, a weak ray of April sunshine fell on a blue canopy erected over an open grave. Clearly the ground had not been used for a burial in many years, as the tangles of weeds were long and unbroken, the headstones tilted and crumbling. The names of the deceased were barely visible on the markers, but the plot was apparently reserved for only a few families, including the Porters.

The place smelled of rain and wet grass, of earth and flowers. A particularly sweet odor issued from the two memorial bouquets placed near the grave.

"Who's that standing with Dennis?" Diana asked. The young man, both feet planted aggressively on the ground, was one of the most handsome males she'd ever seen. He was several inches shorter than Dennis, but his physique was agile and implied power. His custom-made silk suit, designer tie, and Italian shoes proclaimed an aura of privilege, while his face was movie-star perfect: tan with a tiny scar on his chiseled jaw, enhanced by dark hair and eyes. Next to this specimen, Dennis looked as apple-pie common as the boy next door.

"Shit." Liz moaned. "What the fuck is *he* doing here?" She hid behind Diana.

"Who is he?"

"He's Brantley Craven, the developer who tried to buy the Porter place, got chased off with the shotgun. You'll have to do this thing without me," she gasped. "I'm heading back to the car…"

She snagged Liz's arm. "Hey, what's with you and Craven?"

She closed her eyes and let out a huge sigh. "I was stupid blind in love with him, that's all. We were together all last year. He took me to all the best places, and the sex was great. We even went on a Caribbean cruise. He was my dream prince, complete with a Mercedes Sport and his own boat. I was hearing wedding bells when I discovered he was screwing two other women, *and* engaged to marry the third."

Diana tightened her hold on Liz. She'd heard the *love Liz first* rule many times, and knew all about her quest for *Mr. Rich and Perfect,* but she couldn't allow Liz to be intimidated by this guy.

"C'mon Liz, just throw him a sweet little smile and blow him away. You have every right to be here. And what the hell is he doing here anyway? It seems to me that if someone tries to shoot you, you'd think twice before attending his funeral. What's he up to, anyway?"

She gave Diana a wicked grin. "He's up to no good. It's about cash, pure and simple. He's a vulture. He can smell money a mile away."

"Okay, but what's he doing with Dennis?"

"Well, they knew each other at UNC, but when I was dating Brantley, he called Dennis a daddy's boy and a brainless jock. No love lost between them. Dennis told me Brantley was bad news, and for once he was right. Brantley's done so many crooked deals and stiffed so many contractors, that any legitimate company, like Crawford Realty, would get dirty just brushing up against him."

So likely it was about money, and the Brantley/Dennis connection was a partnership of opportunity. She dragged Liz along and smiled at Dennis. When he waved back, Diana was amazed to see tears in his eyes.

She whispered to Liz. "Look, Dennis is crying. Did he know Jed Porter?"

"Never said so, but he was friends with Jed's grandson. He might have met the old man."

Who knew? A public display of emotion was totally out of character for her young boss, but this was a tragic occasion. Also, Dennis had lost his father recently, so maybe he identified. Even tough guys cried. Tough gals, too. For months after her father died, Diana had broken into tears at the slightest provocation.

As she looked around the sad little field, she wondered if only those with a financial interest had come to mourn the friendless old hermit, and the service was about to begin. In addition to the young preacher, who gazed solemnly at the cheap pine coffin poised to drop into a red hole, she saw a middle-aged couple sitting alone beneath the canopy. They too were staring at the pine box.

"Are those Jed's children?" Liz asked.

She looked closely. The man was tall and wiry, with a sharply contoured face and small, close-set eyes. He looked exactly like a weasel. He was rigid, uneasy, and his body language conveyed his impatience.

"I don't think the man is Bobby," she told Liz. "Bobby was estranged from Jed, and I doubt he'd show up. But I'm pretty sure the woman is Amy."

The haggard woman was about Diana's age, but she looked much older. Her shabby dark suit was vintage thrift shop, and her black pumps, while freshly polished, were worn down at the heels. She was definitely not as Clara had described her: *an angel with hair of spun gold.* She was an overweight matron with bleach-damaged hair and a face that had seen too much sorrow. But oh, those eyes! They were red from weeping, but still *big and blue as saucers.* They were open and innocent as the fawn's eyes in *The Yearling*, and Diana loved her instantly. Suddenly she couldn't wait to meet this woman and give her the book, still wrapped in brown paper, safely concealed in her purse.

The service began. The preacher admitted that he'd never met Jedidiah Porter, but was sure he'd been *a good Christian man, born again in our own Baptist church.* Diana tuned it out. What could that young pup actually know about Jed, or his family, or what was waiting for Jed in the Great Beyond? The preacher did know that someone would slip him a little money after the service, and she prayed he also knew enough to keep it short and sweet.

No such luck.

During the Twenty-Third Psalm, dark clouds gathered above the field and the rain began again. She guided Liz under the canopy, but couldn't squeeze under herself. At the same time, two tall men, latecomers to the service, jumped from an old red and white Ford pickup and rushed through the downpour towards their sorry little band. She instantly recognized one of the men. A conservative gray suit and a somber demeanor could never disguise the high cheekbones and intense black eyes of Sheriff Wayne Bearfoot.

She nudged Liz and cocked her head in his direction.

Liz leaned in close. "I bet he's looking for Bobby. Do you think Bobby will show?"

Diana silenced her with a stern frown just as the two men moved in beside them. Bearfoot acknowledged Diana with an almost imperceptible nod, while the other man, a perfect stranger, smiled at her.

"Close quarters, isn't it, ma'am?" His voice was deep and friendly. "Would you care to share my umbrella?"

Before she could protest, he quietly opened his umbrella and guided a warm hand under her elbow. He stepped her back several paces into its shelter. This wasn't the time nor place to make a fuss, so she allowed the familiarity. Frankly, she was pleased to put some distance between the neighborhood sheriff and herself.

She tried to ignore the stranger as the preacher launched into the service. It seemed Jed's daughter and Diana's male companion were the only ones listening, so she took the opportunity to appraise this man with whom she shared intimate space. He was tall, well over six feet and solidly built, a man who had always worked outside, never in an office.

He seemed to be several years Diana's senior, but he wore it well. She couldn't say the same for his suit. His tan coat and chocolate trousers were well-tailored and fit nicely, but they obviously made him uncomfortable. Once he tugged at his dark green tie as though it was a hangman's noose. She pictured him in a comfy old flannel shirt and torn blue jeans.

She peeked at his face. It was rugged and tan, with crinkles at the corners of warm brown eyes and a sunburn line on his forehead, where a cap usually sat on his thick brown hair. Sensing her scrutiny, he glanced at her and smiled. Of all things, she saw tears in his eyes.

Quickly looking away, she took stock of the situation. This was, after all, a memorial service, and it was therefore likely that the stranger had been a friend of Jedidiah's. Was it possible the old fellow actually had friends? At first she had assumed her companion was a deputy, since he'd come with Bearfoot. But now, noticing his hands, with rough skin and a hammer bruise on one finger, she knew she was wrong. Relaxing, she enjoyed the comfort of his closeness.

Dust to dust, ashes to ashes, may our brother, Jedidiah rest in peace...

It was over.

Wayne Bearfoot circled around. "Mrs. Rittenhouse, this is my friend, Matthew Troutman. Folks in these parts call him *Trout.*"

She smiled and shook Matthew's hand. "I don't usually share umbrellas with strangers. But thanks."

"My pleasure, ma'am, and I prefer to meet beautiful women under happier circumstances," he drawled.

"Were you a friend of Mr. Porter's?" Suddenly she felt uncommonly shy. His rich southern accent was charming, and she couldn't tear her eyes from his wide, expressive mouth.

"Well, I guess you'd call us friends. Least I was maybe as close as Jed ever came to having one. But I knew his kids real well. Amy, Bobby, and I went to school together. We've been pals ever since."

His sincerity was disarming. She cast about for something to say. "Your name is *Troutman,* right? Did they name the town after you?" She felt foolish as soon as the words left her mouth.

He cocked his head. "Matter of fact, they named it after my great-granddaddy. After that, I can't take the credit, and I won't take the blame."

For a suspended moment they studied one another. She didn't want him to leave, but he nodded towards Amy.

"I want to pay my respects, Ms. Rittenhouse. Will you excuse me? I hope to see you again real soon."

"Please call me *Diana.*"

"Thank you, *Diana*…"

Matthew smiled down at her, and then up at the clouds, where a brilliant burst of sunshine seemed to banish the rain. When he walked away, she was very cold.

And Wayne Bearfoot moved in. "That's not fair. Trout rates calling you *Diana*, while I'm still in the *Mrs. Rittenhouse* stage?"

Heat rose to her face.

"It's been like that long as I can remember," Bearfoot continued. "Old Trout's the strong, silent type—always gets the ladies' attention. Women take one look at me and run the other way."

"Maybe it has something to do with that gun you carry around."

"No gun today." He smiled.

"Are you here to pay your respects, or is this official business?"

The sheriff pretended not to hear. "If you see Trout again, tell him I'll be waiting for him back at the truck, okay?"

Before she could answer, Bearfoot walked away, and Liz, who'd been grinning throughout the exchange, suddenly stiffened. "Shit! Dennis and Brantley are headed this way. Meet you back at the car, okay?"

She escaped before Diana could stop her, and just in the nick of time.

"Diana, this is Brantley Craven, a developer from Charlotte. Brantley's gonna make some big changes up here in our neck of the woods. Brantley, this is Diana Rittenhouse. We hope she'll be handling the Porter estate."

Brantley was watching Liz's hasty retreat, the corner of his lip curled in amusement. Not until the words *Porter estate* sunk in, did he acknowledge Diana at all.

"Pleased to meet you..." He extended a perfectly manicured hand. His tone was buttered molasses.

His hooded expression was a combination of feigned interest and utter condescension. His expensive aftershave was strangely offensive in this natural setting, and she wanted nothing to do with the man.

But she smiled and shook his hand. "Nice to meet you, Mr. Craven, but if you'll excuse me, I want to speak to Amy Porter before she leaves..."

Both men glanced at the middle-aged woman stumbling away from the canopy on the arm of her weasel-faced escort.

"I'd like a word with Amy myself..." Brantley pushed forward, but Dennis held him back, vigorously shaking his head.

"Let Diana do it," Dennis said. "She's still the best one to close the deal, so don't blow it now."

Ignoring them both, she fast-walked up the hill after Amy. When she caught up, Amy turned to face her, and she laid her hand on Amy's arm. "I'm Diana Rittenhouse..."

"I thought so." She smiled. "Dennis described you very well. Thanks for coming today."

"Why are you here, anyway?" the man with Amy demanded in a gruff voice. "Are you another one of them real estate people after her daddy's land?"

Amy seemed to shrink into herself. "This is my husband, Roger Keene. He's forever thinkin' folks are out to take advantage. Roger, you should be ashamed! Dennis said Diana aims to help us."

Roger was not impressed. "I'd sooner have a *man* lookin' after our interests, someone from these parts who knows the score. No offense, but you're a Yankee, ma'am."

She struggled to keep her temper under control. She'd dealt with sexist clients before, but never one so blatant. Yes, this was new territory, and at times the southern ways left her baffled and confused. Remember, she thought, *I am a professional.*

"I have the experience and expertise to do a good job for Amy."

"Sure you do, lady." He was rude and dismissive as he turned to his wife. "I'll wait up yonder on the road. Don't you sign *nothin'* less you run it by me. You hear?" He shook his finger, turned his back, and trudged away through the field, leaving his wife stranded somewhere between grief and mortification.

"I am so sorry," Amy said through a fresh flood of tears. "Roger don't mean nothin' by all that, he's just too protective, you know?"

She led Amy aside to the shelter of an ancient oak, where they stood side by side near a crumbling stone statue of an angel. Dappled sunlight filtered through the branches. Little showers of moisture blew down from the wet leaves as the breeze passed through.

"Did Dennis tell you I met your father last week?"

Amy nodded and stared back at the deserted gravesite.

"Well, he gave me something for you..." She lifted the brown paper package from her purse as Amy startled with surprise.

"Daddy sent this for *me*? That's impossible! I haven't seen him for years, and in all that time, he never gave me nothin'."

Diana handed her the book. "You weren't supposed to open this until..." She took a deep breath and started again. "Under the circumstances..." Diana glanced at the gravesite. "I suppose you can open it anytime."

Amy cradled the package as though it were as fine and fragile as a butterfly's wing. "I think I'll wait till I get home, Diana. Did he tell you what's inside?"

"It's a book, *The Yearling*. He said your mother used to read from it, and he wanted you to have it."

"You sure?" She held the magical gift to her bosom.

"Very sure."

Before her eyes, the middle-aged woman became a little girl, and her eyes sparkled with delight. "Thank you," was all she said.

Amy tucked the book under her jacket and walked away into her personal, unknown future, leaving Diana to do the same.

TEN

The merry go round...

"Your condo is awesome!" Liz burst through the door ahead of Diana. "Your secret hideaway. No wonder you like to hole up here."

She felt guilty as Liz crossed the hardwood floors strewn with Persian carpets, and then opened the drapes to a view of an intimate patio and Lake Norman. "I would've invited you sooner, but you know how it is..."

"Yeah, yeah, I know." Liz stared at the vaulted ceilings and white walls hung with modern art. "You're selfish, Diana."

"Kick off your shoes and make yourself at home," Diana said. "Don't know about you, but I could use a glass of wine—or two."

"Amen. Nothing like a soggy funeral to build up a powerful thirst."

Diana entered her pristine white kitchen, while Liz explored. In truth, she'd never invited Liz or anybody else to her home. Privacy was a commodity she cherished, so that any visitation seemed like a physical violation. Fact was, she'd become a recluse. Not good.

"It's like a page from *Architectural Digest,*" Liz hollered from the living room. "All your stuff is brand new, right?"

"I needed a fresh start!" She hollered back. An understatement. She had banished every stick of antique furniture, of heirloom china, any scrap of memorabilia that reminded her of her marriage to Robert Rittenhouse. Those things were the baggage from the Philadelphia Rittenhouse dynasty. They'd never been Diana's.

Only the art was truly hers: paintings by a few modern masters and lovingly selected works by talented regional artists. Robert had never cared about collecting, so she'd pursued her passion alone. She'd scrimped, saved, and purchased over the years, so that now the paintings and sculpture seemed like her children. At times she loved them more than her actual children, and that wasn't good, either.

"Haul your ass out here, Diana! Where'd you buy your furniture? What about all these pictures?"

Diana figured she'd better put together some goodies to soak up the alcohol. She emerged equipped with a tray of chilled Chardonnay, two glasses, and a plate of crackers, cheese, and veggies. She found Liz fingering her books.

"Have you read all these?"

"You bet. Some I read again and again."

"Your sound system is rad. You into music, or what?"

Liz's enthusiasm was infectious. But she soon lost interest in the art, literature, and music, and focused instead on the new sofa and window treatments.

"You must've spent a year's commission on all this stuff."

"Not really. I discovered the outlets when I moved down here and found some great bargains. I wanted everything to be bright, cheery, and easy to clean."

"I'm checking out the bedrooms…"

Before Diana could warn her, Liz barreled into the master suite.

"*Mother fucker!*" the voice barked out a loud greeting.

"*What* did you say?" Liz was stunned.

"*Piss off, stupid bitch!*" the voice screamed again.

Diana doubled over with laughter to see Liz's beet red face. "It's not *me*, it's *him!*" She pointed to the large cage mounted near her bedroom window.

"What is it?"

"He is Perry..." Diana approached the silvery white creature peering out from behind bars. "Perry's an African Gray, the nastiest parrot on earth."

"*Shut up, bitch!*" Perry squawked.

Liz gaped at the bird. "Yeah, I can see it's a parrot, but Jesus, Diana, did you teach him to talk like that?"

"It's a long story, but I promise you, I'm not to blame."

"You should wash his mouth out with soap."

"Yeah, but with my luck, Perry would develop a taste for soap. C'mon, let's go out to the patio." She handed Liz the tray, unlocked the French doors opening from her bedroom, and they stepped outside. "Take the wicker chair, Liz, it has the best view of the lake."

Liz let out a low whistle. "You ain't a kidding!" She dropped into the chair and propped her feet on the low wall surrounding the colorful tile floor. She gazed out at the four-mile reach of Main Channel, where the water was cobalt blue in the late afternoon sun. "This is a killer view, the best on the lake!"

"Now you sound like a Realtor, but you don't have to sell me. I know how lucky I was to find this place." She filled their glasses to brimming, pushed off her sandals, and settled in. A few white sails dotted the horizon, but soon the boaters would return home for the happy hour. "Drink up!"

"*Fuck you!*" Perry shouted from the bedroom.

Liz rolled her head towards the sound. "Hey, girlfriend, explain your parrot. What's his story?"

"Yes, dear, sweet Perry. Would you believe I inherited him? Back in Pennsylvania, I sold a house for an old man a lot like Jed Porter. The geezer had such a foul mouth, I had to chase him away before I could show it. Long story short, he took a liking to me. When he died several years later, a messenger brought the parrot right to my office."

"No shit? What did you do?"

"What could I do? African Grays can live to be eighty years old, or more. Perry was about my age when he arrived. I identified with him."

"How could you, Miss Squeaky Clean, identify with that filthy- mouthed creature? Hardly a match made in Heaven."

She didn't appreciate being described as *squeaky clean*, but chose not to argue the point. "I was lonesome. My divorce was final, my children had moved out, and I figured Perry would keep me company. Over the years, I've considered wringing his scrawny neck…" She squinted at Liz. "I fully expect the bird will outlive me. Mind if I remember *you* in *my* will?"

"Don't even think about it," Liz groaned. "But, hey, at least Perry would bring some male companionship into my bedroom. Haven't had much of that lately."

Diana refilled their glasses and arched her eyebrows. "What about Danny Capelli? Doesn't he count?" She knew Liz was sleeping with the guy.

Liz's face matched her hair. "You're right, Diana. I fell off the wagon. You remember meeting Danny?"

"Tall, curly-headed young man who visited our office? Yes, I liked him very much."

"Really?" Liz averted her eyes. "I know Danny doesn't fit my agenda. He'll never be rich, so it'll never work out between us… but, hey, what can I say? The man's hot."

Secretly, Diana hoped Liz would stick with Danny. Compared to the other vermin she'd dated, like Brantley Cravin, Danny was pure gold.

Liz filled Diana's glass. If they weren't careful, they'd both be looped before sundown.

"Your turn, Diana…" Liz said. "What about your love life? Danny thinks you're super sexy. He thinks you should get out and play."

Diana fiddled with the seedlings she'd transplanted to her patio box. "Do you like gardening, Liz?"

"Hey, don't change the subject. You've never said one word about the men in your life."

She stared out at the sunset. "After a long marriage and a bitter divorce, I'm off the merry-go-round."

Liz upended the bottle and shook it out over the lake. "That's one dead soldier. More in the fridge?" She headed towards the kitchen. "Let's get shit-faced, girlfriend. When I come back, we'll have a heart-to-heart."

Perfect. Just what she needed. First the ordeal at the cemetery, and now this. She wasn't about to spill her guts to this well-meaning child.

Liz toasted with fresh Chardonnay. "Women get divorced. Big deal."

She braced for a pep talk. No point telling Liz about her husband's secret infidelities, or the sweet young thing who became his wife. Or their oh-so-civil relationship after the divorce. Most of all, Liz didn't need to know, at her tender and optimistic age, that even true love dies.

But Liz pressed on. "I think you're scared, Diana. If you give yourself a chance and start dating, who knows? You might enjoy it."

"If you fall off the horse, get back in the saddle…" If she had to endure this lecture, she might as well utilize her favorite equestrian cliché. "Tell me, Liz, do you know of any white knights just waiting to carry me off into the sunset?"

"What about Matthew Troutman?" Her green eyes twinkled. "I saw you two together today, and he seemed really interested. What a hunk! And he's an eligible bachelor. Since his wife died, women from three counties have been chasing him. I've never seen him respond to anyone, though. Not until today."

Ridiculous. "What do you know about Matthew Troutman?"

"Are you kidding? I've known Trout forever. My parents used to bring us to the lake when we were little. We always stopped at Trout's Place, that store on River Highway? I know you've seen it, Diana. It's a gas station, general store, and auto repair shop all rolled into one. They sell everything from bait and tackle, to hardware and groceries. Trout gave all us kids free ice cream, so I fell in love with him years ago."

Diana had indeed seen Trout's Place in her travels, but she'd never been inside. She recalled Matthew's strong hands and shy smile, so she could easily picture him handing out goodies to children—but they came from different worlds. "I shared an umbrella with the man. End of story."

"He was into you," Liz insisted. "He's quite a catch."

"If he meets all the criteria for the *love Liz first rule*, why don't *you* go after him?"

"If he was ten years younger…" Liz licked her lips. "He's rich, that's for sure. Owns a couple of boats, not to mention, cars, trucks, and a house on the lake. He's one of the good guys, Diana. Folks think highly of Trout. He's generous with his time and his money."

"Not my type."

Liz's eyes narrowed. "Not good enough for you, Miss Diana?"

"It's not that..." Yet she suspected she'd have little in common with a bait-selling, story-swapping quintessential southern male.

An uncomfortable silence grew between them as they finished the second bottle of wine. She hadn't meant to offend Liz. Maybe they were both feeling the effects of the alcohol after a particularly difficult day. Far as Matthew was concerned, she found herself remembering his warm hand on her arm, his gentle voice, and the kindness he had shown. Just being near him had overpowered her with a sense of well-being.

"Be patient with me, Liz," she spoke at last. "I know I'm a mess, especially when it comes to trusting the opposite sex. I keep telling myself I need more time."

"So you'll take my advice and get out more?"

"I'll think about it, okay?"

They shared a pot of strong coffee, and when Liz finally said her goodbyes and hurried off to Danny, Diana was left alone with her thoughts. She'd heard far too much truth in the girl's words. What good were paintings, books, and music? Even the beautiful sunset lost its impact when the only one to share it with was a foul-mouthed parrot.

She got busy and whipped up a tuna salad.

Before moving to North Carolina, she'd made several half-hearted attempts at dating that left her tired, discouraged, and more lonesome than ever. The rules of engagement had changed since she'd been out of commission. Sex on the first date was almost expected. If that test drive didn't work out, one moved on to a different bed the next day, and Diana couldn't get with that program. Now, living in a brand new state that seemed at times like a foreign country, the idea of meeting men was even more daunting.

She buttered two rolls to go with the salad and switched on the local news. Even the newscasters remained strangers, and the local issues failed to engage her. This was her fault. She should make an effort to understand what was going on in her new backyard, and she needed to meet new people. But she was gun-shy about everything, so how could she meet new people, let alone begin a relationship?

"*Fuck, fuck, fuck!*" Perry hollered from the bedroom. The TV always stirred him up, and at the moment, she agreed with his sentiments.

Purchasing a king-size bed had been her biggest mistake. It had seemed like a good idea at the time, because the oversized master bedroom was begging to be filled. But she had not anticipated the emptiness, how small and alone she would feel under an acre of covers. She missed the warmth of another human being holding her in his arms. And yes, she missed the sex.

She turned back to the TV, where the weatherman had finishing his portion of the broadcast and promised a late-breaking story. Suddenly a close-up of a familiar face flashed onto the screen, jarring her into harsh awareness.

Iredell County Sheriff, Wayne Bearfoot, made the arrest early this evening at the Days Inn in Statesville...

She dropped her fork and watched as Bearfoot led a frail, frightened-looking man in handcuffs towards the Hall of Justice, apparently to jail.

The suspect, Mr. Bobby Porter of Barium Springs, is being held for questioning in the drowning death of his father, Mr. Jedidiah Porter...

Having lost her appetite, she gaped at the prisoner. The middle-aged man looked rough in a wrinkled shirt and baggy trousers, like he'd been sleeping in his clothes. He covered his face and tried to hide from the camera, and the gesture tore at her heart. Where was hope in a world where a son kills his father? And in that same world, where was there hope for love?

ELEVEN

Make a change...

The phone shattered Diana's sleep at seven the following morning, and she groped in the dark for the receiver.

"Hello?" she croaked, her mouth dry from too much wine.

"Is that you, Mrs. Rittenhouse? I hate to be callin' so early, but your home number's right here on your card, and ..."

The woman's voice was vaguely familiar. She struggled upright in the pillows and snapped on the bed light.

"I just know I woke you up, but I didn't want to call you at the office..."

"It's okay," she muttered. Clients called at all hours, it went with the territory.

"You want to fix you some coffee, then I'll ring back later?"

"It's fine, really. How can I help?" The caller's face was beginning to take form in her mind: big blue eyes red from crying, dappled sunlight and wet leaves...

"When we met yesterday, Mrs. Rittenhouse, I knew I could trust you. And to tell the honest truth, I'm so mixed up it's like my head's on backwards."

The image shifted into sharp focus, and suddenly she was wide-awake. "Calm down, Amy, and please, call me *Diana*."

"Well then, Diana, I got to say, everything's goin' to hell on a handcart. My daddy just laid to rest, my husband gone crazy, and now Bobby's in jail! Did you see it on the news?"

She took a deep breath. "Yes, I saw, but let's take it one step at a time."

"Don't know where to start. Roger's driven' me crazy about selling Daddy's farm, but I ain't even one hundred percent sure it's mine to sell. He's been talkin' to some lawyer who claims I'm the one in charge, but..."

"Are you the *executrix*?"

"That's the word the lawyer used, but what about Bobby? He's kin too, but now...with all they've been sayin' on TV..."

The poor woman was sobbing, and Diana's heart went out to her. She longed to give her a big, motherly hug, but that was impossible over the blasted telephone. "Let's get together and talk, Amy. Maybe it's not as bad as it seems."

Her words of comfort rang false. How could things be worse? Amy's father was dead, her husband was desperate to get his hands on the money, and her brother was in jail under suspicion of murder.

"I'll meet you tomorrow in my office," Diana said. "We'll have a nice cup of coffee and put our options down on paper."

"No!" Amy wailed. "Not at the *office*. What if Dennis is there? I love that boy like a son, but him and Roger are thick as thieves. Even before all this happened, they was talkin' behind my back about Daddy's land. Please, Diana, I don't want my husband to know I'm meetin' you. Please?"

So against her better judgment, she agreed to meet Amy secretly for lunch the following day at a little restaurant in Mooresville. It was mid-way between Amy's house in Salisbury and Diana's office in Cornelius. When Dennis called, pushing her to follow up and get a listing from Amy, she told him nothing about this plan. Maybe she was paranoid, but whatever worried Amy about the Dennis connection, worried her twice as much.

Dennis had implied that Amy had already hired him, but that was obviously a lie. If Diana was putting her job in jeopardy, so be it. And if misleading one's broker was a mortal sin, then she'd burn in hell.

Later that afternoon, Diana was feeling almost human. She showered and dressed for her customary Friday night dinner with Mama, but because it was such a beautiful day, she left early to drive around in Ruby. She hoped the fresh air would blow the cobwebs out of her brain.

She was proud of herself for daring to drive on Interstate 77, and proud of her defiant decision to meet in secret with Amy, but what she really needed was some honest self-evaluation. Was she too insular? Liz had hit a nerve when she'd said that Diana liked to *hole up* and keep her life under wraps. She hadn't always been that way, and she wasn't exactly *scared* of relationships. It was just easier not to get involved.

She got lost in self-analysis and completely missed enjoying her favorite view of Lake Norman. She'd sailed across the bridge, never noticing the glistening blue water or the floating white clouds. Typical. She'd set out to savor the spring day, and then ignored it.

Make a change, girl!

She steered off at Exit 36 and turned west on River Highway, moving in the opposite direction of Mama at Shady Oaks. She was heading towards the lake, and Matthew Troutman's store. The plan was not premeditated, and she needed an excuse. Well, Mama *did* need batteries for her CD player, and surely they sold batteries at *Trout's Place*. And if Matthew just happened to be there…

Her heart was beating double-time when she spotted the store coming up fast on the right. She pulled into a parking space, turned off the engine, and rolled down the window to take it all in. Her senses were heightened. It seemed she could read history in the magic light of late afternoon.

The original store appeared to have once been a one-roomed log cabin. It was set back from the road in a large open field surrounded by a pine forest. The structure was older than the lake itself, and she could almost imagine a teenaged Matthew working there. A rustic covered porch sheltered an ancient steel ice chest, once filled with soda pop. She saw an enormous steel tank filled, no doubt, with live minnows. An abandoned gas pump with a big red *Amoco* star on its cracked globe transported her back to childhood road trips, from an all-but-forgotten past. A *Hardware* sign was nailed to the roof, and she could almost smell the dust, the oil, and the feel of a cool, damp interior.

A modern convenience store had been constructed closer to the highway, with standard plate glass windows and a brightly-lit food mart inside. Several customers were outside pumping gas.

Finally, between the old cabin and the modern store, stood a dilapidated barn labeled *Garage and Auto Parts*. It was entirely enclosed by a chain link fence. Cars of every make, in every stage of disrepair, rested in the fenced yard along with a few boats. She spotted a familiar red and white Ford pickup parked directly in front of the garage, and her heart stopped beating altogether.

Dear God, Matthew *was* there! Unable to contain her panic, she started Ruby's engine, shifted into reverse, popped into drive, and peeled out. She was miles down the road before she realized she was still heading in the wrong direction, away from her appointment with Mama. To put it kindly, she was behaving like a goose with a screw loose.

No words were harsh enough to describe her shame. Liz was right, she was a coward. She'd come to see Matthew, but couldn't face him. She was like a silly schoolgirl with a bubblegum crush. Someone should shoot her, put her out of her misery. Impulsively, she veered left onto one of the many roads leading down to the cottages along the lake. She knew a few of these streets, but on a lake with over five hundred miles of shoreline, most roads were still a mystery—including this one.

She stopped and switched off the ignition. Time for a reality check. If she didn't turn around that instant, she'd disappoint Mama, so she twisted the key and pressed the accelerator.

*Thunk, thunk, thunk...*said Ruby.

She tried again.

*Thunk, thunk, thunk...*nothing. The battery was stone cold dead.

Sweet Jesus, what had she done to deserve this? She watched the minute hand jerking round and round on her watch as the sun set in the sky. And of course, she'd forgotten her cell phone.

She closed her eyes and listened to the faraway traffic on River Highway. Everyone was speeding home to dinner with loved ones. Not Diana. Thanks to her own stupidity, she could either walk towards the lake hoping to find a friendly cottager before some murderer found her, or she could stay put, lock the doors, and hope for the best.

She opted for the second choice. Worrying about a killer on the loose was a bit extreme, but after the events of the past two weeks, who knew?

Suddenly a white flash of headlights bounced off the rearview mirror, blinding her. A large vehicle pulled off on the grass directly behind her car. The driver killed the engine, but left the lights on. A door slammed, and heavy footsteps scattered gravel as they approached.

Now what? Hopefully this was a Good Samaritan, not a stone cold psycho, and as she tried to swallow her fear, a tall, dark figure rapped on the window. Taking a deep breath, she was determined to show a little trust and courage for once this day, and powered down the window inch by inch.

"Hey, ma'am…" a deep voice spoke. "Looks like you could use a little help."

Diana's voice froze in her throat as she peered up at the crooked smile and friendly brown eyes of Matthew Troutman.

TWELVE

Some explaining to do...

"Diana?" Matthew's brown eyes widened in surprise. Pulling an ancient green fishing hat off his head, he peered through the partially opened window. "Didn't expect to see you again so soon. Must be my lucky day."

"Hello, Matthew..." She hastily powered the window all the way down. "No reflection on you, but this is not *my* lucky day."

"Car trouble?"

Before she could protest, he reached through the window, brushing her arm with the sleeve of his flannel shirt, and popped the hood.

"Not sure I can fix it, but it can't hurt to have a look..."

This wasn't happening! The gods were out to get her. She'd been stalking him, and this was her punishment. Mortified, she watched him fumble with the hood. In her long, stormy relationship with Ruby, few men, even experienced mechanics, had cracked the secret of lifting the old Subaru's hood. Matthew was no exception.

"Let me help..." She climbed out to join him. "There's a trick to this, see?" She reached under the lip, just left of center, and tugged the hidden lock.

"Oh yeah, now I get it." He stepped forward to lift the heavy lid.

She watched in silence as he heaved and heaved, but couldn't get the hood to stay up. Each time it flopped down, she suppressed a giggle.

"Very funny. I suppose there's a trick to this, too?"

"Matter of fact, there is." She fingered the grimy underbelly of the hood and found the support rod. Jerking it loose, she slipped its end into the prop slot near the engine. "See, it's just like a tent pole," she crowed.

"How 'bout that?" He grinned. "Very impressive, Diana."

Usually she enjoyed inflicting a little blow to the male ego, but with Matthew, it gave her no satisfaction. Besides, she got the distinct impression he'd known how to open the hood all along.

"I suppose you know what's wrong with the car?" he said.

"I think it's the battery."

"Yeah, but it could be the starter. Hop inside and crank her up…"

She did as she was told.

Thunk, thunk, thunk…

"Right again." Matthew smiled. "Your battery's deader than yesterday's roadkill. Climb into my truck. We'll go to my place for some jumper cables."

"I can wait here…" Yet she followed him to his Ford. "I am a member of *Triple A.* Loan me your cell phone, and I'll call them."

"Don't have one. I hate the fool things." He frowned as he wiped the grease off his hands onto his jeans, and then boosted her into his cab. "Am I crazy, not owning a cell phone?"

A kindred spirit. She hated them, too. "I require one for my job, and usually carry it with me. But…" She preferred peace and quiet when she was out on the road, and often "conveniently" forgot the phone when she wasn't driving for business. A shrink would have a field day analyzing her phobia.

As they drove away, he grinned at her. "Fact is, Diana, if you had to have a breakdown, you met up with the right guy. I fix cars for a living."

Nervous breakdown more like it. As they rounded a curve, she peeked at the side mirror and saw Ruby grinning like an evil Cheshire cat. Obviously this was her idea of a joke.

"My house is down at the bottom of this hill," he continued. "What were you doing way out here, anyhow?"

If he only knew. "Well, I've never explored this part of the lake."

"So you were lost."

"Guess so." As he sped through a series of hairpin turns, each bump caused her to jolt against his thigh, and the contact was disconcerting. She gripped the armrest and hung on hard.

"Your Subaru's too old to have GPS, but I thought all Realtors carried maps, in case they forgot their cell phones," he teased.

"How'd you know I'm a Realtor?"

"Wayne Bearfoot told me."

Of course he did. Had he also told Matthew that her business card was found on the murder victim? Her new home was proving to be a very small town, so forget keeping secrets. She looked away from him and concentrated on the view outside the truck. The land was rugged, with shaggy pines and hardwoods flanking both sides of the road. Through the darkening filigree of trees budding into leaf, she caught glimpses of the lake shimmering in the sunset. She saw no signs of cottages, no rural mailboxes, and no friendly lights gleaming through the woods. This stretch had to be one of the last undeveloped locations on the lake, and if Matthew Troutman owned even a small part of it, he was, as Liz had implied, potentially very rich indeed.

"Yes, I own the whole peninsula." He read her mind. "My wife and I bought it when it was cheap, and before you ask, *no*, I'm not interested in selling."

"That's good, because I'm not interested in buying." She smiled sweetly.

"Were you on your way to an appointment?"

"No, I was on my way to see my mother. She lives in a retirement community in Statesville. We eat dinner together every Friday night. Too late now."

"If she's anything like my mama, God rest her soul, she won't be happy about that."

"No she won't." By now the gang at Shady Oaks would be pushing away from the dinner table, and Mama would be way beyond mad.

"Nothing you can do about it now," he said. "Sit back and relax. You can phone her from my place."

"I'll relax when you slow down."

"Sorry."

He immediately eased up on the gas, and she began to enjoy the aroma of pipe tobacco, coffee, and good old-fashioned sweat that permeated their space. The cracked upholstery was patched with clear packing tape, and the floor was littered with paper cups and fast food bags. His vehicle felt lived in, much like a truck she'd owned back in the day, when she hung around horses and stables. It felt like home.

"You're not in a hurry now, right?" He cocked an eye at her, then braked as they pulled into a wooded driveway.

She forgot to answer as miles of gold and crimson sky opened before them. The image she saw in the sunset clouds looked like the mythical, burning phoenix, its fiery wings spread in splendor above the darkly churning waves. The breath caught in her throat.

"Beautiful isn't it?" he whispered. "See that line of bright red lights across the lake? That's the River Highway Bridge."

He cut the engine and they sat in silence, seduced by the wonder of the scene before them. The bridge lights formed a long ruby necklace stretching between two points of black shoreline, and as she lowered her gaze to Matthew's back yard, she could just make out the shape of his house. It was a low, rambling structure at the water's edge, with a dock complex and gazebo silhouetted against the flaming sky beyond.

"*Beautiful* doesn't begin to describe this, Matthew. It is *magical*, nothing less."

He climbed from the cab and stretched, his eyes never leaving the panorama before them. "I agree. It's a miracle. I've lived here more than thirty years, and each sunset is different." He came around and opened her door. "C'mon inside and I'll give you the three-penny tour, but I warn you in advance, the place is a mess."

She felt the warm pressure of his hand under her arm and stiffened. "No thanks. I'll wait out here. You've done too much already, and it's getting late…"

She sensed his disappointment, but held her ground.

"Suit yourself. I'll be back in a jiffy with the jumper cables."

She watched him sprint down the long path to his house. He knew his way in the dark, navigating the trees and bushes with a certainty born of familiarity. The screen door slammed and the lights blinked on, one by one. And as he moved from room to room, she tried to pick out the details of the interior, but she was too far away for successful snooping.

Suddenly, she was furious with herself for being so stubborn. She should have gone in. She was dying to see his place, and she really should use his phone to call Mama. More urgent still, she desperately needed to pee. The half- gallon of iced tea she'd drunk hours ago was threatening to bust loose, so waiting was not a smart option.

Still cursing her hard-headedness, she climbed from the truck and picked her way through the night. The stone pathway was uneven, and her sandals caught in the matted grass cover. Finally, she saw Matthew's screened porch looming in the glow from the kitchen window. If only she could make it to the steps, she'd be fine. Stretching her hands out in front like a blind woman, she groped her way forward.

Then, from the corner of one eye, she spotted a big black lump, likely a bag of garbage piled near the bottom of the stairs. Too late! Her toe caught, she tripped over the heap and went flying. She flailed at the night, groping for a handhold, and at the same time, the garbage bag shrieked and started to move. She landed in the azalea bushes face down, the wind knocked out of her.

She screamed when something hot and wet slobbered on her ankles, and she twisted around to fight off her attacker. The creature was not human, and as she beat against its taut chest, it whimpered, but didn't fight back.

The screen door slammed, and she heard Matthew's boots. Once her eyes adjusted to the gloom, she saw a huge black head and white fangs. Its lips were pulled back in a hideous grin.

And as two pale eyes stared into her terror, she knew precisely where she'd seen this creature before.

"Dear God!" Matthew gasped. "What happened?"

She was swimming in sensations, not knowing whether to laugh or cry, as he reached down to lift her. She'd skinned her hands and elbows, but the pain was secondary to the fact of his hands stroking her hair and face. "I tripped over the dog!" she choked.

He shouted at the dog. It backed away, hanging its head. "Ursie wasn't lying there when I came in," he said. "I'm so sorry, Diana. She must've come round for her dinner."

Matthew seemed devastated. Even in the dark, she saw his face was drained of all color. She found her balance and pulled away, her emotions crazily conflicted. His concern was well and good, but what was this particular animal, which obviously meant no harm, doing at his house? "Is this *your* dog?" she demanded.

He shifted from foot to foot, averted his gaze. Stalling for time, he whistled. When the dog leaned against his jeans, he scratched its ears. "How should we answer her question, Ursie?" He rubbed its head. "You live here now, don't you, girl...?" He faced Diana. "Of course, she's my dog."

Ursie slinked up beside her, whining and licking her hand. Okay, they were friends, but all the canine love in the world couldn't convince her. In the wake of this bald-faced lie, Matthew Troutman had some explaining to do.

THIRTEEN

An innocent man...

He gave her a fresh towel and washcloth. She locked herself in the bathroom and scowled at her reflection in the mirror. What the hell had she gotten herself into? She'd set out to simply say hello to Matthew at his store, and here she was, using his john and dirtying his sink. She looked more closely. Aside from a tiny scratch on her chin, scuffed hands and elbows, and heavy -duty stains on her favorite pants, the damage to her person was minimal. All and all, she'd fared much better than when she'd first encountered the demon dog of Porter Farm.

But why was Jedidiah's dog here? What was Matthew's connection? The questions troubled her so much she failed to snoop through Matthew's medicine cabinet, or note how his towels were folded, or sniff his brand of aftershave. One can tell a lot about someone by the state of his bathroom, and this one was immaculate—no dust balls on the gleaming floor, no rings around the bathtub, and no streaks on the mirror. He was very neat, or else he had a maid. Either way, he was a liar.

She washed her hands and face and considered her predicament. He must have taken Ursie from Jed's farm. But when? After the murder? The implications sent a shock of fear down her spine. Her hands trembled as she pressed the towel to her scratches. Her skin was clammy. After all, what did she know about this man? Other than some glowing propaganda from Liz, absolutely nothing.

"Hey, did you drown in there?"

His hesitant knock made her jump.

"Sorry, but I was getting a mite worried. I hope Ursie didn't hurt you. You'll find peroxide and band aids in the cabinet."

"I'm fine."

"If you say so…" his deep voice continued. "Want to call your mama? The phone's in my bedroom, just down the hall."

"Thanks, I'll call her." At least her voice sounded calm and collected. She had to get her jitters under control, because she sure couldn't stay in a locked bathroom forever.

The moment his footsteps retreated, she scuttled down to the master bedroom. Sure enough, he'd tossed a phone onto the big bed. She quietly closed the door and resisted the temptation to lock it. He'd turned on the bedside lamps, and an intimate glow filled the charming room. Jumpy as she was, she had to admit the place was cozy, with two dark wood easy chairs upholstered in a masculine plaid. The heavy dressers and antique desk near the window were also clearly chosen by a man. But a woman had lovingly chosen the bedspread and frilly curtains. After years in real estate, she had an instinct for these things and couldn't help wondering…who was the woman? Someone from Matthew's past, or his present? Was she the one who kept his house so clean?

Sitting gingerly on the very edge of his mattress, she took a deep breath and dialed her mother. Mama was furious, of course, when she told her about the car trouble. Vivian had been nagging for years, telling her to trade Ruby for a new American model. She could have admitted that she was sitting in a strange man's bedroom, and Mama would have been tickled pink. She also would have kept her on the line all night, fishing for details.

When Diana finally said goodbye, she looked more closely at the framed photograph on the bedside table. The woman gazing out at her had a dark, soulful expression. Her lovely pale skin contrasted dramatically with her long, brunette hair. A gentle quality to her eyes offset the wry humor in her smile. She looked like someone Diana would like to know. Her intuition said that the woman in the photo was Matthew's deceased wife, so she turned the picture away, ever so slightly, so as not to be confronted with the reality of Matthew's deep loss.

Once her emotions were under control, she walked out to the kitchen and found him bent over the stove. He had set out two plates, two tall mugs, and a pitcher of sweet tea on a big red tray.

"What are you doing?" she asked.

"Everyone has to eat, Diana. I know you missed supper with your mom, and I'm hungrier than a bear in the blueberry patch, so I figured I'd make us a meal."

The aroma of searing pork exploded hunger pangs in her stomach. "You didn't need to do that, Matthew."

"It's no trouble..." He opened a bag of potato chips and pulled a package of buns from the breadbox. "I have leftover Carolina barbeque and slaw."

She had skipped lunch, and the package of peanut butter crackers she'd eaten was past history. "I really shouldn't..." she protested weakly.

He glanced at the dog staring up at him. "Then I'll give your share to Ursie."

"Okay, you win."

"It's settled, then. How many sandwiches can you eat?" He heaped mounds of juicy pork onto two buns for himself. "That'll get *me* started, but I'll make three for you."

"Don't you dare. I couldn't possibly eat more than one." But she was hooked. It wasn't an issue of *whether* she would eat, only how much.

"Well, I'll fix three anyhow." He shoved the pitcher of tea into her hands, hefted the tray laden with food, and led her through the house onto the front deck. "It's too pretty to stay inside. We'll eat in the gazebo."

He hit a bank of switches, illuminating the pathway through the yard to the dock and gazebo, which twinkled with small globes of pale light. "It's like a fairyland, isn't it?" he said.

"More like a scene from a romantic movie." Why on earth had she said that? She clamped her mouth shut and followed her tall host into the gazebo. Ursie trotted close behind, her nose lifted to the tray of barbeque.

They gobbled the food and gulped the iced tea. Normally she wouldn't touch such a high cholesterol spread, but this was the best meal she'd eaten in ages. Waves lapped against the rocks below, and the *Catawba Queen*, an old Mississippi-style riverboat, churned past a hundred yards out. It was strung with colorful lights and alive with music.

"Now that *is* right out of a romance movie." He licked his fingers and winked. "Don't you agree, Miss Diana?"

His observation caught her with a mouthful of the third sandwich, which she'd sworn not to eat. The best she could manage was a pig-like grunt.

"I like a woman who enjoys her food," he said. "None of that prissy, picky-style eating for us, eh? But you best save a bite for poor Ursie. She's been patient as Job."

She nearly choked on her last bite of pork, and with as much lady-like dignity as she could muster, she extracted a bit and set it discreetly aside on the edge of her plate. Right on cue, Ursie poked her long nose out and eyed her wistfully.

"What kind of dog is she, anyway?" She offered the morsel, which Ursie accepted, dainty-as-you-please.

"She's a full-blooded Doberman." He ruffled the dog's head. Ursie whined, and then held up one paw for Matthew to shake.

"I thought so, but what's wrong with her ears? They flop over. Aren't they supposed to be pointy?"

"Yeah, I guess so. Seems like someone got round to bobbing her tail, but plumb forgot to clip her ears. And take a look at her paw…" He passed her the paw he was shaking, and Ursie seemed to approve the transfer by laying her head in Diana's lap. The paw was deformed, curled up and knotted.

"What happened?"

Matthew hesitated. "Ursie took a bullet between her toes. Near took her leg off, from what I understand."

In spite of the jovial meal they'd just shared, her earlier doubts came flooding back. A chill descended as the last rays of sunset died in the sky. She looked closely at Matthew. "How do you know all this about Ursie?"

He shrugged, pretending to wipe crumbs off his shirt.

Her chest tightened. The romantic movie faded to violent reality. "Ursie belonged to Jedidiah Porter, didn't she?"

He nodded, but didn't look up. He took a pocketknife from his jeans and began opening and closing the blade.

She tried not to look at the knife. "Listen, Matthew, you can't just ignore this. For starters, who shot Ursie?"

"Jed claimed she wandered in one day, all shot up from a hunting accident. He swore he anesthetized the dog by pouring a gallon of whiskey down her throat, and then he cut the bullet out himself."

She shuddered. "And you believed him?"

He finally met her eyes, a grim expression on his face. "Nope, I didn't believe him. Not to speak ill of the dead, but I think Jed shot Ursie himself. He was always trigger-happy, and I suspect he was trying to chase the dog out of his garden. But he was a strange old coot. I think he had a change of heart, patched her up, and kept her for his own."

She was inclined to believe his theory, but it still didn't answer the big question: why did Matthew have Ursie? She stared at him, a shroud of sadness settling around her shoulders as he continued.

"Jedidiah used to come 'round my store once a month, to buy supplies and what not, and he always brought Ursie. He tied her up outside and grumbled about what a nuisance she was, but I could see he loved her."

"Was Jed a friend of yours, Matthew?"

"Hell, no!" He snapped the knife shut and jammed it into his pocket. "But I was real close to his kids. We grew up together, went to the same little school, and we've been friends ever since. It's a wonder they survived to adulthood, Diana. Jed near killed them a time or two."

His angry outburst made her tremble, but she summoned all her courage: "Why do you have Ursie now?"

"Doesn't matter," he grumbled.

Suddenly her patience and fear evaporated. "Of course it matters, Matthew. Jedidiah's been murdered! Did you go to his farm and take his dog?"

"Nope."

"Then how'd she get here? Someone will recognize her and call the police. Don't you care?"

"Nope." He rose abruptly and turned towards the house. "I'll get us some coffee."

"Skip the damn coffee!" She pounded her fist on the table. "How'd you get the dog, Matthew?"

He sighed and dropped back into his chair. "You're one hell of a pushy woman, Diana Rittenhouse. What's it to you?"

"If you must know, this morning Jed's daughter asked me to help her. I like her, and I promised I'd do what I could, but I need to know what's going on. She's at her wit's end."

"I'm truly sorry to hear that." His face softened. "Amy's a dear friend, and I'd do anything to help her."

"Then tell me the truth about Ursie."

He cleared his throat. "If *you* must know, Bobby Porter brought her by and asked me to look after her."

Now that was front-page news! The images from television, of a frightened little man hiding from the cameras, replayed in her mind. "When was this?"

"The night his daddy died."

Her heart leaped into her throat. "God, Matthew, don't you know Bobby's been arrested? Did he bring Ursie to you *after* he killed his father?"

"Nope." Matthew's eyebrows dipped in a frown and he crossed his arms.

"I don't understand…"

"No, you sure don't understand, lady. No one does. Point is, Bobby wouldn't kill anybody. Those brainless idiots are holding an innocent man. If you really want to help Amy, then butt out of it. And when you see her, tell her not to worry. I know Bobby's innocent, and I aim to prove it."

96

His passion rendered her speechless as she struggled to piece it together. "But if Bobby brought Ursie here, he must have known his father was dead."

"I guess he knew, but that doesn't mean he killed him. He was a wreck when he got here, talking nonsense. Yes, he was upset and in one hell of a hurry, but that proves nothing."

She kept her radically different opinion to herself. Friendship had clouded Matthew's judgment. "Did you tell Sheriff Bearfoot what happened?"

"Nope."

"You didn't turn Bobby in?"

"Nope. Even if I'd known where Bobby had run to, I wouldn't turn him in. Wayne and I go back a long way. He can track his man without help from me, or anyone else."

Matthew's stubborn defiance made him an accessory to the crime, and his misplaced loyalty could get him in serious trouble. "Maybe *I'll* tell the sheriff," she said. "He should know that Bobby brought Ursie directly after the murder."

"Mind you own business, Diana!" His dark eyes flashed anger. He struggled to get his temper under control. Then very gradually, his eyes softened, and she saw something new, a hint of tenderness.

"Please don't tell Bearfoot," he said at last. "Give me a chance to help Bobby and Amy. Trust me on this."

Trust him? Why should she? For all she knew, it was Matthew, not Bobby, who visited Jed's farm the night of the murder. She knew nothing about his motives or his history with the Porter family. He obviously had a protective nature and a powerful fondness for Amy.

"And another thing…" He placed his hand on hers. His touch burned her icy fingers. "I want you to walk away from this

97

mess, Diana. Whoever murdered Jed is still out there, and if you go poking your nose where it doesn't belong, you'll be in danger, too."

Was that a threat, or was he really concerned about her welfare? All her instincts told her to trust him, and yet, she'd been so very wrong before. Her track record was abysmal. She was a bad judge of character when it came to the men in her life, but then, Matthew wasn't in her life. Was he?

Suddenly she was very tired. "It's late. I should get home."

"But I made coffee, and we have cake for dessert."

"Sorry…" She got to her feet and started walking away.

"Hey, aren't you forgetting something…?" He reached into his pocket and pulled out the keys to his truck. He twirled them on one finger and grinned. "How do you plan on getting home? You still have a dead battery, and I charge double for after-hours roadside assistance. Let's compromise, okay? If you sit a spell and have coffee with me, I'll let you borrow my truck. What do you say, Miss Diana? Do we have a deal?"

FOURTEEN

The cycle of abuse...

Carolina Bell Café was a large, one-story brick box. From what Diana had seen so far, this style was North Carolina's architecture of choice for everything from residences to commercial structures. The restaurant was located on North Main Street in Mooresville, surrounded by a parking lot. It seemed out of place in a lovely established neighborhood of gracious old homes. Yet what did she know? Hodge-podge development was the rule of thumb in her adopted state, and no one, not even the frantic town commissioners, seemed able to control it.

For her lunch date with Amy, she'd chosen a pleated skirt, silk blouse, and a tailored blazer. Mama had purchased this outfit because it *brought out* her blue eyes. She felt silly all dressed up in Matthew's pickup, which was still littered with coffee cups and sandwich bags. And she was very nervous about this meeting. Over dessert last night, Matthew had told her about Amy's difficult marriage, and she doubted she could convince her to sign a listing agreement, against her husband's wishes.

Nevertheless, she tucked a contract into her big purse and scanned the parking lot for a car that could be Amy's. The lot was packed with everything from compacts to workmen's vans. She even saw an Iredell Sheriff's patrol car out back, like the one Wayne Bearfoot had driven. Obviously the little café had a good reputation with the locals, so she was anticipating a succulent, home-cooked meal.

She passed through a glass entranceway into the *no smoking* dining room, which had been recently redecorated. The pastel motif was pretty, with country patterns and flowers. The place was alive with animated chatter and the homey clank of silverware on china.

As she searched the faces, a smiling waitress took her elbow and guided her towards a table in the far corner. "She's waiting for you, ma'am..." the woman explained.

"Hey, Diana..." Amy rose with a shy grin. "Is this table okay?"

"Looks just fine." Alarm bells sounded when she noticed that her friend was wearing dark glasses in this very dim part of the room. "Sorry I'm late."

"You're not," Amy said as they slid into their chairs. "I'm always early, always first to the party. My kids tease me about it. I'm always first to chow down the food, so I end up washin' dishes while the rest of them's still at dessert."

"I'm afraid I have the opposite problem," she admitted. "I can't be on time to save my soul, and *my* kids tease *me* about that." She hoped to establish some common ground right off the bat.

"How many kids do you have, Diana?" Amy twisted one napkin to shreds, then pushed it aside to start tearing another.

"I have two, one boy and one girl, but they're actually adults now. My daughter's in Florida and my son lives in Pennsylvania."

"Me too! I have twins." Amy brightened. "Only my two ain't never gonna grow up. My girl's already married, with a baby of her own, but she's the one acts like the baby. And my boy don't have a clue. He still lives at home with Roger and me, and he can't keep a job more'n a month at a time. He's the one went to school with your boss, Dennis. Now he's got this bee in his bonnet about goin' to Mitchell Community College. Problem is, he expects Roger and me to foot the bill."

"I understand. It's expensive to send a child to college."

They paused to order their meals. The waitress placed an enormous pitcher of iced tea between them, along with a plate of lemons and two tall glasses. Diana pretended not to notice when Amy tried to pour, but splashed tea on the tablecloth. Wearing those dark glasses, it was a wonder the poor woman could see a thing.

"The service is real fast here, and the food's special," Amy jabbered.

"Thanks for inviting me."

Amy had also dressed for the occasion. Her pale rose blouse had survived many washings, but every ruffle was starched and ironed to perfection. It was troubling, however, that on this warm spring day, her sleeves were buttoned down at the wrist, and her collar was secured way up at the base of her neck by an antique brooch. "That's a pretty blouse..." Diana offered gently.

"You really like it? I bought it at a thrift shop in Troutman." Her voice dropped to a whisper. "I buy all my clothes there, stuff for the kids, too. It's real cheap, but some of the clothes have designer labels. All them rich ladies from the lake bring in their things not hardly worn at all. Would you like to go there with me sometime?"

"I'd love it, and my mother would love it, too." Diana and her mama had spent many happy Saturdays combing yard sales and thrift shops for treasure, so she knew Viv would jump at a chance to visit Amy's favorite thrift shop.

Soon the food arrived. They'd both ordered the daily specials, but the huge helpings of country-fried steak, fried okra, grease beans, mashed potatoes, corn, apple crisp, and hot biscuits were more than Diana had bargained for.

"This is too much!"

"Told you so." Amy dug right in. "Eat up, Diana. Business and digestion don't mix. Eat now—talk later."

She had no problem with that philosophy, but last night she'd gorged on barbeque with Matthew, and now she was chowing down again. She tended to stay skinny, but if she wasn't careful, this Carolina lifestyle would put on the pounds. Yet somehow the food disappeared, the waitress cleared away the plates, and another pitcher of tea appeared like magic.

"Now, Amy, it's time to talk. How can I help?" She couldn't bring herself to shove the listing contract under Amy's nose right away, because the woman now seemed more like a friend than a client. She decided to ease into it. "Did your father leave a will? Or did he write anything down about how he wanted to settle his estate?"

Amy shook her head and punished another napkin. "That's funny, Dennis asked me the exact same thing at the funeral. But Daddy didn't leave no will. I told you how Roger went to see some lawyer? The lawyer said that since I'm the oldest child, I'm in charge."

That sounded reasonable on the surface, but the law didn't work that way. If someone died intestate and didn't name an executor, often the court took matters into its own hands unless the siblings could agree on a representative. Also the siblings would have equal say and equal shares in the disposition of the real estate.

"Did this lawyer say how you should proceed with the sale of your father's land?"

"Well, he said it might get hung up in court a long time, and that made Roger hoppin' mad. He also said we could speed things up considerable if we was to get something down in writing from Bobby saying it was okay to put me in charge." Amy's voice thickened with emotion. "But how are we supposed to do that, with Bobby in jail, and all?"

"Can't Roger go to the jail and talk to him?"

"No way! Roger would as soon kill Bobby, as look at him."

"Is he violent, Amy?" She had to ask, but she didn't expect the flood of tears the question provoked.

Amy lifted off her dark glasses and wiped her eyes. Even thick makeup couldn't disguise the bruises—some fresh, others yellowing with age. Someone had used her face as a punching bag.

Her temper flared. "Did Roger do this to you?"

Amy sniffled and looked away. "He don't mean nothin' by it. He just gets so angry and frustrated, you know? He don't rightly know what he's doin' when he gets like that."

"The hell he doesn't!" Diana could not conceal her outrage. A chubby deputy seated nearby glanced up at her outburst, but then quickly looked away. "Listen to me, Amy, you don't have to put up with abuse. Does it happen often?"

Her look of pure misery said it all. She pushed away from the table, nearly toppling her chair. "That tea went right through me…" Her small hands fluttered. "I'm going to the ladies' room. Be right back, Diana…"

Helpless, she watched Amy's back as she fled.

103

The deputy smiled. His nametag said *Doug*. "Is there a problem?" he asked

She composed herself and smiled back. "Thanks, officer, we're fine."

"Well, if there's anything I can do…"

She shook her head, toasted him with her glass of tea, and he went back to his meal. Sure, there was plenty he could do, if Amy pressed charges. He could slap a restraining order on Roger or throw him in jail. But likely Amy would not press charges, victims rarely did. The cycle of abuse was never ending, or so it seemed. Battered children chose abusive mates, and then they beat their own kids. Diana had heard about Jedidiah's violence to both Amy and Bobby, but must it follow that his daughter becomes a battered wife, his son a murderer?

The food churned in her stomach as she recalled her own brush with abuse. It had happened only once, that awful night when she first learned of her husband's infidelities. Robert had been drinking when he hit her. She remembered how the floor had tilted, and then she heard the crack of the coffee table against her head.

It had happened a lifetime ago, and yet she'd never confessed the shameful secret to anyone, not even to her mother. But in Diana's case, it happened only once. She'd kicked Robert out of the house that very night and filed for divorce the very next day. Unlike Amy, she'd never blamed herself for her husband's misconduct. Yet after all these years, it still hurt, so she was more determined than ever to help her new friend.

The dark glasses were back in place when Amy returned, and Diana decided to try a lighter approach. "Did you read the book your father gave you?"

104

Amy looked blank, but then she remembered. "Oh yeah, *The Yearling*. Would you believe I misplaced it, Diana? I reckon it'll turn up…"

"Yes, I'm sure it will." Diana was shocked. She never would've lost something her father gave her, especially a gift that turned out to be a deathbed bequest. "Speaking of things being lost…" she continued. "Guess who's taking care of your father's dog?"

"What dog? Daddy never had no dog. He hated all animals, 'less you could cook 'em up and serve 'em for dinner. Bobby and me always wanted a puppy, but Daddy wouldn't hear of us havin' no pets. Once when the geese come in from the lake and got in his garden, he shot 'em all. Shot the ducks too, and they wasn't even…"

"Please stop!" Diana interrupted. "But let's say your father *did* have a dog, would you like to have it?"

"I told you, Daddy didn't have no dog. Even if he did, I couldn't take it. Roger hates dogs worse'n Daddy did."

Why wasn't she surprised? Undoubtedly, Amy's twins had also enjoyed a pet-free childhood. She found herself hating Roger Keene more with each passing minute. "What does your husband do for a living?"

"Long story. When I met him, he was a trucker for a furniture company in High Point. He's been a driver for one company or another ever since, till two years ago…" Amy hesitated.

Last night Matthew had told her what happened two years ago. After stealing several loads of furniture from his employer and moonlighting for extra cash, Roger had spent five years in prison. He was paroled for *good behavior,* but his

105

criminal record made him virtually unemployable in the furniture industry.

Amy sighed and continued. "After a spell, Roger saved up the down payment for a truck of his own. Now he mostly goes around to the outlets and takes in closeouts...seconds, you know? Then he sells them direct to offices, or to folks in them rich neighborhoods."

Matthew had told it a little differently: Roger had gotten his down payment by putting Amy to work as a night waitress at Denny's, a job she still held. Roger's tactics were strictly *hit and run*. He would knock on some sucker's door, close a deal, and then disappear around the block before his mark discovered the goods were damaged.

"Tell the honest truth," Amy continued. "He's not much of a salesman. That's why he's so hateful at times. He's way behind on the truck payments, and with our boy set on college..."

Tears gathered in Amy's eyes, and Diana steered the conversation away from poor Roger's lack of business acumen. "It'll all work out, you'll see. Once we get the estate settled and sell your father's land, your worries will be over."

Amy took up a fresh napkin and smiled. "Sure hope so, Diana. Thanks so much for meeting me here today."

"No problem. Why didn't you want to meet at my office?"

A flash of fear crossed her face. "I told you before, Roger's funny about all this. He don't want me talkin' to you, and Dennis would tell Roger, sure as you're born. Roger would kill me if he knew we was meeting like this."

Kill? There it was again. The very thought of Roger had put Amy into another panic. Roger was getting in Diana's way, too. "Does your husband mistrust me because I'm a woman, or is there some other reason why he doesn't want us to do business together?"

"I don't want to talk about it."

With that, Amy slipped a generous tip onto the table and hurried towards the cash register. Their lunch was definitely over, and what had Diana accomplished? Other than packing in upwards of a thousand calories? Absolutely nothing.

FIFTEEN

A little misunderstanding...

Before Diana could protest, Amy paid the bill and escaped into the blinding afternoon sun. Diana was hot on her heels, shucking her blazer as the heat hit her. "Wait!" she called, but the plea was unnecessary, for as she struggled out of her second sleeve, she bumped full force into Amy's back.

Amy gripped her arm. "Oh my God! Help me!"

"What's wrong?" Her terror was contagious. Diana followed her gaze across the parking lot, to where a dazzling black cab and silver semi-trailer idled with its engine running.

"It's Roger, don't you see? He followed me here."

Stalked her, more like it. Amy's fingernails bit into her arm as they huddled together. The truck had a vanity plate: *Roger's Rig.* Stenciled across the trailer's walls: *Deals on wheels---wholesale furniture---discount direct to your door.*

Sure enough, the little weasel she'd met at Jed's funeral hopped down from the cab and sauntered towards them. He took his time, making each step in his platform cowboy boots count for a full measure of terror. She glanced at Amy, whose face was drained of all color. When Diana looked back at Roger, she noticed his snide grin revealed a sinister gap between his two front teeth.

Under different circumstances, she would have laughed at the little rooster's show of bravado, but as things were, she wanted to turn tail and run, dragging Amy along with her.

"Well, well, lookee here…" Roger drawled. "If it ain't my lil' wife and the real estate lady. Didn't I tell you to steer clear of this woman?" He shoved at them, breaking them apart.

"Leave us alone, Roger," Amy squeaked. "We was only eatin' lunch together."

"*We was only eatin' lunch together,*" he mimicked in a rude, high-pitched voice. He stepped in close and grabbed Amy's wrists, twisting hard.

"Back off, Roger!" Diana stepped between them.

"Shut up and mind your own business, lady!" He shoved hard, causing her to stumble into a parked car. "I reckon I'll do as I see fit with my own wife."

She looked on in horror as he pinned both of Amy's wrists in one hand and delivered a sharp slaps to both sides of her face. Amy cried out and tears rolled down her cheeks. Her agony goaded him on, inspiring bolder atrocities as he gripped Amy's shoulders and shook until her bones rattled.

Diana cast around looking for a pipe, a stick, any object to bash the bastard's head to a pulp. And then she remembered the crowbar stashed behind the seat in Matthew's truck.

At the same moment, she spotted the chubby deputy leaving the café. "Over here, Doug!" she screamed. "Please help us!"

It all happened so quickly, she didn't know how much the deputy had actually witnessed. Everything shifted to slow motion as he ran across the lot, his hand on his holstered pistol.

First Amy melted, onto the hood of a blue car. Then Roger seemed to vanish before their eyes. Common sense told Diana that he'd climbed back into his truck, because the rig was pulling away fast. Next someone was shouting into her ear.

"Are you all right, ma'am?" Doug helped Diana up from the pavement. "Did that guy hit you?"

She wasn't sure. She thought maybe she'd fallen on her own. Mostly she was relieved to see Amy still in one piece, supported on the deputy's arm.

"Was that man harassing you ladies?"

"Harassing?" Diana fumed. "Try criminal assault! That *man* was this woman's *husband,* and he was beating her to death!"

The young officer blinked and stared at Amy. "That guy your husband? Is it true what she said? Was he trying to hurt you?"

Amy began to hyperventilate. "No, it wasn't like that! We was just havin' a little misunderstanding. It was all my fault."

Diana's mouth fell open in disbelief. She stifled an urge to wring Amy's neck. "Look at her face, officer." Any fool could see the red imprint of Roger's fingers on Amy's cheeks.

Doug squinted, then frowned. "It appears your *little misunderstanding* got a mite rough. Would you like to press charges, ma'am?"

"No, no!" Amy wailed. "Just go away, you hear? I already said it was my fault!"

The deputy looked to Diana for confirmation, and she rolled her eyes. "*I'll* be happy to press charges."

"No, Diana!" Amy pleaded. "Just forget it, okay?"

In a perfect world, Deputy Doug would have gone after Roger, guns blazing, but as it was, he shook his head and turned back to Diana. "Did the man hit *you,* ma'am?"

Again, she couldn't remember. Damn it! Even she'd wanted to lie, Amy was obviously distressed for her husband's sake. So she pressed her lips together and held her tongue. Like it or not, this was a domestic squabble, and Amy was entitled to her own martyrdom, if that's what she wanted."

"So, no one wants me to follow up on this incident?" Doug asked.

Amy vigorously shook her head, and Diana shrugged. "Guess not."

He looked at Amy. "I'll be on my way, then, but I intend to catch up with your husband and escort him out of town. I'd feel mighty bad if he took a notion to turn around and continue this *little misunderstanding*, know what I mean?"

Even Amy did not argue with the deputy's decision to escort Roger out of town. They watched in silence as he walked around the restaurant to his patrol car and drove away, but then Diana turned on Amy.

"Shame on you!" She latched onto Amy's arm and dragged her to Matthew's truck. She opened the passenger door, boosted her up, and locked her in. "We both know what happened out there, and now we're going to discuss it."

By the time Diana climbed into the driver's seat, her temper had cooled, but only a fraction. She yanked the dark glasses off Amy's nose and searched her frightened blue eyes.

"Good Lord…" Diana said. "What *are* we going to do with you?"

SIXTEEN

Go directly to jail...

Ruby purred contentedly as Diana pulled into a parking space across from the Hall of Justice. She suspected Matthew had supplied more than a new battery to coax this surge of pep out of her old car. He'd also washed her, waxed her, and detailed her interior. All Diana had done in return was fill up his gas tank before swapping vehicles, so she was already feeling obligated before she'd asked for the enormous favor that brought her here today. And he had accepted without a moment's hesitation.

Monday morning, ten o'clock, the gleaming new Hall of Justice bustled with activity. Only a few years ago Statesville, the Iredell County Seat, had been a sleepy little town with no money to build a municipal complex of this magnitude. The lake and sudden prosperity had changed all that, and if the big new prison was any indication, the boom had also grown a new crop of crime for the area.

She searched the parking lot for Matthew's truck. She'd gotten herself into this, but at least she wouldn't have to face the ordeal alone. But where was he? They had agreed to meet at ten sharp, and she was only a few minutes late. Was Matthew already inside? Not likely. His pickup was nowhere in sight, and it was his damned truck that got her into this predicament in the first place.

It had begun the moment she locked Amy into the truck, after the dreadful incident at Carolina Bell Café:

"Lord have mercy, this is Trout's truck! Why on earth are *you* drivin' it, Diana?"

She'd tried to sidestep the issue. "We were talking about Roger. You can't let him to treat you this way."

A knowing twinkle sparked in Amy's teary eyes. "You can't fool me. I know Trout better than most, and he don't lend out his precious truck to anyone, let alone a woman."

"Roger's behavior is criminal abuse." She refused to be side-tracked. "I know people who can help you..."

But Amy's mind continued to race down the wrong track, she was on a roll. "I ain't seen Trout with a woman since his wife died. I can't believe it! Are you dating him, Diana?"

"Mr. Troutman is fixing my car, that's all. His truck is a loaner."

"Yeah right," she scoffed. "Hard to see the two of you together, but they say opposites attract."

Amy had jumped to all the wrong conclusions, and one thing led to another. When she found out Diana intended to switch vehicles with Matthew soon, she made a request. Since Amy and Matthew were such good friends, she decided that Matthew and Diana should visit Bobby in jail. She wanted them to get the release Amy required to proceed with the sale of her father's land.

Oddly, it had made sense to Matthew, too. Though he still thought Diana should steer clear of the trouble, in the end he agreed they would go together. And he had promised: *I'll be with you each step of the way.*

So where the hell was he?

A patrol car pulled up beside her in the parking lot and a young officer stepped out. He wore an ominous uniform: black shirt, black gun and heavy black boots. But when he peered curiously into her car and tipped his cap, he was just a rosy-faced kid.

"Morning, ma'am. Can I help?"

Did she look lost? Was she this Boy Scout's good deed for the day? "I'm looking for the jail." The word "jail" stuck in her throat, and she felt extremely nervous. She'd never visited a prison before, so maybe she was entitled to the jitters.

"You've come to the right place." He gestured towards a sprawling white stucco structure connected to the Hall of Justice. "I'm headed there now. Can I show you the way?"

"No thanks, I'm waiting for someone."

He smiled and lumbered off, his gun belt jangling and his boots creaking, leaving her alone once again. She should have gone with the officer, because it was ten fifteen, and they were late for their appointment. Silently cursing Matthew, she decided she'd have to do this thing alone. She exited the truck, and putting one foot before the other, made her way towards the jail.

Like most folks, her only knowledge of prison protocol came from the movies. Naturally, it held a grim fascination, but her knees turned to jelly when a guard passed her through a metal detector, searched her purse, and then waved her inside. Matthew had made advance arrangements with Sheriff Bearfoot over the weekend. Apparently getting an interview with Bobby was serious business, and she dreaded facing him alone.

She walked down a concrete ramp to a door, took a deep breath, and then pushed into the visitor's lounge. She found herself standing in a small waiting room, sparsely furnished with several rows of steel office chairs with blue upholstered seats. A handful of people were scattered about in the chairs. A little girl, who was waiting with her mother, waved a doll at Diana, and in turn her teenaged brother, with elaborate dread locks, scowled at Diana. The brother wore a Snoop Dog T- shirt and had gang tattoos on his upper arms.

An eerie hush filled the space. Except for a large sign stating that visitors and their belongings could be searched at will, the place resembled a bus station, with the usual complement of weary travelers.

"You have to sign in, ma'am." The muffled voice came through little holes in a Plexiglas window.

As she approached the booth-like office and peered through the dark glass, she saw a female officer with a pen poised above a register book.

The woman frowned. "You have an appointment?"

Evidently she didn't look like one of the regulars. "Yes, I'm Diana Rittenhouse. I'm here to see Bobby Porter."

"No shit?" The woman giggled. "You hear that, Ricky? Bobby's got *another* girlfriend lined up."

Ricky stepped from the shadows at the back of the office and entered the lobby through a steel door. "Aren't you the lady from the parking lot?"

The Boy Scout she'd met outside was laughing at some private joke, and obviously she was the brunt of their humor. "What's so funny?" she demanded.

"Sorry, it's just that some other gal's in with Porter right now, and I was saying, *what's Bobby got, I ain't got?* Get it?"

The woman inside the booth said, "Where's Matthew Troutman? He's supposed to be here, too."

115

Diana emphatically agreed. At the same time, someone knocked on the other side of a white steel door to her left, which Ricky quickly opened.

"Okay, Mrs. Rittenhouse, it's your turn now…"

As she moved towards the door, a small woman exploded out from behind it, bumping into her full force.

"Shit!" The woman's dark eyes sparked. "Excuse me!"

Ricky faced the woman. "Slow down, lady. You couldn't wait to get in, now you can't wait to get out." He winked at Diana. "You *sure* you want to see Mr. Porter, Mrs. Rittenhouse?"

Before she'd recovered her balance, the female dynamo spun around: "You're here for Bobby? Who the hell are *you*?"

She spoke with a Mexican accent. She wore high heels, tight jeans, and a low cut halter-top. An antique gold locket dangled conspicuously in her cleavage, compelling Diana to stare.

"What do you want with my Bobby?" The woman yanked a pack of cigarettes from her waistband and lit up.

"Hey, no smoking!" Ricky warned.

She gave him a *screw you* look and kept on puffing, blowing smoke into Diana's eyes. "What do you want with my Bobby?" she repeated.

A little pulse began twitching under Diana's left eyelid, a sure sign she was about to do something she'd later regret. She dragged her gaze away from the woman's bosom and looked calmly into her flashing eyes.

"Not that it's any of your business, but Bobby's sister asked me to visit."

"Well, fuck Amy! Fuck the whole damned family! They don't give a shit about Bobby!"

"Watch your language, lady." Ricky plucked the cigarette out from between the woman's lips. "Now step aside and let Mrs. Rittenhouse pass, you hear?"

Ignoring the officer, the woman pushed in close and glared at Diana through a cascade of raven black hair hanging nearly to her waist. "You're a lawyer, right? Amy and her asshole husband want to get their greedy hands on Jed's money, right?"

Close up, she could smell the woman—a distinct, acrid odor she couldn't identify. Then she realized the girl reeked of the chemicals used to give permanents. Yet her hair was ironing-board straight.

"No, I am not a lawyer." She pushed past the obnoxious woman.

At the same time, Ricky took Diana's elbow with one hand, while clumsily fingering the smoldering cigarette with the other. Finally, he dropped the butt onto the floor and ground it out with his boot. "I'll clean it up later," he apologized, blushing furiously. "But first I'll take you in to Bobby, okay?"

As the heavy steel door clanged shut behind them, she was almost relieved. The space they next entered was glaringly bright, no wider than a closet. More like a long, windowless, concrete box that made her instantly claustrophobic. Six interview stations and a narrow stainless steel shelf ran the length of the wall. Each station included its own privacy wings, a sealed window the size of a microwave oven, and a small round steel seat affixed to the floor on a pod. Black phones were mounted beside each window. The place was unnaturally cold and smelled like fear, and as the walls closed in, she gripped Ricky's arm.

"Don't worry, ma'am," he gently reassured her. "You'll be okay, and no one will disturb you. Usually these seats are filled during visiting hours, but that's all changed since Porter got here."

She remembered the little girl with the doll and her tattooed brother. "But what about the others? They were waiting before I got here."

"To be honest, ma'am..." He lowered his voice. "We don't get many murder suspects, and it doesn't hurt to take precautions. Besides, we have a room just like this one on the other side of the lobby. Long as Porter's housed with us, those other folks will meet their kin over there."

She sank onto one of the stools, feeling light-headed. Was Bobby Porter that dangerous?

The young officer touched her shoulder. "Don't worry. You're perfectly safe, Mrs. Rittenhouse. The prisoner can't get to you. He can't even hear you unless you pick up one of those phones. The glass is bullet-proof, so nothing bad can happen."

For the first time, she dared to peek through the window. Much to her horror, a violent struggle was taking place as a man in an orange jumpsuit wrestled another man into a seat directly across from her.

"The guy in the orange suit is a trustee," Ricky explained. "The other guy is Porter. Looks like he doesn't want to talk to you. His last visitor must've pissed him off."

If Bobby didn't want to see her, then she wanted to see him even less. She groaned as his face swam into view and stared angrily into her eyes. She felt like she was peering into an aquarium, because the creature seated across from her looked for all the world like a pale, slack-jawed fish.

Ricky rapped on the glass to get the prisoner's attention, and then he gestured for Bobby to pick up the phone. Next, he handed a phone to Diana. "You're all set now, ma'am. I'll leave you two alone to do your thing." He smiled and retreated. "Remember, just holler if you need me."

With that, the heavy door closed, leaving her alone with a man clad in black and white stripes. She prayed her head would clear and begged the little pulse under her left eyelid to cease its infernal twitching.

She did not anticipate a pleasant chat.

She forced herself to focus. The man was wary and hostile, with a day's growth of whiskers on his sunken cheeks. Those eyes! Where had she seen them before? They were deep blue and fathomless, like Amy's, yet infinitely more sinister. She recalled an old table by lamplight and an elderly man with thick glasses seated across from her, like Bobby was right now. That was it! The abyss, the evil. This man was Jedidiah Porter, come back from the dead.

The unhappy prisoner picked up his phone, raised his thick eyebrows, and scowled. "Where's Trout?" he growled into the receiver.

"I'm sure he's on his way," she stuttered. "But in the meantime, my name is Diana Rittenhouse. Your sister, Amy, asked me to see you."

For a fleeting moment, she sensed a softening in Bobby's eyes, but just as quickly, those eyes became flat, simmering pools.

"Amy sent you. So what?" He abruptly hung up the phone.

The interview was over

SEVENTEEN

A pack of lies…

Matthew saw Diana's old Subaru parked in the lot and knew he had no time to lose. Of all days to be late! He sprinted down the ramp towards the Hall of Justice and cursed Bearfoot for playing phone tag all morning, for making him late. Once he'd finally connected with the sheriff and tried to get a bead on Bobby's situation, Wayne kept stalling:

"Wayne, I love you like a brother, but will you please give me a straight answer? Has Bobby been charged, or not?"

Bearfoot mumbled through a mouthful of breakfast. "The judge got an Affidavit of Probable Cause over the weekend, and I suspect the arraignment's happening about now."

"You mean *right* now? This morning? Diana and I are meeting Bobby at ten."

"I know that, Trout. I'm the one who set it up, remember?" He gulped some coffee. "Don't worry, it'll be over by the time you get there."

"How bad is it?"

Reluctantly, Bearfoot had detailed the damaging evidence compiled against Bobby. "What it all boils down to? It don't look good for your boy."

Without actually breaking into a run, Matthew rushed through security and shoved through the door to the visitor's lounge, nearly toppling a woman who was making a hurried exit.

"Oh, sorry…" He lifted his arm and held the door open as the tiny woman ducked underneath. At the same time, he recognized her. "You're Juanita, right?"

Bobby had brought Juanita to his store a couple of times, but from the blank look on her face, Matthew had not made a strong impression. "I own Trout's Place out on River Highway. Don't you remember me?"

She ignored his extended hand.

"So, how's Bobby?" he persisted. "You've been to see him, right?"

"How the hell should he be?" She spat out the words. "And if you're planning a visit, you better buy a ticket. There's some woman in with him now."

Matthew's heart plunged. Diana had gone in without him, and she'd be hopping mad. She'd chew him up and spit him out, and who could blame her? He shoved past Bobby's truculent girlfriend, leaving her to deal with her own devils, and then he tapped on the receptionist's window.

"I'm Matthew Troutman…"

"Your friend's already inside with Porter." A young guard said, and then led him through a steel door. "I know she'll be happy to see you."

He sure hoped so. He felt suddenly claustrophobic, jammed against a wall of windows, standing under glaring lights, yet all he saw was Diana—the defeated slope of her shoulders, her phone held mid-air. Beyond the glass wall, a man in orange was leading Bobby away.

"Hey, wait!" He rushed to the glass and pounded hard. And then, in suspended animation, the prisoner turned and saw him, his mouth slack with confusion. When Bobby started back towards the glass, Diana put down her phone and locked eyes with Matthew.

"Glad you could make it." Her voice dripped sarcasm.

In a flood of tenderness and shame, he longed to close the space between them and fold her into his arms. He'd known her only a short time, but her spirit and strong will were as welcome as a long lost friend. Yet he couldn't bring himself to touch her. Instead, he sensed her fear, her defeat and felt guiltier than ever.

"I'm so sorry, Diana…" Any excuse sounded lame, under the circumstances. He lowered himself onto a steel stool and searched her face. Across the glass, Bobby gestured wildly for him to pick up the phone.

"Use mine…" Diana sighed.

Their fingers brushed as he accepted the phone. Was that a smile tugging at the corner of her mouth? He fiddled with the buttons and managed to change the phone to speaker, so they both could hear what Bobby had to say for himself.

"Hey, Bobby…" Matthew began. "I see you already met my friend, Diana. Mind if she listens?"

Bobby scowled. "Don't know, man. Amy sent her. What the hell does Amy want after all these years?"

"Let's all talk, and maybe you'll find out."

Bobby eyed Diana suspiciously, his mouth compressed. Finally, he relented. "If she's your friend, I reckon she's okay. But I'll only talk to you."

Diana moved away, assuming the role of passive listener.

"You sure *they* ain't listenin', Trout?" Bobby whispered. "Maybe they have one of them recorders planted somewhere."

"I think it's okay, Bobby. Lawyers talk to clients here all the time. It's against the law to listen in." He wouldn't have spoken with such assurance if he hadn't asked Bearfoot the same question that morning. Even so, Bobby's paranoia was contagious, and Matthew wasn't sure anyone should trust the cops.

Bobby leaned close to the glass. "No one knows about the dog, right?"

"Well, Diana met Ursie. They get on like fire and brushwood."

Bobby snorted his displeasure. "Well, don't go tellin' no one else. They're makin' up a pack of lies. They need a fall guy real bad, and I'm it."

Matthew said, "They found your fingerprints, Bobby. They were all over Jed's house, even on the coffee can."

"*Coffee can?*" Diana snickered.

Bobby's lip curled in a snarl. "What do the dumb cops expect? I grew up in that friggin' house. Of course, they found my fingerprints."

"They found *fresh* fingerprints, buddy. They can tell the difference."

"So what?"

"I hate to break this to you, but Sheriff Bearfoot spoke to your girlfriend, Juanita. She told him you went to Jed's the night of the murder to steal money from a coffee can."

Bobby's face went dead white. "She wouldn't do that.'"

"I'm afraid she did. After you were arrested, she tried to take it back, but the damage was already done."

Bobby groaned. He slumped in his chair and stared at the ceiling. Matthew glanced at Diana and saw her forehead creased with concern, her eyes filled with a question.

He dragged his attention back to Bobby. "Listen carefully. I can't help you unless you tell me the truth. Understand?" He nodded, his face a study in misery. "You visited your daddy's farm the night he died, right?"

He nodded.

Diana's fingers reached under the shelf. She gripped Matthew's knee.

"Did you steal money from a coffee can?"

Bobby nodded again.

Diana dug in hard and pressed her lips against Matthew's ear. "Should we be hearing this? If he confesses, we'll be obliged to tell the authorities."

"No, we will not." He took her hand and held firm. "Whatever he says here goes no farther, agreed?"

"But, I…"

"If you don't agree, Diana, you should leave right now." He held his breath, kept a steady grip on her hand. He prayed his instincts were right, prayed she wouldn't leave.

In the meantime, Bobby became increasingly agitated. His pallor was replaced with a red blotchiness around his eyes. He roared into his mouthpiece. "Hey, talk so I can hear you, or I'll get that ape to take me back to my cell!"

"Easy, Bobby," Matthew softly urged. "You can trust us, can't he, Diana?"

She exhaled. "Yes, you can trust us, Bobby. I promise not to tell anyone."

She turned to Matthew, as if to say: *there, are you satisfied?*

The hard knot in Matthew's chest eased. He let go of her hand and mouthed a silent *thank you.* Then he tried again. "Did you see your daddy the night he died?"

Bobby squeezed his eyes shut, shrugged his shoulders, and opened his hands. Matthew looked to Diana for guidance, but she too seemed nonplussed by the drama being played out behind the glass.

"Did you see Jed, or not, Bobby?"

Bobby leaned so close he was almost kissing the glass, then mouthed the words, *He was already dead.*

Diana gasped, and Matthew was jolted speechless. They stared at Bobby in disbelief.

"You sure?" Matthew asked at last.

Bobby's laugh was sharp and bitter. "Course, I'm sure. A man don't make a mistake 'bout somethin' like that. You sure it's safe to talk?"

At that point, he wasn't sure of anything, but he urged Bobby to continue.

Bobby shot a warning glance at Diana, then hunched over the phone and shaded his mouth. His words were barely audible—eerie, muffled, raspy.

"I know'd somethin' was wrong soon as I come up on the porch and the door was hangin' open. Daddy always locked up, like the whole world was fixin' to steal him blind. Inside, everything was too quiet, you know? But I didn't call out to him. I just walked to the cupboard and took out the can."

"How much money did you take?" Matthew asked.

Bobby's eyes narrowed to slits. "Don't matter. Took the whole roll of bills and stuffed it in my pocket."

Matthew glanced at Diana. She lowered her eyes and shook her head. He decided not to press about the money. "Then what?" he prompted.

"If I'd had the sense of a mule, I'd a high-tailed it outta there, but I'm curious, you know? I figured Daddy was out in the shed, but then this crazy dog come to the door. She was barkin' and carryin' on like she was fixin' to bite my leg off....

"I'd seen that dog a time or two in town, waitin' in the old man's truck. She wouldn't go away. She kept on barkin' and runnin' into the yard, like she wanted me to go with her, you know? Well, like a fool, I followed her down to the dock..."

Bobby got quiet and stared into his lap. When he lifted his eyes, they were filled with tears.

"Damn it, Trout..." He choked. "Daddy was just layin' there face down in the shallows. His arms was spread wide open, like Jesus on the cross. He looked kinda peaceful, with the waves rockin' him against the shore...

"Then the dog run into the water, whinin' and cryin' and pawin' at Daddy's coat. I climbed down over the rocks and waded into the water with my shoes on. First off, I was scared to touch him. But then I rolled him over and he stared right up into my eyes. I swear, Trout, he looked alive and as mad as always, like he was about to lift his fists and start beatin' on me, you know?

"Of course, I seen he was dead, but I scrambled up them rocks and watched a spell—just to make sure. All the while that crazy dog stayed in the water and kept lickin' Daddy's face."

Diana was trembling. Matthew reached out and took her hand. "I'm so sorry, Bobby. What do you think happened?"

"When I come to my senses, I seen one of the oars from the rowboat floatin' in the weeds. Then I went out on the dock and seen the other oar was still in the boat. I figured Daddy was goin' fishin'. He maybe dropped one of the oars, reached out to fetch it, then fell in and hit his head."

"Did you see anything else?"

Bobby hesitated, and then shrugged. "Found an old locket. Don't rightly know what it was doin' there, but it caught the sun and sparkled real pretty. It was wedged between the boards, and when I pulled it out, the chain was broke."

"You broke the chain?" He didn't know why it mattered, but Bobby's story was getting more bizarre by the moment.

"It was already broke," Bobby insisted. "Don't know what my old man was doin' with a trinket like that."

"Maybe it didn't belong to your father," Diana piped in excitedly. "Maybe it belonged to the murderer. If he dropped it there, it's an important piece of evidence."

Matthew squeezed her hand. The idea was far-fetched, but who knew? He fixed on Bobby. "What did the locket look like?"

Bobby grinned ear to ear. "It's one of them sweetheart lockets, with a gold heart. You keep one, and your girlfriend keeps the other, you know? I seen such things at yard sales, and this one was real old. I reckon it's worth a pretty penny, if one was to sell it."

"What else about the locket, Bobby?" Diana seemed hooked. She released Matthew's hand and rummaged through her purse. Taking out a pen and a notepad, she sketched a jagged heart on a chain and pressed it against the glass so Bobby could see. "Did it look like this?"

Bobby squinted. "Yeah, that's it, only it had a little red ruby up in one corner and engraved initials on the backside."

"What were the initials?" Matthew and Diana chimed in unison.

"C- R- A. I can see them letters plain as day"

"Were there periods after each letter, or were they part of a name?" Diana was drawing *C* and *R* and *A* in various combinations on her little pad.

"Don't remember nothin' else." Bobby frowned. "Ain't that enough?"

"Where is this locket?" Matthew asked.

He clamped his mouth shut and crossed his arms.

"C'mon. Did you tell Bearfoot about the locket?" Bobby was stubborn as molasses in January, but they'd gotten this far, now he wanted the whole story.

Bobby snorted. "I may be dumb, but I'm not stupid. Tell the cops I stole the money? Tell 'em I took the locket and fled the scene? Shit, Trout. They'd throw away the key."

"Well, maybe they *should* throw away the key. Where's the damn locket, Bobby?" He wanted to reach through the glass and shake some sense into him.

Diana squirmed on her stool. "Wait, Matthew, I know where it is. He gave it to his girlfriend. I bumped into her as she was leaving, and she was wearing that very locket around her neck."

Bobby glared at Diana. "Yeah, I gave Juanita the locket. So what? While I was holed up at the Days Inn, my face was in all the papers, on TV too. Nosey maid who cleaned my room was the one turned me in. She was a snoopy bitch, so I packed up the money *and* the locket and mailed them to Juanita at Sylvan Acres."

Matthew groaned. "Smart move. That's the last you'll see of the money *or* the locket."

"Screw you, Trout! What do you know? Juanita loves me. When she come by just now, she told me she'd already paid off the loan on my lawn equipment. Every penny. Plus, she went out and bought a new chain for the locket. It looked real pretty, too."

Matthew sighed. "Okay, I hope you two live happily ever after, but you still have to tell the cops."

"In your dreams, man. What's done is done." Bobby wasn't budging.

"Okay, what happened after you found your daddy?"

He rolled his eyes. "I pulled the dog off Daddy and put her in my truck. Couldn't just leave her to starve, could I? I did see other tire tracks in the drive, but after all that rain, they was a muddy mess. So I split and brought the dog to you. End of story."

"Did you make a phone call?" Diana gently inquired.

Bobby's eyes widened.

"Sheriff Bearfoot said someone called 911," she continued. "Was it you, Bobby?"

He let out a long breath. "Couldn't just leave Daddy like that, could I?"

The three sat in silence, watching one another.

At last Bobby spoke. "This morning a judge said I'll have to stand trial."

"Yeah, I know," Matthew said. "That was your arraignment, Bobby. The preliminary hearing comes next."

"Whatever..." He stared at the floor. "I'm in deep shit, Trout. Will you help me?"

"Not unless you tell the sheriff exactly what you just told me."

Bobby lifted his eyes, the eyes of a hunted animal. "Please, Trout."

He paused, hating the next step. "I'll help you, if you help Amy. She's asked Diana to represent her, and they need some papers signed..."

Diana kicked him under the table and vigorously shook her head. Seemed she'd decided it wasn't the time or place to conduct business, but he pressed on anyway. "Amy wants your permission to sell your daddy's land…"

He signaled Diana to hand over the waiver papers. At first she didn't comply, but he reassured her with a firm nod of his head. Finally, she fished the forms from her purse. He held them up for Bobby to see. "I'll leave these with the guard. You sign, then we'll talk. Understand?"

Bobby neither confirmed nor denied as he stood and signaled the guard.

Clearly blackmail was not ideal between friends, but Matthew knew no other way.

He took Diana's arm and guided her into the perfect April day. The sunlight was warm on his face, the air brisk and clean as they escaped to freedom. It felt strange, and very good, to have a woman on his arm. Diana was taller than his wife had been, and she walked with long, graceful strides. Her perfume, a hint of jasmine in the breeze, intoxicated his senses, and it was great to be alive.

"You didn't have to do that," she told him. "It could have waited."

"It's done. I did it for Amy, as well as for you. We'll have to wait and see what he does."

"Thanks, Matthew."

He breathed deeply of the day. "Lord, how can Bobby stand it? I'd go crazy being locked up, even for an hour."

"Yes, well…" When she smiled, little sun creases gathered around her amazing blue eyes. "Maybe Bobby deserves to be locked up."

Throughout the interview, he'd sensed her skepticism, but he knew Bobby was innocent. He'd stake his life on it. But the evidence against him, motive and opportunity coupled with his truculent attitude, did little to inspire confidence. Bobby was his own worst enemy, but he didn't deserve to be caged like a wild animal. Maybe he could convince her over a meal?

He screwed up his courage. "Listen, Diana, there's this great Chinese restaurant out near the highway. Want some lunch?"

Her laugh was deep and throaty. It filled him with joy. "Wish I could, Matthew, but it's my afternoon to sit floor time. Give me a rain check?"

Suddenly he felt very old, and the warmth went out of the sun. He'd lost the knack for this kind of thing. Maybe he shouldn't have tried? He walked Diana to her car and opened the door for her.

She laughed "Wow. Nobody's done that for me in years. I thought old-fashioned manners had gone out of style."

He brushed a lock of pale hair off her forehead. "That's me—old fashioned and out of style," he mumbled as she fastened her seatbelt and pulled the door shut.

She winked, then twisted the ignition. The old Subaru's engine jumped to life. He'd spent two hours tuning that car, all new plugs and points. At least he was good for something.

"See you later…" he called.

She waved, and he watched until she was out of sight.

Then he crossed the street to do what he should've done instead of tripping all over his big feet asking for a date. As he entered American Bail Bonds, he calculated his life savings. Bearfoot had already hinted it would cost a small fortune to free Bobby, should he be held over after the preliminary hearing. The judge had set a figure for the bail, but he had to hear the bad news for himself.

"Hey, buddy…?" he asked the man across the desk. "Can you phone the Court House and find out how much it's gonna cost me to spring a fellow out of jail?"

EIGHTEEN

Danger becomes you ...

"Who the hell do you think you are, *Nancy Drew*?" Liz grumbled.

"What a surprise! I thought Nancy Drew was before your time. My mother read those books when she was a little girl."

"Yeah? Well I watch the new series on Prime," Liz smirked. "But if you expect me to go along with your crazy scheme, think again."

Diana loved teasing Liz, and she'd had the upper hand all morning. First she'd described her assault by Amy's enraged husband, then her evening at Matthew's, and finally, her trip to the jail. Liz couldn't believe any of it. She'd given Diana a hard time about Matthew, asking if they'd had sex, but she was seriously impressed by Diana's dances with danger. Beneath her bluster, she was jealous, and this gave Diana's fragile ego a boost.

They were driving Liz's car, on official real estate business, but Diana was behind the wheel, so she was boss. "Where's your sense of adventure?" she pressed. "Isn't this more fun than the weekly Tour?"

Every Wednesday Crawford Real Estate agents teamed up in shared cars to visit the newly listed homes in their inventory. The idea was to preview each house and come up with the best sales strategy. Over the years, Diana had been there, done that, so she was bored sick with the routine. Plus they were required to wear their perky little Crawford Realty blazers, which was doubly annoying.

"Danger becomes you, Diana," Liz said as Diana parked outside The House of Beauty. "But I still think you're nuts."

Maybe so, but she hadn't felt so alive in years. That morning she'd eaten Godiva chocolates and whistled in the shower. Matthew was a big part of her happiness, to be sure, but the action and excitement addicted her like a drug. She couldn't wait for her next fix.

Liz frowned at the beauty salon. "Bad idea. Don't expect me to go in with you."

The noonday sky was bruised yellow. A fitful wind sent clouds streaking across the horizon as the weather tried to make up its mind. With some basic sleuthing, Diana had discovered where Juanita Cruz worked, so she was high on her detective abilities.

"This is none of your business, Diana. Can't you leave it to the police?"

Fair question. Matthew had promised Bobby they'd keep the secrets he'd confided at the jail, and she intended to keep that promise. She'd given Liz only enough information to string her along, and scare her to death. But Diana had also promised to help Amy, so unless she screwed up the courage to enter the beauty salon, she couldn't help anyone.

She jabbed Liz in the ribs. "Remember what I said about Juanita's big boobs? Aren't you the least bit curious?" Liz prized her large bosom, so any competition in that department piqued her interest.

"Okay, you win. I'll check her out." Liz jumped from the car, slamming the door behind her. "But don't let this woman give you a manicure. If she's half as vindictive as you say, she'll file your fingers off."

Diana's bravado drooped when they came face to face with Juanita behind the counter. Her dark eyes glittered as she recognized Diana.

"What do *you* want?" she snapped.

Liz was focused on the woman's breasts. "Look! She's wearing the locket!"

The comment prompted Juanita to flaunt the gold heart on its cheap chain. She twirled it around her finger and tucked it deep inside her halter blouse, out of sight.

"May I see it?" Diana held out her hand. "Please…?"

Juanita ignored Diana, but turned cold eyes on Liz. Her stare was dry ice as she stepped out from behind the counter and stood breast to breast with Liz.

Liz backed up a few paces, seriously upstaged. "Hey, don't look at *me*. I'm just along for the ride." She scuttled backwards and sank into a chair at the far end of the room.

"Please cooperate, Ms. Cruz." Diana said. "That locket might prove Bobby's innocence. It might even belong to the killer!"

Juanita turned her back and lounged against the counter. When she turned around again, Diana noticed a lethal-looking pair of stylist's scissors resting on the counter. Juanita began spinning them with one blood red fingernail.

"Please believe me," Diana pleaded. "I want to help Bobby. I saw him at the jail, remember?"

Juanita casually picked up the scissors. "Yeah, I remember, Mrs. Real Estate Lady. You don't give a flying fuck about Bobby. I know what you want. He told me all about it. You're working for that bitch, Amy."

Diana's eyelid twitched. She backed away when Juanita stepped forward, scissors in hand.

"Mucho dinero, senora? Si, *I* know. Money, money, money! You forced him to sign his name, and now his sister gets it all." Juanita advanced, lazily snapping the scissors into the air.

Liz jumped from her chair and came to Diana's defense. She grasped Diana's arm and eased her backwards, away from Juanita. "Diana really wants to help..." she squeaked.

"Bobby's a big boy. He can help himself," Juanita hissed. "When he finds out you came here making trouble..." Her eyes smoldered as she inched forward, her knuckles white around her weapon. "He'll be loco, comprende? If I was you, I'd watch my back!"

Diana felt herself being propelled backwards as Liz dragged her towards the door. "Hey, thanks for the hospitality, Juanita," Liz yelled as they made a brisk exit.

Diana trembled with fury as Liz pushed her into the passenger's seat, and then locked the door. Liz floored the accelerator, and they were miles away before she regained enough composure to speak. "Well, that went well."

"Think so?" Liz pounded the steering wheel. "You almost got us killed! Now Bobby will be gunning for you, since his girlfriend didn't manage to stab you first. If Bobby fails, Amy's maniac husband will finish the job."

"If I'm such a liability, then drop me off right now, Liz. You don't want to be in close proximity when the bullets start to fly."

Liz's jaw dropped. "Very funny, but since you offered..." She swerved into the parking lot of a neighborhood shopping center, cut the engine, and then unlocked the door. "Okay, get out, Diana."

"I beg your pardon?"

A smile quivered at the corner of her lips. "Run into Grub Pub, will you? Get me a taco salad for the road. You're buying, right?"

They were at Liz's favorite lunch spot. "I guess I owe you one," Diana muttered.

"You owe me more than one, girlfriend, so move your ass. And take your time, will you...?" Liz took out her cell phone. "I'll call Danny and tell him I won't be home for dinner. We'll finish this stupid Tour, then head out for drinks and dinner. We'll get wasted. You're buying, am I right?"

"Don't push it!" She headed into Lakeside. When she glanced back, she saw Liz talking with Danny. She'd put her phone into its cradle on the dash, and her hands fluttered in animated conversation.

She placed their orders and imagined Danny getting an earful. The episode at The House of Beauty could have escalated to real violence, and she regretted putting Liz in the crossfire. But the girl had a good head on her shoulders, and they made a great team.

She went into the Ladies' Room, swallowed two Tylenols, and then sat at the bar near the cash register to wait for the take-out.

"Mind if I join you, Mrs. Rittenhouse?"

A distinguished-looking, white-haired man in an impeccable custom-tailored suit moved down two stools to sit beside her. Her mind drew a complete blank.

"You don't remember me, do you?" the stranger continued. "I'm Harold Havers from Wells Fargo. We met at a zoning meeting last month."

"Sorry, I didn't recognize you, Mr. Havers."

He laughed. "Don't worry about it. Your Crawford Realty blazer was *my* first clue, and your nametag filled in the blanks." He nodded at Liz's car parked outside the window. "Besides, Corkie and I go back a long way. We've survived many a closing together."

Yes, Harold Havers was a very big fish indeed. He oversaw all the local Wells Fargo branches.

"By the way," he said. "How's Dennis Crawford doing these days? Is he fixing to pack it in, or will you folks tough it out a few more months?"

Her mouth dropped open. She had no idea what he was talking about.

"C'mon, Diana, don't play coy with me. After all, it's no big secret." Harold paused to sip the drink cradled in a napkin on his knee. "Only mystery, far as I'm concerned, is where would Dennis get enough cash to stay in business?"

She smelled alcohol on his breath and realized this pillar of the community was a wee bit tipsy. Her face burned with embarrassment for him, and for herself.

"Everyone knows the land your office sits on is worth a small fortune, what with Jetton Village across the way and commercial development pushing in on both sides. Any banker would jump at a chance to buy Dennis out. Lord knows, I was happy to give Dennis a second mortgage. And not just because his dad, God rest his soul, was a good friend...."

"No, ma'am, lending young Crawford the money was a sound business move." Havers signaled for another drink. "It's too bad, though. Everything the kid touches turns sour—like that cotton mill deal. Dennis' daddy would flip in his grave if he knew my bank was ready to foreclose. It's a crying shame."

Havers had rendered her speechless. Wouldn't she know if her own company was headed for Chapter 11? "Look, I'm sure Dennis has his finances under control."

The banker arched his bushy white eyebrows. "What do you know about his new project, Diana? He claims he's onto something big. If it comes through, then no more worries, he'll be rolling in cash. If you have an inside track on this, I wish you'd share it."

She inched away. His breath smelled like a brewery. "To be honest, I don't know what you're talking about."

"Of course not." He smiled. "I respect your loyalty, Diana."

The gods were watching, and her food arrived before the conversation turned ugly. She made a hasty retreat and tossed the two Styrofoam lunchboxes on the seat of Liz's car. She pointed at Havers, who was making a wobbly exit. "Do you know that obnoxious man?"

Liz squinted. "Sure, that's Happy Harold, the blitzed banker. He's okay when he's sober. In fact, he's an investment wizard. But whoa, after a three martini lunch, watch out!"

"Tell me about it…" She told Liz about her conversation with Havers as they drove to their next listing. "Could there be any truth in what he said?"

Liz wiped taco salad off her lapel with her free hand. "Don't know, but it makes sense, in a weird kind of way. You know Dennis has been acting funny lately. He canceled the cleaning service, and last Sunday morning I saw him out behind the office mowing the grass himself."

"He jumps each time the phone rings," Diana added. "Maybe it's bill collectors." She sipped some iced tea, but the chill made her temples throb. "Havers mentioned a new project. Do you know anything about it?"

"Not really, but last week he hired a locksmith to install a security lock on his desk. He carries the key around everywhere. What's he hiding, Diana?"

"Search me, but I hope it's not as dire as Havers implied. I'm not ready to go job-hunting again. I just got here."

Liz's eyes grew enormous. "Shit! I was going to suggest we skip the afternoon tour, but I've changed my mind. If I'm gonna be out on the street, I plan to sell each and every one of these new listings. So settle back, partner. We still have a long day ahead."

Diana figured the day could only get better.

NINETEEN

Thief in the night...

Boy, was she wrong! The day got worse.

Lightning flashed across the dark sky and the first drops of rain fell the moment Liz dropped her at the office door. Diana needed to pick up some homework, so they'd decided to eat at Tito's, a great little Spanish restaurant right behind Crawford Realty.

"I'll park close as I can," Liz said. "But if it pours, you'll have to make a run for it."

"No problem. I'll join you in a few minutes."

Diana huddled on the covered porch, rummaging through her purse for her office keys. The place was closed for the night, completely dark except for a yellow security light burning in the deserted lobby. Damn! She'd left her keys in Ruby's glove compartment, and her car was parked around back. Now she'd get soaked, along with everything else.

She snaked around the building, hugging the walls beneath the overhang, and slid into Ruby's front seat. Thank heavens for small favors. Ruby's door locks had been broken for years. Otherwise, considering her state of perpetual absent-mindedness, she'd have been left out in the rain more than once.

She ran her fingers through her damp hair and blew her nose. She'd agreed to have dinner with Liz, when all she really wanted was to snuggle up with a good book. Yet, she needed to get out more. Ever since her divorce, she'd been retreating from society. Now even the simple act of enjoying a restaurant with bright lights, chatter, and other members of the human race was a challenge.

As she located her office keys and regretted her antisocial behavior, she noticed that Dennis' silver Lexus was parked beside Ruby. She figured he must be out in a client's car. She also spotted a shiny new Mercedes SUV in Crawford Realty's private lot. Another wealthy client?

Thunder exploded as she dashed to the rear entrance and let herself in. She couldn't locate the light switch, so she stumbled dripping through the dark hall and groped her way to her desk. As she felt along its cluttered surface for her lamp, she saw a flicker of light from the corner of her eye.

She hesitated. Something was amiss. As her eyes adjusted, she saw a watery green glow coming from Dennis' office and decided he must have left his antique desk lamp on by mistake. Yet, as she peered through the smoked glass wall that separated the boss from his underlings, she saw movement.

Diana froze. Clearly she wasn't alone. Two figures were bent over Dennis' desk, and as they moved back and forth in the shadows, she recognized one of the faces. Thank God, it was only Dennis! But why was he here so late? It violated his relaxed work ethic to burn the midnight oil. And why hadn't he turned on the overhead fluorescents?

Fascinated, she kept very still and watched as he lifted something from his drawer. He opened the thing, which appeared to be a large plot plan, then spread it open on the table. The other person, a man in an expensive silk suit, seemed equally engrossed by the plan and kept running his hands across the paper. She still couldn't see the other man's face.

All at once, her heart did flip- flops and she fought an unreasonable urge to hide. Ridiculous. She wasn't a thief in the night. This was her office, too. She had just as much right to be here as Dennis and his guest, so why did she feel like an intruder?

Enough of that nonsense. She snapped on her desk lamp, flooding her room with light. At the same time, the men startled like a bomb had been set off. Dennis' face blanched with fear, and then stiffened with anger as he recognized her. The stranger quickly closed the map and nudged Dennis, who in turn, hastily stashed it into his drawer and slammed it shut.

It all happened so fast. She saw the stranger's face: dark complexion, a tiny scar on his jaw. His hair was jet black and his eyes smoldered like fiery coals. Brantley Craven! She'd met him only once, at Jedidiah's funeral, and once was enough. That day she'd decided she wanted nothing more to do with the man, yet there he was, sauntering towards her like he owned the place.

Dennis was close behind. "What are you doing here, Diana?" he demanded.

"I work here, remember?"

Brantley parked his rump on her desk. "Hey, Dennis, don't complain when one of your employees shows some initiative. Obviously she has nothing better to do than work late."

Rage rose like bile at the back of her throat. "I guess that makes two of us, Mr. Craven. What are *you* doing here?" Not that it was any of her business, but questioning him was more acceptable than ramming her pen into his perfectly creased trouser leg.

Brantley glared at her. If looks could kill, she'd be stone cold dead. But then he smoothly shifted gears. His snarl transformed into a crooked smile, and he chucked her under her chin. "Get a life, lady."

Lucky for him he moved away, because to hell with the pen. She'd select her lethally sharp letter opener as her weapon of choice. At the same time, poor Dennis looked lost. If he didn't deal with Diana's impertinence, he'd lose face. He'd just opened his mouth to chastise her, when an enormous crash shook the walls and jolted all three of them out of their skins.

"What the fuck?" Brantley roared.

It sure as hell wasn't thunder. They all rushed to the window in Dennis' office, for obviously the crash had come from the parking lot. When Dennis rolled up the shade, the scene was sheer bedlam.

"Oh God!" he moaned.

"Fuck!" Brantley cursed.

Both men ran out the door before she could fully process the disaster. She pressed her nose to the glass as chaos reigned in the parking lot. Apparently, an elderly couple had been leaving Tito's in an ancient clunker of a station wagon, when they backed out and crashed into both Dennis' Lexus and Brantley's Mercedes. As luck would have it, Ruby was unscathed. Her old car sat there smiling as the clunker wagon detached itself from the two expensive vehicles, dragging both sets of bumpers along with it.

Diana was delighted. She jumped up and down, whooping and clapping for the beautiful irony. At the tearing of metal, Dennis and Brantley began their own little dance: stomping, cursing and waving their arms.

The elderly husband told his wife to stay in the wagon, while he bravely confronted the two maniacs. He tried to explain how the torrential rain had impeded his vision, but clearly a resolution would take a long time.

This stroke of fate caused Diana to notice Dennis' key lying unattended on his desk. She'd never planned to pick it up, let alone unlock his drawer, but was guided by forces beyond her control. Even as she slipped her hand inside and pulled out the secret map, she knew it was wrong. But as long as she could hear the men shouting outside, she knew she was safe.

Possessed by demons, she took the precaution of not turning on the overhead lights. Instead, she hunkered in the dim glow at Dennis' desk, spread open the document, and quickly oriented herself. Just as she'd suspected, it was a plot plan, a blueprint detailing a major development.

Years of experience allowed her to absorb the details of a plot plan faster than she could read the Sunday funnies. In a glance, she saw that Loftus Company, a firm of architects and landscape artists often employed by Crawford Realty, had designed the plan. In addition, the Brantley Craven Corporation had commissioned the blueprint.

Her pulse raced as she continued to read. Craven Corporation had been hired by—no, this could *not* be true—*Mrs. Amy Keene?* She blinked and read it again. No way! Every instinct told her Amy knew nothing about this plan. Amy would have told her. Why would she lie?

Diana looked more closely. At first the development seemed much like any other resort community, but on a massive scale. It offered a golf course, country club, condominiums, and a neighborhood of single-family residences. It included an upscale shopping center and a yacht club on a lake. *What Lake?*

Before continuing, she glanced out the window. The parking lot drama was still in full swing, so she had more time. But even she couldn't memorize the intricacies of such an ambitious undertaking. She required a duplicate. Rushing down the hall, she turned on the power at the oversize copy machine. *Please, God,* she prayed. *Let it warm up fast.*

While she waited, she squinted at the small print. As she suspected, the lake in question was Lake Norman, and the resort was to be built on an enormous peninsula. A red circle had been hand- drawn on the map, on the site of a future county club. In the same red ink were the words: *site of the former Porter household.*

She gulped for air. She'd already guessed this, of course, but hadn't been prepared for the date printed at the bottom of the plan: January 9th of this year. Dear God! Someone had planned to develop the Porter estate exactly three months before Jedidiah's death!

She nearly stumbled as she raced to the machine and made one copy. She flew to her desk, located her briefcase, and shoved the contraband duplicate inside. Next she sprinted to Dennis' office, peeked out the window, and confirmed that the injured parties were wrapping it up. The gray-haired wife had stepped out of the station wagon to hold an umbrella above her husband's head as everyone exchanged insurance information.

Brantley climbed into a tow truck hitched to his battered Mercedes, while Dennis folded a scrap of paper into his wallet. In a matter of seconds, she'd be caught red-handed.

Then she panicked. She smoothed the original plot plan out on Dennis' desk, but for the life of her, she couldn't fold it in the proper pattern. Blast these maps! Reading them was one thing—getting them back together right was impossible.

To hell with it! She yanked the drawer open, slid the crumpled plan inside, and then shoved the drawer shut. She noted it locked automatically upon closing.

And accomplished all this not a second too soon.

Dennis was stomping on the welcome mat, knocking water off his shoes, and she was determined to replace the desk key exactly where she'd found it. But where was the stupid key? She dropped to her hands and knees and crawled around searching the floor. Nothing.

This couldn't be happening! She remembered seeing the key on its red plastic ring. It had been lying in plain view on Dennis' desk when she first opened the map, so where did it go? She mentally traced the key's imagined trajectory, and then she understood. Dear Lord, what had she done to deserve this? The key had fallen into the drawer along with the map, and the drawer was now locked.

How could she explain her way out of this one? That was easy. Since she *could not* explain, she *would not* explain. But the Fates who lured her into this fiasco must have been watching over her, because she managed to escape from Dennis' office and slide behind her own desk nanoseconds before he rounded the corner.

"Jesus, Diana, are you still here?" His short blond hair stood out in wet little spikes, like a baby duck with apoplexy.

"I'm sorry about your car, Dennis," she mumbled. "I was just leaving…"

Before he could comment, she snatched up her briefcase and bolted for the door. Glanced back over her shoulder, she saw two things: Dennis standing over his desk, scratching his head in confusion, and the green eye of the oversize copy machine glowing in the dark.

She stepped outside and closed the door behind her. How could she be so stupid? Their secretary never *ever* forgot to turn off the copier. Worse still, this copier recorded the time and date of every copy made. The only data the infernal machine did not report was *what* got copied and *who* copied it. But then, Dennis was no fool. Would he doubt for one second that she was the guilty party?

She lifted her face to the storm, and lightning flashed. She'd sure enough stepped in it this time. As she scampered to the restaurant, she wondered: *should I start typing employment resumes tonight, or is tomorrow soon enough?*

TWENTY

Everyone has a motive...

Liz was on her second margarita when a white-coated waiter led a dripping Diana to her table. "What happened?" She teased. "You need to tumble dry—twenty minutes on wash n' wear."

"Make that *worse for wear,*" Diana groaned. "I'm off to the ladies' room. Order me a vodka martini."

"Hey, Diana, leave your briefcase. Why lug it to the restroom?"

But Diana gave her a strange look and hugged the briefcase to her chest. "I'll be right back..."

She noticed the defeated slope of Diana's shoulders as she strode away, then took a big gulp of her margarita. Something was definitely wrong. Diana had been in the office for at least half an hour. She doubted the delay had anything to do with the fender bender out in the lot. More likely, Diana was putting off their dinner together.

She hoped the dinner would go well. Lately Diana seemed more reluctant than usual to socialize, and that wasn't healthy. They needed to knock back a few drinks and forget all their worries. After all, Liz had given up a cozy evening with Danny to be here. On the other hand, she needed some space from Danny. He was getting too serious. She could read all the signs. Any day now he'd propose marriage—again—and their relationship would go south, history repeating itself.

The waiter arrived with Diana's vodka martini and the plate of quesadillas Liz had ordered for them to share. She licked her lips and bit in, enjoying the rush of warm cheese and spinach on her taste buds. And then Diana returned and deflated into a chair, like the weight of the world was on her shoulders.

She hoped Diana wouldn't spoil their evening.

"Here's to you, Diana!" She raised her glass in a toast. "Super sleuth of the century!"

"Please don't call me that," Diana moaned. "I've messed up big-time."

Diana had toweled the rain off her face and tamed her short blond hair, but she still looked wilted. Liz pushed the martini into her hand. "What's happened?"

Diana took a long drink and a deep breath. Outside the storm raged, pelting steadily on the roof. People's conversation buzzed louder, with excessive clattering of silverware, to prove they were having fun in spite of Mother Nature. But when Diana confessed what she'd done at the office, Liz was appalled.

"Holy Mary Mother of God! What were you thinking? You might as well resign right now. You know Dennis will figure it out."

Diana nodded.

"How will he get his desk open?" Liz's mind reeled. "He'll have to call the locksmith. When he pulls out the drawer and finds the key inside and the plot plan folded all wrong, he'll freak. You sure you left the copier on?"

Diana's face was a study in misery.

"Well, that cinches it. Dennis won't need a road map, he can only drive in one direction. He'll run you down, Diana."

"Hit and run…" Diana signaled for another martini. "I think I can handle Dennis. It's Brantley I'm worried about."

Liz's mouth went dry as an all-too vivid image tortured her brain. She'd told Diana about her affair with Brantley, but she'd never confessed the full horror to anyone. Throughout their relationship, he'd manipulated her with subtle mental cruelty. In the end, when he tired of her, the abuse got physical. She couldn't admit, even to herself, how degrading the damage had been. She'd escaped with minor bruises and a broken spirit, but Brantley was capable of unspeakable violence.

"Brantley's bad news, Diana. Stay clear of him, no matter what. If he's involved, even a little, you better start running right now."

"He's in it up to his eyebrows," Diana whispered. "Dennis couldn't mastermind a project this complex on his own."

They fell silent when the waiter approached and took their orders. Liz glanced nervously over her shoulder, like maybe the Devil himself was about to walk in from the rain.

"I'm scared," she confessed once they were alone. "Why would Dennis get involved? He knows any partnership with the snake is poison. His father never would have associated with the likes of Brantley. What's happening?"

Diana leaned in close. "Remember what Harold Havers said today? He claimed Dennis was deeply in debt. Could the Porter project be the big deal he's counting on?"

"But why bring Brantley in on it? The Loftus Company was listed as the architects, right? They're a reputable company. They'd never work with Brantley."

A light ignited in Diana's eyes. "I bet we have it backwards. What if *Brantley* brought *Dennis* in on the project? We know Brantley's been trying to buy the Porter land for years. Bringing Dennis in gives him an entree with Amy and credibility with the Loftus Company. But I still don't see why Dennis didn't just go it alone."

They quit talking when the waiter brought their meal. Diana smiled at her steaming bowl of *zarzuela Espanola,* while Liz dug right into her *filete en salsa cobrales.*

"Does Brantley have influence at any particular bank?" Diana asked through a mouthful of seafood in sherry sauce.

Liz's grilled filet mignon was topped with a creamy bleu cheese. Her mouth watered when she tried to eat and speak at the same time. "Not really. In fact he always complained because bankers rejected him. He'd done so many crooked deals, no one trusted him."

Diana drummed her fingernails on the table. "So what does Brantley have that Dennis needs? There must be something...?"

Liz nearly choked as the answer surfaced. "I've got it! I always thought it was bullshit, but Brantley used to brag about how he had the Iredell Planning Committee in his pocket. He swore any project he wanted passed was a done deal."

"How could a jerk like Brantley Craven control a planning board?"

Liz rolled her eyes. "Bribes? Blackmail? Three of the members are women. Maybe he's screwing them all?"

Diana laughed. "Well, however it happened, both men stand to get rich and retire in luxury."

"Not to mention Amy." Liz frowned. "You said her name was on the plot plan. Maybe that bitch Juanita was right. She said Amy was after the money."

Diana lowered her eyes and pushed away her plate. "No, I refuse to believe Amy's mixed up in this. She's a decent, honest human being who's had more than her fair share of trouble..."

"Stop, Diana," she interrupted. "Think what you're saying. You told me Amy's desperate for cash, right? Her husband Roger is a bastard, her brother's a psycho, and her son wants to go to college. So we have Dennis, Brantley, Bobby Porter, Roger Keene, *and* Amy. Everyone has a motive for murder, or so it would seem."

"Liz, you're wrong about Amy, so you might as well take her off that list. Besides, not everyone had the *opportunity* to kill Porter."

Liz sighed. It was useless to argue with Diana about Amy. She was blinded by friendship. And as she considered the issue of opportunity, she realized that one suspect could be eliminated immediately. "Dennis didn't do it," she said.

Diana blinked in surprise. "How can you be so sure?"

Liz didn't have to stretch, the memory was clear. Jed had been murdered Friday night, April ninth, the day after she began sleeping with Danny. She turned to Diana: "I called in sick the morning before Jed died. You called in sick too, remember? But I had floor duty later that evening, and you went to have dinner with your mother…"

The memory made Liz blush. The last thing she'd wanted that night was floor duty at the office. Every muscle in her body had ached from lovemaking, and she longed to spend the entire evening recovering in Danny's bed.

"Anyhow…" she continued. "That night the Iredell Chamber of Commerce was meeting, and Dennis was their keynote speaker. The second I set foot in the office, he made me type his speech and practice with him. What a drag. He was so nervous he kept leaving out whole passages of the presentation. He changed jackets three times and went nuts trying to choose a tie. Make a long story short, he left for the meeting on time."

"Yes, but are you sure he got there?" Diana was determined to play devil's advocate.

"Sure, I'm sure," she replied with mounting irritation. "The next morning he made me send promotional packets to all the new Chamber members, like I was his personal secretary. He'd collected those names at the meeting."

Diana chuckled. "Okay, that's one down. What was Brantley doing that night?"

"Do I have a crystal ball? How the hell should I know what the snake was up to? Chances are it wore a skirt. In fact, I'd put money on it."

"Good. Since you're in a gambling mood, I bet twenty bucks you can find out whether or not Brantley visited Jeb's farm that Friday night. You know his habits and where he hang outs better than most, and…"

"Excuse me, Ladies…" Suddenly their waiter came up from behind. He pulled a chilled bottle of wine out from under his towel and ceremoniously placed it on their table.

"We didn't order that," Liz protested. "You've made a mistake."

"No mistake, ma'am." He added three sparkling glasses to the table and gestured. "It's complements of the gentleman at the bar…"

Liz and Diana stared at one another. Liz held her breath and sneaked a peek at the tall, smiling young man with curly brown hair. He waved sheepishly and shifted from foot to foot.

"Thank God, it's only Danny." She exhaled. "Sorry. I didn't invite him, but…"

"But what's a girl to do?" Diana finished the sentence.

Danny pulled up a chair, propped his elbows on the table, and blushed with the bashful charm of a naughty teenager.

"C'mon, Corkie. You didn't invite me to *dinner,* but you didn't say anything about *dessert.*"

Liz laughed. She couldn't stay mad at him, but she could do plenty about the way he was eyeing Diana, like a lovesick puppy. She kicked him under the table.

"It's nice to see you again, Danny." Diana smiled and poured the wine. "Please do join us for dessert, but I'm buying."

"Yeah, I know." He grinned. "Corkie said you owed her dinner and drinks, after that crazy adventure at the beauty salon. Lucky that Mexican chick didn't stab you with those scissors."

"No secrets between you two, eh?" Diana gave Liz a hard look.

"Nope, Liz tells me everything," he continued. "You two are like Cagney and Lacey. We discuss your exploits over dinner each night. Makes for lively conversation."

She avoided Diana's eyes. She'd promised not to tell anyone what they were up to. She was supposed to be a friend and confidante. Now Diana knew she was merely a blabbermouth.

"Well, then, Liz…" Diana frowned. "You might as well fill Danny in on the next installment."

Liz was mortified, yet lost no time telling him what had just happened at the office. When she finished, he gaped in disbelief.

"Jeez!" He exclaimed. "When Dennis leaves and sees your cars in the parking lot, he'll storm in here and kill you both!"

All three heads turned in perfect sync towards the door.

"He wouldn't have the nerve," Diana said with finality. "Now hush up and eat your dessert."

Like obedient children, Liz and Danny sampled their hot flan with caramel sauce, but then Danny reached under the table.

"Can I see that plot plan?" Before Diana could object, he grabbed her briefcase and lifted out the map. "Whoa..." He whistled softly and spread it open on the table. "North Carolina's answer to Disney World!"

"Put it away!" Liz hissed through her teeth. "What if someone sees us with that thing?"

Diana's lips flattened as she tried to snatch the plan and hide it out of sight, but his palms were firmly planted on the corners. "All right, you can look," she conceded. "But make it snappy!"

Liz was furious, but what could she do? Change the subject, maybe? She fixed on Diana. "All right, then, what do you want me to find out about Brantley?"

"His alibi, of course. Visit his office and discover where he was the night of April ninth."

Liz's stomach lurched, but Diana was right—she still had connections. The secretary at Craven Corporation had become a good friend. Like Liz, the woman was one of Brantley's ex-lovers, so they shared a common grievance. "When should I do this?" she asked.

"How about tomorrow?" Diana's eyes sparked with excitement.

"Do what?" Danny looked up from the map.

"None of your business." Liz was firm. She hadn't told Danny much about Brantley, and aimed to keep it that way. But if she were to do this dangerous favor for Diana, then Diana would have to share the pain.

"I have a job for you too, Diana," she said. "Since you're in a gambling mood, I dare you to meet with Amy and find out why the hell her name's on that plan."

Diana seemed to understand that turnabout was fair play. "You drive a hard bargain, but tomorrow's my day with Mama, and she's been begging me to take her to this thrift shop Amy told me about. I guess I could ask Amy to meet us there…"

"Deal!" Liz reached across the table. They shook on it.

"What can I do?" Danny said. "It's not fair. You guys get all the fun…"

Both women shushed him as the maître d' approached their table. He pointedly glanced at his watch, then walked towards the front door. As he began locking up, thunder clapped and the door flew open, allowing one last guest to rush in from the night.

"God, it's Dennis!" Diana gasped. "Hide the plot plan!"

Three sets of hands fumbled to fold the plan, scattering napkins and spilling coffee. At the last moment, perhaps too late, Diana wrestled it under the table just as Dennis arrived.

"Isn't this cozy?" He glared directly at Diana. "How come you girls didn't invite *me* to the party?"

Liz noticed with alarm that her boss's face was flushed red under his dripping blond hair. He looked freaky, like he'd been drinking or doing drugs. Was it her imagination, or was he staring down at Diana's lap, precisely where the plot plan had disappeared?

Danny climbed to his feet, towering above the stocky football-player-gone-to-seed. "Hi there, I'm Liz's boyfriend." He gave Dennis a playful jab in the shoulder.

The glaze of fury cleared from Dennis' eyes and he focused on Danny, weighing his options. "Mind if I join you?"

Danny scratched his chin. "Tell you the truth, buddy, this is a private party. It's not what you'd call *work related*, understand?"

Dennis assessed the turn of events. Liz could almost hear his tiny brain processing the situation.

"Hey, I'm no party crasher," he said, "but tonight something funny happened back at the office…" Again he stared at Diana. "Tell you what, I'll grab a quick drink for the road and come back to your table. Maybe you girls can shed some light on the mystery."

Before they could stop him, Dennis scurried to the bar, leaving wet footprints across the floor.

"Now the shit's gonna hit," Liz said.

"Maybe not, take a look…" Diana pointed to their little waiter. He was confronting Dennis, placing his body between Dennis and the barman.

"Cool!" Danny said. "They're refusing to serve him."

Their waiter whispered something into Dennis' ear, and then led him to the door. Without further conversation, he pushed him out into the storm. A gush of wind sighed behind him and the door locked.

Danny gave the waiter a *thumbs up*, then turned to Diana. "You better leave that guy a humongous tip."

TWENTY-ONE

No way out...

Liz stepped off the elevator on the ninth floor and calmed herself. This mission wouldn't easy. In fact, it could be a nightmare. The foyer of Craven Corporation was exactly as she remembered: silent with the hush of wealth and privilege. Brantley had designed the space to impress and intimidate, and the floor-to-ceiling picture windows, which looked out on the Charlotte skyline, made her feel small indeed.

Soaring, phallic skyscrapers of glass and steel thrust into the clouds, reminding everyone that this was a young, virile, primarily male city. They rode bareback on the wild banking industry or held the reins of runaway development. They were the gods of the future. Once she'd believed Brantley was such a god, and that she, little Liz McCorkle from West Charlotte, had the horse by the tail.

Wrong. She ran nervous fingers through her mane of red hair, which had been hopelessly tangled by the wind tunneling in the streets below. She smoothed the wrinkles from her new green silk suit. She knew she looked hot in her ass-hugging short skirt and high heels, so if Brantley was there (and she fervently hoped he was not) she might hold some advantage.

She checked her reflection in the window, then looked beyond to where an odd orange cloud hung in the northern sky. She figured the cloud was floating right above Lake Norman, and she imagined Danny sitting on a roof, watching the cloud. He'd put down his paintbrush, open his lunchbox, and think about how much he missed her. The vision was a comfort.

Mustering all her courage, she pushed through an oak door to the receptionist's desk. If she'd timed this right, her old pal Sheila would be poised to leave for her lunch break. Liz would get the information she needed fast, then leave before the snake spotted her.

So far, so good. Sheila's purse lay open on her desk. She was peering into her mirror compact and applying fresh lipstick when she heard Liz's high heels click across the floor. She'd hate having her lunch break delayed, but as Liz drew near, the secretary gasped and gave her a friendly smile.

"Jeez, Corkie, what are *you* doing here?"

She dropped into the chair across from Sheila, just like old times. They had history and some common ground, because both were Brantley's jilted ex-lovers. That experience had devastated Liz, but Sheila had taken it in her stride. An aging beauty, Sheila had been discarded long before Liz came on the scene, so jealousy was never an issue. In fact, Sheila had turned her rejection into a victory of sorts by landing a permanent position as Brantley's private secretary, which paid quite well.

"I know you're leaving for lunch, so I won't keep you…"

"What's up, Cork?" Sheila snapped her compact shut and looked her up and down. "You look good, kiddo, but I gotta say…you're the last person I expected to see walkin' through that door."

Liz knew it was a revolving door, at least where women were concerned. Undoubtedly Brantley currently had at least one new mistress, so her assignment was tricky. Sheila tended to keep her mouth shut. She was protective of Brantley's relationships, because that kind of loyalty translated to a very big paycheck.

But Liz was determined to take her best shot. She'd practiced any number of lies and concocted several stories that might convince Sheila to confide, but in the end, she opted for the direct approach:

"Look, Sheila, I'm asking a big favor. Where was Brantley the night of April ninth?"

Sheila blinked three times. A little rumble started deep in her throat. It bubbled up and exploded as laughter, as heat crawled up Liz's neck.

"Get real, Corkie. You expect to waltz in here and get an answer to that?"

She wanted to slide under the desk and hide. How could she be so stupid? She'd hoped for pity, maybe a little soft spot for a sister in need. Instead, Sheila consulted her watch. The lunch hour was ticking away, and her stomach was growling.

Still Liz held her ground. If nothing else, she'd force the woman to starve.

Finally, Sheila cleared her throat: "You must want this real bad, kiddo. Tell me the honest truth, and I might reconsider."

Liz gulped. "Sorry, Sheila. The truth is, it could benefit Brantley if I knew where he was that night. More to the point, it could prove he wasn't *somewhere else*, where he shouldn't have been."

"What kind of double talk is that?" Sheila chuckled. "As it happens, I recall exactly where he was that night, because I made the reservations myself..." She pulled a planner from the drawer and thumbed backwards through the month. "I'm only telling you this because one thing you said made perfect sense. Where Brantley *wasn't* sure as hell can't hurt him, and he was *nowhere* around here. He spent the night in Atlanta, The

Peachtree Hotel. I arranged it all, paid by American Express, and drove him to the airport myself."

"You sure?"

"Ask him yourself. He's standing right over there…" She nodded at a point behind Liz's back, and then she left.

Liz spun around in her chair and saw Brantley lounging against the wall. A sickly smile twisted his lips as he folded his arms across his chest.

"Was there something you wanted to ask me, Cork?"

Her knees trembled as she pulled herself to her feet. Brantley was gorgeous, as always, in black pleated trousers and a crisp white dress shirt. His sleeves were rolled up, exposing his strong forearms, while his burgundy silk tie was yanked loose at the collar, revealing his muscled neck. Every black hair on his head was slicked in place. In short, he was two hundred pounds of sheer power and menace—every ounce directed at her.

"I was just leaving…" she said.

But he moved across the room and placed his body between her and the door. "Did Sheila tell you everything you needed to know, doll?"

His tone was buttery smooth, the prelude to big trouble, but she saw no way out. She was trapped. Fear closed her throat. In a blind panic, she turned and fled down the hallway, heading for the women's restroom. The bastard wouldn't dare follow her in there.

She pushed through the swinging door and turned around to throw the deadbolt, but was too slow. He flung himself against the door with all his weight. The force sent her flying across the room to crash against the sink. The impact sent a shock of pain up her spine.

"Get out! Leave me alone!"

"Leave *you* alone?" he snarled. "Why won't you leave *me* alone? What the hell are you doing here, anyhow?"

Her back throbbed and her legs were jelly. His face was contorted with rage. The scar on his jaw was blood red and a vein pulsed in his left temple. She moaned. She'd seen it all before. "Please don't be mad, Brantley," she begged in a tiny voice. "It's nothing, really. Sheila and I were just talking."

"Yeah, I heard. You were talking about me, and you were asking where I was the night of April ninth. Did I get that right?"

She began sinking. She was locked alone with a madman, with no help in sight. "Please don't hurt me," she whimpered.

"C'mon, doll, would I hurt you?" He tugged at his tie, pulled it loose, and then twisted it taught between his two fists, like a garrote. "Dennis told me something's missing from his office. You wouldn't know anything about that, would you?"

She backed against the cold porcelain sink as he closed in. She couldn't tear her eyes off the tie. He could strangle her or snap her neck in a heartbeat.

"Folks who steal stuff get punished, isn't that right, Cork? I know that bitch Diana stole the item in question, but you gals are tighter than ticks on a hound, am I right?" He flexed the tie tight and snapped it in the air. "You'll give Diana my love, won't you?"

She tried to squeeze back the tears, but they ran hot and salty down her lips and onto her neck. "Please leave her out of it," she sobbed. "I don't know what you're talking about."

"The hell you don't!" Suddenly he pinned her. He reached around and bound both hands behind her back with the tie.

She struggled, but her efforts only increased his excitement. "Brantley, I beg you, please don't do this!" She choked on her words as his mouth closed over hers. The searing heat of his erection pressed against her thighs, and the familiar scent of his aftershave triggered a flood of adrenaline to her bloodstream. She brought up her knee to deliver a vicious blow to his groin, but he blocked the move and laughed.

"Relax, doll, I thought you liked it rough…"

One hand tore at the buttons on her new blouse, while the other tightened on her throat. Next he found her waistband, and his hot fingers began a forbidden exploration.

Please God! She said a silent prayer for intervention, and then closed her eyes.

TWENTY-TWO

A raging bull...

Diana drove towards Interstate 77 and glanced up at the odd orange cloud hanging in the sky. The weird cloud had been following her around like the harbinger of doom, and sure enough, nothing had gone right today. First Mama had been under the weather, so she couldn't come to the thrift shop. Amy had arrived, but her boss at Denny's had scheduled her for the afternoon shift, so she only stayed a few minutes. Diana only hoped Liz was faring better on her mission.

On the other hand, her meeting with Amy hadn't been a total loss. Amy had claimed she knew nothing about the plot plan. In fact, she was genuinely surprised and angry that someone had gone behind her back to propose such a development. She said her signature on the document was a forgery, and since her brother had given his permission, she'd actually signed a listing contract with Diana, making her the exclusive agent to market the Porter estate. So why was she complaining?

She glanced at Ruby*'s* glove compartment. After much deliberation, she'd decided it was the safest place to store the stolen plot plan, so she'd locked it away. She didn't know what the eventual consequences of her theft would be, but she'd worry about that later.

For now, her only concern was making it back to the office, and Lordy, she hated Interstate 77! It was like a racetrack, where all the drivers were bent on suicide. Steeling herself, she eased up the entrance ramp. Ruby had zero pickup. No matter how far away the on-coming cars in the right lane might be, they were never far enough. Every time she pulled out, her gas pedal pressed to the floor, Ruby crawled like a drugged turtle. And each time the speeding traffic filled her mirror, she braced for a rear-end collision.

Whew, she made it! The Force was with her! When she cast a grateful prayer to the sky, she saw it was again—that strange orange cloud. She wasn't the least bit superstitious, but she had a mystical respect for the weather. When he was little, her son, Robbie, loved boating and was forever chanting the sailor's credo:

Red sky at night, sailor's delight...
Red sky at morning, sailors take warning.

Did this bizarre orange cloud foretell a threat? It was strangely segmented, like a shrimp salad gone sour. She hadn't lived in North Carolina long enough to read weather phenomena, but even she knew this cloud was trouble.

She checked the rearview mirror. Now what? Instead of a receding black highway, a giant grid of steel bars filled her vision, and she had a sudden sense of prison and enclosure. A band of fear tightened around her throat as she dropped her eyes to the speedometer. Ruby was running at full steam—sixty miles per hour. She couldn't go any faster.

Thank heavens the tailgater dropped back, allowing her a full view of the grill and hood of an enormous silver truck. An unpleasant memory flickered at the edge of her mind, and then she spotted the vanity plate: *Roger's Rig!*

No way! But then she remembered the telltale click on the telephone line yesterday, and how Roger had eavesdropped on her conversation with Amy. He likely overheard every detail of their plans to meet at the thrift shop. His intrusion had been infuriating, but once he was off the line, Amy had brushed it off: *Don't worry, he does that all the time.* Don't worry? Roger was a professional driver. He knew the territory, and today was no coincidence. This was an ambush!

She gripped the wheel and tried to stay calm. The orange cloud had become an ugly bruised canopy, weeping torrential tears onto the pavement. Why, in God's name, hadn't she replaced those wiper blades? Oncoming headlights and retreating taillights glowed yellow and red through gray wax paper, while fog steamed up the inside of her windshield. The defogger hadn't worked well for years.

A pounding headache throbbed behind her eyes as she strained to see. She knew the truck was breathing down her bumper, because two blinding yellow suns filled the blackness of her rear window. If she slowed, even a fraction, the monster truck would crush her like a bug under a steamroller.

Up ahead, the traffic began to slow. The red taillights directly in front rushed at her with alarming speed. She prayed and thought fast. Unless she changed lanes, in a matter of seconds she'd be the meat in a crushed steel sandwich. Without signaling, she jerked into the left lane and braced for the impact.

But God was good. Miraculously, the left lane was traffic-free, and for the moment, she was spared. In those blessed seconds, she was gliding solo and wiped off the steam on her windshield with an open palm. It didn't help.

Suddenly, the blinding twin suns of Roger's headlights were behind her again, bearing down and closing fast. She switched on her emergency flasher lights, but knew damn well the maniac would not slow down.

The first hit was a little love tap, but the force sent her chest into the steering wheel. The second bump caused Ruby to buck forward and skid wildly from left to right.

Diana screamed. The man was trying to kill her! The traffic in the right lane was still crawling along bumper to bumper, leaving no space for her to pull in. Roger began honking his horn. It was the crazed bellow of a raging bull, and it filled her with red hot fury.

How dare he? Her blood pounded as she imagined the impact of a speeding locomotive. She imagined steel sparking against steel, and how it would feel to fly over the guardrail. She saw herself falling over the edge of a cliff and catapulting into oblivion, a fireball in the night.

She ground her teeth and promised to sell her soul to the Devil for one last chance. If only she could make it into the right lane! Somewhere in the back of her seething brain, she recalled that an exit was coming up. If her calculations were right, the exit to Barium Springs was dead ahead, and if Satan saw fit to let her escape, she was his for life.

Roger's next assault caused Ruby*'s* bumper to shriek and tear. Her head whipped forward, lashed back, and white-hot pain shot through her shoulders. It was now or never…

Maybe the Devil decided her soul was worth the effort, because the right lane cleared and she made her move. She jerked the steering wheel, and before she knew what had happened, Ruby was floating up the off- ramp.

Was it a gift from Hell, or Divine Intervention? She blinked and swallowed hard. She was trembling so much her teeth chattered. Her guardian's magic hand waved a heavenly wand, and the rain stopped as suddenly as it had started. A ray of sunshine beamed through the clearing clouds and illuminated a red steel building at the crest of the exit. *Cheap Ed's Fuel Stop* was a humble gas station, but to Diana, it was salvation.

TWENTY-THREE

Years of blind obedience...

Sheila left the elevator at the Skyway, a network of covered walkways that bridged the streets of Charlotte and offered a glorious potpourri of restaurants and specialty shops. It was one of the many amenities she adored about the city. She could shop, choose lunch from foods of all nations, and even leave her dry cleaning for one-day service. All this—parking lot to office—without once stepping outside and risking the disturbance of a single hair on her perfectly coiffed head.

As she passed through a glassed-in passageway, she noticed that the funky orange cloud that had been hovering all morning was gone. Instead, a black thunderhead and little zigzags of lightning flashed between the skyscrapers.

Damn! Today she'd hoped to eat wiener schnitzel in the outdoor patio beneath the Nations Bank tower and enjoy their special attraction. All week a band of roving polka dancers had been performing, and the patio was decorated like a German biergarten. She'd openly lusted after all those rosy-cheeked blond boys in their tight little shorts, but in this rain, their lederhosen would be soggy as spaetzle soup.

Oh well. She'd settle for two shrimp egg rolls and save little bites for her cats. She paid the vendor, who handed her a white paper bag with extra duck sauce and mustard, and then found a single table near the window.

She was opening one of the little cellophane packets with her teeth when an unpleasant thought pushed into her head. She didn't want to dwell on it, because she'd already decided to look the other way. She got paid good money to do just that. But she couldn't get Corkie's wide green eyes out of her mind. It took guts for the girl to show up like that at Craven Corporation.

Sheila knew better than most how rough the breakup had been. Brantley had seduced Corkie, chewed her up, then spit her out without ceremony. At the time, Sheila had pretended to be unaffected by her boss's arrogance, but in fact, the cruel incident had almost convinced her to resign.

Yet she didn't leave the company. How could she? She couldn't afford the emotional or financial cost, so she didn't get involved. She took one bite of egg roll, but it tasted bitter in her mouth. Suddenly, she folded the white bag into her purse and started to run.

Her heart skipped when she missed the elevator speeding up to the ninth floor. She saw the trappings of her life—nice clothes, the Uptown condo, the car payments—all breaking off and drifting away. At the same time, she visualized a scene of unspeakable violence and prayed she wouldn't be too late.

She prayed even harder that the whole scenario was a figment of her imagination, but when Sheila finally made it upstairs and burst through the oaken door, she saw Corkie's purse had fallen to the floor. Her head pounded with fear. At first she heard nothing. Then, like the thudding of her heart, a thumping came from down the hall at the restrooms.

She found door of the ladies' room was locked, but the struggle inside was obvious. The rage began in her belly and boiled up to her fists. She beat on the door.

"Open up, God damn it, or I'll call the cops!" She screamed again and again. She kicked at the door with her high heels.

Suddenly she heard silence, then scuffling, and then muffled sobbing. Finally the door swung open, and Brantley stood there. He was flushed and breathing hard, fumbling as he tried to tuck in his shirttail. He walked over to where a disheveled Liz lay on the floor and unknotted his tie, which had bound her hands.

"What the fuck?" Sheila hissed. She shoved her boss aside and rushed to where Corkie had wilted. Buttons had been torn from her blouse, and her skirt was hiked up around her waist. "Jesus!" she gasped.

The girl's beautiful eyes looked stunned, like she was in shock. She reached up. Sheila took her hand and carefully helped her to her feet.

"Christ, Cork, did he rape you?"

The girl seemed unsteady and dazed. She thought a moment, and then shook her head. "No, but he was working on it."

"Did he hurt you?"

Suddenly Liz came to life and hobbled into the hall, favoring one hip. *"Hurt me?"* she cried. "That asshole almost *killed* me!"

Brantley retreated several paces, laughing nervously. "Don't listen to her, Sheila. Hell, you know how it is. Corkie came on to me, and things got a little rough."

All the years of blind obedience churned up like venom in the back of Sheila's throat. *"A little rough?* Is that what you call it, asshole?" She turned to Corkie. "I hope you press charges. I hope they lock him up for a million years!"

Brantley stopped laughing. He turned his back and walked towards his office, all the while smoothing his hair and fiddling with his tie.

In the meantime, Sheila slipped her hand under Corkie's elbow and guided her towards the exit door. On the way, Corkie retrieved her purse and tucked it under her arm. Clearly the girl was in pain, but she didn't cry, and her heart went out to this brave creature.

Brantley turned abruptly and said, "You're fired, Sheila. Anything you want to take from your desk?"

He lit a cigarette and blew perfect smoke rings at the ceiling. His eyes were cold, blank pools.

"There's nothing I want here, Mr. Craven. Not now, or ever again." The words tasted surprisingly sweet on her tongue, as Corkie squeezed her arm.

And they left together.

TWENTY-FOUR

Cat and mouse...

Diana breathed a long sigh of relief and switched off the ignition. Steam rose from Ruby's overheated hood like smoke, while mysterious parts inside the engine gave off little death rattles. She climbed stiffly from the driver's seat, rubbing her sore neck and shoulders, and then walked around to inspect the damage.

Surprisingly, the bumper was still attached, but it canted downwards at an angle dangerously close to scraping the tires. It easily could have torn away on the highway, causing a fatal accident—hers.

Had she really made a pact with the Devil? As she lifted her eyes and gazed out at the Interstate, sunlight streamed through the mist, and yes, she saw a rainbow. Was it in honor of her near-death experience? Or maybe her soul was Satan's pot of gold at the end of that rainbow.

Frankly, she was too shaken to care. Her headache had escalated to a full-fledged throbber, and she wanted to swallow a whole bottle of aspirin. But mainly, she was relieved to see real-life, sane people milling around at the gas station and restaurant right next door. Strength in numbers, right? And wonder of wonders, the place had a pay phone mounted on the wall near her shoulder. Which was a blessing, because like a stupid fool, she'd forgotten her cell phone again. But who should she call? Would she tell the cops she was rear-ended on the Interstate, but the truck got away? How would Amy feel if she implicated Roger? Did she need to call Triple A?

She leaned against Ruby and gulped air. The oxygen rush gave her strength to dig through her purse and locate the little tin of Tylenol she kept for emergencies. Okay. She'd huddle inside Brenda's Bar-B-Q, find a glass of water, and hopefully get her head screwed on straight enough to make a plan.

The moment she entered, she was time-warped back to the 1950's, a time when her parents were courting, and she was only a gleam in their eyes. Pink and purple hula- hoops hung from the ceiling, and *45* rock n' roll records dangled from the hula-hoops. Pictures of Elvis, Frank Sinatra, and vintage baseball teams graced the walls, while ads for the Swiss Army Knife and Morton's Salt were taped to the counter.

Under better circumstances, she'd be planning an outing with her mother to this fun place, but as it was, she made a beeline to the bathroom, the one with a Patsy Cline poster on the door, instead of the one with James Dean. She used the facilities and swallowed three pills.

When she returned to the dining room, a teenaged waitress with a ponytail and a poodle skirt gave her a dirty look that said: *if you pee, you pay*. So she ordered a Classic Coke and sat down in a gray Formica booth near the window.

Her hand trembled as she lifted the glass. She was still too rattled to think straight. As she scanned the tiny café, the only other customer was an old man hunched over a pile of half-eaten French fries. He worked his false teeth and stared mournfully at his plate, like his fries held the key to eternal life, a key he did not possess. A teenage waitress and a dispirited old man—no help there.

She sipped the Coke. The icy liquid gave her a brain freeze and her headache returned with a vengeance. Should she call Matthew? He'd be furious—first with Roger, and then with her. She could almost hear his voice, as his worry about her safety translated to anger. He'd warned her to steer clear of trouble, and he was helpless to protect her. She decided she'd sooner take her chances with 911.

She took another sip, but did not swallow. Instead, she held the liquid in her mouth to warm it up and lifted her eyes to the clearing skies. From this vantage point, she could see the Interstate and the exit where she'd made her escape. At the moment, very few cars cluttered the highway, but a lone silver truck had pulled over about fifty yards beyond the exit ramp. It was slowly backing up along the berm, as though it had overshot its mark. Wasn't that illegal?

She coughed and nearly choked as she recognized the truck. Roger had lost her in the storm, but had not given up. Like cat and mouse, he'd spotted his prey and was returning for the kill.

Dear God in Heaven! The monster truck crawled up the exit ramp, into the lot and parked directly behind Ruby. Again she cast about the room looking for help, but the little waitress had disappeared, and the old man was asleep on his arms.

The moment was déjà vu, a rerun of her lunch date with Amy. Today, when Roger crawled down from the cab of his *Deals on Wheels*, he still looked like a weasel—from his egotistical saunter, to his platform cowboy boots, to the sinister gap between his two front teeth. Amy had told her that Roger was a slimy, abusive husband. Now, after the attack on the highway, she also knew he was capable of murder.

It was the most surreal moment of her life. The magnificent rainbow still hung in the sky, and the man who had just tried to kill her was silhouetted against the clouds. He seemed confused and slightly disoriented as he looked first at the Fuel Stop, and then at the café. At the same time, Dion's *Runaway Sue* blared from the jukebox, a tune she'd heard the day she got her first period.

"Another Coke, ma'am?" The perky little waitress reappeared at her elbow, talking through her bubblegum.

"Do you have a cell phone?" Diana heard the panic in her voice.

The waitress shook her ponytail. "Sorry, customers have to use the pay phone." She glanced out the window. "But some guy's talking on it now."

Sure enough, Roger was leaning against the wall, speaking into the receiver. What the hell was he doing? Calling for backup? Telling Amy he'd be late for dinner?

Suddenly her temper flared. Why hadn't the Tylenol kicked in? Why was Roger hogging the phone? And what the fuck was she doing just sitting there? She paid the waitress, did not leave a tip, and then left the safety of the restaurant.

She stomped right up and tapped Roger on the shoulder; "Hang up, it's *my* turn…"

He feigned surprise at seeing her, and then covered the mouthpiece with his hand. "Hey, I'm talkin' to a trucker buddy of mine. He run into a similar situation out on the highway. This lady driver who didn't know nothin', almost run him off the road. He called the cops, and guess what happened…?"

She stared at the gap between his teeth.

"Well, doggone if they didn't take her license away!" He grinned.

She refused to react to his juvenile bluff. Instead, she'd have a go at his jugular. "You want to play, Roger? Where were you the night Amy's father died?"

His eyes narrowed to slits. He slammed down the receiver and started slinking away. She grabbed his sleeve and held on tight. "Where were you, asshole?"

His weasel face flushed crimson. Hatred flashed in his beady eyes. She braced herself as he clenched and unclenched his fists. At the same time, several passersby noticed their altercation, and he backed off a few paces. Slowly he got his anger under control and growled, "Can't rightly remember where I was."

"Maybe I can help?" she calmly replied. "Mr. Porter died Friday night, three weeks ago."

"Yeah, so what?"

At least she'd wiped the stupid grin off his face. The muscles in his jaw tightened.

"Did you take a little ride out to the Porter farm that night, Roger?"'

In spite of the onlookers, his reaction was swift and violent. He gripped her arm, his fingernails biting into her flesh.

"You sayin' *I* killed the old man?"

Somehow she kept from screaming. "Where were you?" she gasped.

He let go of her arm and shoved her away. "For your information, I was out of state. I was up in Virginia, makin' a delivery." His gaze was icy and unflinching.

But his answer seemed too practiced. She didn't believe one word. "All right, let's say you *were* in Virginia during the day. Where were you *that night*?"

Roger got in her face. He stank like cigarettes. She knew his next move would be considerably more violent than his first, so she quickly backed away. At the same moment, a young couple strolled up and gave Roger a warning look. He too backed away.

"You deaf, lady?" he whispered, his breath like rancid hamburger grease. "I was in Virginia day *and* night. Got me a motel room and never come home till the next day."

She should have cried out for help, because the young couple climbed into their car and drove away, leaving her alone with a psychopath. There was no turning back. "Can you prove it?" She steeled herself for the punch that never came.

Instead, he leaned into her ear. "Don't need to prove nothin', bitch. Not to you, or nobody else. You hear?"

Loud and clear. She retreated a few more steps. His eyes were void of all human expression. "Move away. I need to use the phone…"

He pulled back his upper lip and snarled like a rabid dog. "Sorry, bitch, the phone's broke!" With one violent jerk, he reached around her and yanked the cord right out of its base, then threw the receiver on the pavement.

As she recoiled in horror, he settled the big Stetson on his head and sauntered to his truck. He climbed into the cab and waggled his fingers at her. But after firing up his diesel engine, he made no move to leave the lot.

Her knees wobbled, paralyzed by fear. Why on earth had she challenged this maniac? All her bravado of a moment before vanished, leaving her suspended in fathomless dread.

Then the silver cab started gliding towards her. For an instant, her emotions were strung out in sheer terror, and then adrenalin kicked in. He intended to run her over, and all she could think to do was head for Ruby. She sprinted for the driver's seat. At the same time, Roger made a subtle change in direction, picked up speed, and aimed for Ruby's open door.

The giant wheels screeched, and the glittering teeth of the grill bore down like flying fangs. She screamed and flung herself out of harm's way, across Ruby's hood. At the moment of impact, Ruby lurched like a drunken sailor, and she swore her dear old car cried out in pain.

Roger shifted into reverse and backed away from the carnage. Seconds later, he eased the truck around, picked up speed and fled the scene.

People rushed from the café and the gas station, but the silver truck was a blurred memory, its red taillights fading on the northbound horizon of the Interstate. In other words, he got clean away.

"You all right, ma'am?" Little Miss Ponytail lifted her upright. She patted Diana's head and stroked her hair. She was grateful to the child, but pulled away.

"I'm fine, don't worry..." She waved reassuringly to the stunned crowd. She'd make her damned phone call when she got home. She'd call the cops and file criminal charges against Roger. But for now, she needed to hide herself away for a good long cry.

She tugged at Ruby's door, but the driver's side was bashed in, welded shut. She limped around to the passenger's side and eased herself inside. Ignoring the curious stares, she lowered her aching head onto the cool dashboard.

"My poor little Ruby," she crooned. "You're such a brave girl. Do you think you can carry me home?"

TWENTY-FIVE

Old married couple...

Matthew fiddled with the menu, but couldn't concentrate on the selections. Instead, he watched Diana across the table. She was lovely in candlelight. Her jacket, a blousy affair, put him in mind of a faded garden. It fell open at the collar, exposing her slim pale neck and a sparkling gold chain. Her earrings sparkled too, like fireflies in a nest of silken blond hair. Her skin was translucent in the glow, and when her blue eyes caught the light, he saw fathomless reflections in a secret pond.

"Thanks for coming, Matthew..." She glanced up from her menu. "I know this restaurant wasn't your first choice, but I..."

"No, it's great," he quickly reassured her.

She buried her face in the menu again.

He was concerned. Clearly she was down, and who could blame her? They hadn't discussed it, but he already heard the whole story. News traveled fast in their little community, and this morning Wayne Bearfoot had filled him in. Diana had pressed charges against Roger Keene, and the sheriff had already obtained a warrant to examine Roger's truck. But until she was ready to talk about it, he wasn't going to press.

"Are you hungry?" She smiled.

"Yeah sure. What's good here?" He hated to see her like this. She kept pulling tissues from her purse and daubing at her nose. Her beautiful eyes were red around the edges, and he was sure she'd been crying.

"I'm having the quiche and soup," she said.

"You call that food? Why don't you order something to put some meat on those bones?"

She cut him a warning glance. "You sound exactly like my mother."

Not good. The last thing he wanted was to be anyone's mother. He would have preferred taking Diana to Big Papa's, a steak and seafood place up near his house, where you could get a real meal. But if she enjoyed this yuppie food, he'd jolly well make the best of it.

The waiter arrived and took Diana's order, and then he turned to Matthew. "What about you, sir?"

The kid had a Yankee accent, probably a Davidson College student moonlighting to make some extra cash. "I'm hungry, son. What do you suggest?"

"How about the *Mate's Filet and Shrimp*? You get six ounces of beef, and the shrimp comes grilled or Cajun."

"That sounds real good. I'll take the shrimp grilled, and can you bring me sweet tea?"

"Don't you want a beer, or something, Matthew?" Diana interrupted.

"Nope, tea's just fine."

When the waiter left, he debated with himself. He didn't drink. Should he tell her? It wasn't a moral decision, just personal preference. He grew up in a dry household and had never developed a taste for the stuff. Same with cigarettes. But some folks thought his abstinence was weird and old-fashioned. Some figured he was an alcoholic on the wagon. Should he give their relationship some time before confessing his eccentricities?

She'd said she wanted a favor. He expected it was the real reason she'd invited him today. Bearfoot had told him that somehow Diana had driven her wounded Subaru home from the highway, but the old car needed major body work. He figured that was the favor she wanted. "So, can I help?" he asked, cutting to the chase.

But she pulled deeper into her shell. "Can we discuss it later, Matthew? After we eat?"

He'd been too abrupt, too direct, but it was the second time in one week she'd asked for a favor, and he was just plain curious. First she'd asked him to accompany her to the jail, and afterwards he'd asked her out to lunch. She'd said no. The jail was Monday, now it was Sunday, and the interim seemed like a year. How many times had he dialed the number for Crawford Realty, only to hang up before the first ring?

"Something to do with your car?" The suspense was killing him.

Again she shrank from his question, and he thought he understood why. He imagined she didn't want to talk about anything having to do with Roger Keene.

"Never mind..." he quickly amended. "You'll tell me after dinner."

Gradually, they both relaxed. The food was actually quite good and the atmosphere was cozy. "Nice place," he conceded.

"I was hoping you'd like it. It's convenient for me because my condo's right up the hill. I come here at least once a week, when I'm too lazy to cook."

"Yeah, I get it." As a longtime widower, he empathized. He wasn't bad in the kitchen, but eating alone every night, without the companionship of another human voice, got old real fast. But it hadn't bothered him that much until he met Diana.

183

"I love my new condominium," she continued. "But I still feel a little claustrophobic with so many people living all around me."

He got that, too. She lived in the Lakeside Condominiums. The homes were charmingly situated at water's edge, with a view of a marina filled with expensive boats. The complex was the first of many that had cropped up like malignant mushrooms, replacing unspoiled forest and farmland. He had mixed feelings about the so-called progress. It wasn't his world, but he admired Diana for trying to make it hers.

"Don't get me wrong," she continued. "My new place is nice, but I used to live in the country. Back in Pennsylvania I rode my horse through empty fields, and I had a great big garden. God, I miss my garden."

He nodded in sympathy. It had been dark when she'd visited his house, so she hadn't seen his pride and joy—the working garden he'd created on his land. He had lovingly hauled away the rocks and enriched the red clay with topsoil, and his efforts yielded enough vegetables for year-round consumption. Maybe she'd enjoy helping him with spring planting? Her obvious love of nature was a common cord between them, maybe a lifeline.

"Now I have strangers living on the other side of my bedroom wall," she said. "Take that couple over there… They live across the hall, but we work different hours, so I never see them. Don't even know their names."

He followed her gaze to where young lovers sat two tables away. They were lost in intimate conversation, their hands entwined on the table, their knees touching.

He was struck by a powerful loneliness. "Newlyweds?" he asked.

She winked. "Don't think so. I'm pretty sure they aren't married."

He chuckled. "Out for a test drive, I reckon. Making sure everything works before they buy."

Diana laughed, and he wondered where she stood on the issue of cohabitation. He had no problem with it, but for him a more traditional relationship was the only option.

"Well, they seem happy. That's what counts," he said.

"I agree." She laughed and touched his hand. "Do you ever feel like the world kept changing and left you behind?"

If she only knew. The more time he spent with her, the more he wanted to know what made her tick. He sensed they shared many ideas and ideals. She was a mystery he very much wanted to solve.

He drank the last of his iced tea. Across the aisle, the young woman reached under the table and touched the man in a very intimate way. Had Diana seen it, too? He searched her face, and by the way she avoided his eyes, yes, she'd seen. At the same time, her cool fingers closed around his hand. The contact made his heart contract with an unfamiliar tenderness. She seemed so fragile, but he suspected that was an illusion. Still, he longed to hold her, protect her, and feel her heart beating against his chest.

"Want some dessert?" was all he could manage.

"No thanks. I don't have much appetite for some reason. How about you?"

"I'll order another glass of tea, but let's take it outside. A beautiful sunset's heading our way. It would be a shame to miss it."

She wanted to pay, he argued, but in the end, she won—an example of how she wasn't so fragile, after all. Her stubborn streak was alive and well, and he admired that. She did allow him to leave the student waiter a generous tip, and then he followed her out to the patio. Sure enough, the sunset was putting on a good show. The warm breeze off the lake promised summer, but Diana was shivering. The time had come to talk, and she seemed jumpy as a chipmunk two laps ahead of the dog.

They sat at a small white table, and he wrapped his jacket around her shoulders. "I'm all ears…" he gently coaxed.

Her story took some time to work itself loose, but once she began, the dam broke and it poured out like a tidal wave. Like Bearfoot had said, she'd been the victim of a vehicular assault, curtesy of Roger Keene. As she spoke, he experienced red hot waves of anger. It was one thing to hear it from Wayne Bearfoot, quite another to watch Diana relive the agony.

He pulled closer, elbows on his knees, head bowed to hide his fury. He could almost see that bastard's truck bearing down in the storm, and when she told him how Roger had ripped out the phone and tried to run her down, his muscles tensed and he lusted for vengeance. Holding the iced drink against his forehead, he tried to control his temper.

"So, that's what happened," she finished with tears in her voice, and then glanced at Matthew. "I shouldn't have told you."

"Why'd you wait so long?" He was jealous that Bearfoot had known before he did. Why hadn't she called him for help? He would have brought her home safe, and dealt with her old junker later. Plus, he'd warned her to steer clear of the Porter mess. He suppressed an impulse to scold her for putting herself in danger. Like a father helpless to protect or avenge a hurt child, he ached to punish someone.

But Diana was no child. "I'm so sorry," he said, his voice rough with emotion. "How can I help? Want me to kill the bastard?"

"The idea is appealing." She choked out a laugh and latched onto his arm. "But I had something less extreme in mind."

Matthew was not a violent man. He didn't enjoy hunting and had never owned a gun, but this situation had him reexamining his values. They sat in silence. Gradually, she loosened her grip, but couldn't quite stop crying.

The young lovers emerged from the café. They passed close to Diana and Matthew and gave them a look of curious disapproval.

"They think we're having a fight." Diana sniffled.

"Yep, like an old married couple with nothing better to do on a Sunday night."

His remark made her smile. She wiped her eyes and blew her nose with what appeared to be her last tissue.

"Here, use this…" He reached into his jacket, still draped on her shoulders, and extracted a clean cotton handkerchief. "It's an old southern custom. Every mama teaches her son to carry one, in case of an emergency."

She flashed him a watery smile and used the hankie. By the time she finished, she was her old self again. "It seems like I'm always thanking you, Matthew, for one thing or another. Now, about that favor…"

He listened intently while boats bobbed gracefully at their moorings and the first stars filled the sky. The lovers spread a blanket on a patch of new grass and engaged in some serious kissing.

"You say this was *Liz's* idea?" he interrupted.

"Yes, she said you'd know how these things work."

He hardly knew Liz, but she'd been coming to his store since she was a little kid, and he really liked the woman.

Somewhere along the line, she must have learned that among his many past pursuits, he'd once been a truck driver.

"But how does Liz figure I can check Roger's alibi?"

"She wasn't very helpful with the details..." Diana's face clouded. "She was having a very bad day herself."

He wondered about Liz's problems, but his only concern was Diana, who'd begun to shiver again.

"Look, I have an idea..." he began, "but it's a long shot. Big rigs like Roger's are required to check in at a weigh station when they cross state lines. I have a buddy who works the station on North 77, just our side of Virginia. If Roger was heading home after a delivery, he'd have checked in there."

Diana's eyes brightened. "That's perfect! He can tell us whether Roger was really out of state the night of the murder."

"Maybe..." He shook his head. "Truckers are required to keep their own logs, called Bills of Lading that describe what they're hauling and where they're taking it. They check the Bills of Lading at the weigh station, but they don't necessarily write down time, license plate—that kind of thing."

Her face fell.

"On the other hand, my buddy's an observant guy, with a great memory for details. The way you describe Roger's truck, the vanity tag *Deals on Wheels* would stick in his mind."

"You'll ask him, then?"

"You bet." He closed his eyes, put his arm around her shoulders, and hugged her close. He would keep his promise and ask his buddy, but whatever the result, he'd settle this score with Roger his own way.

"Still cold?" He pulled her closer.

"I'm better now." She got to her feet.

He stood up beside her and wrapped his arm around her waist. The familiar scent of her jasmine cologne both soothed and excited him, and as they walked up the hill together, the young lovers glanced up from their blanket and smiled.

"Now they approve of us," he whispered.

"Shall we give them something to talk about?" Her eyes sparked with mischief as they reached her door. "Will you come inside for some cognac, Matthew?"

He leaned his cheek into her hair. "Got any iced tea?"

TWENTY-SIX

Scene of a crime...

He remained surprisingly calm as Diana fumbled through her purse for the key. Since his wife died, many women had made overtures. They brought covered dishes and lingered at his store. They invited him to dinner and hinted that he needed someone special in his life. Somehow he'd been immune—until now.

She inserted her key in the lock, but the door fell open before she twisted. "That's funny, I'm sure I locked it."

Suddenly tense, he guided her around behind him. He didn't want to alarm her, but he couldn't allow her to enter the dark space first. "Where are the lights?" he whispered.

Instead of answering, she seemed to be listening to something. He heard it, too, an eerie thumping sound, like an animal was loose in the house.

"Oh my God, it's Perry!"

"Who?" He slipped into her hallway and groped along the wall, feeling for a switch.

"*Mother fucker!*" a tinny voice shrieked.

"What the hell?" He stiffened as she shoved him aside, and guided him in. She hit the lights, blinding him, and at the same time, a dark object flew at his face, clawing and nipping at his skin.

"No!" she screamed.

When he lifted his hands to defend himself, he got tangling up with Diana. But in seconds it was all over, as she pulled his attacker away.

"Oh Mathew," she cried. "I'm so sorry!"

He blinked and rubbed his face. Something warm dribbled down his chin, and an enormous gray bird clung to Diana's arm. She wrapped his jacket around the creature, and the action seemed to pacify the thing. Its sharp yellow beak began slowly opening and closing, while its beady yellow eyes glared at Matthew.

"What is it?" he gasped as he took out his hankie and daubed a spot of blood from his chin.

"My parrot," she moaned, stroking the bird's head. "How did this happen?"

"Does he always greet your friends this way?" He was still shaken, but the bird closed its eyes, lulled by Diana's touch.

"Don't you see, Matthew? Someone let him out of his cage. Maybe they tried to hurt him. Look around, for God's sake!"

For the first time since the assault, his eyes focused. Diana's home must have been beautiful, before the hurricane hit, but now the condo was a shambles. The intruder had overturned the antique furniture and pulled the cushions off the sofa. Books and CDs were strewn everywhere, and all the paintings were cockeyed on the walls.

He was speechless as she dropped to her knees, still cradling the bird. She touched an African sculpture that had been knocked off a table. The impact had scarred the hardwood floors, while the sculpture's head had broken off and rolled away.

She rocked on her knees and wailed, "Who would do this?"

He had a fair idea. The image of Roger Keene bubbled up like hot tar. First the asshole had tried to run her off the road, and now this. The sick bastard was out of control, and Matthew felt utterly powerless.

"I'm taking Perry back to his cage," Diana said.

He intervened and grabbed her shoulders. "Let me look around first. What if someone's still here?"

She seemed shocked by the idea, but she didn't protest when he started searching her house.

He moved room to room, determined to keep his temper under wraps. Pots and pans were scattered across the kitchen, and the refrigerator door hung open. The guest bedroom had been trashed, but the master bedroom, Diana's private space, was truly violated. He clenched his fists. The obscene destruction of the bedroom was tame compared to what the monster had done in the bath.

He supported himself against the cold sink, his heart pounding with helpless rage. The image of Roger smirking made him want to punch the gap in the asshole's two front teeth until he had no teeth left.

He gulped for breath and splashed cold water on his face, washing away the last drops of blood from the parrot attack. He had never intentionally hurt any living thing, but Roger deserved a taste of his own medicine. He'd stayed silent through the years, though he'd suspected that Roger was abusing Amy, but this atrocity marked the end of his pacifism. Feelings for Diana exploded painfully in his chest, just as a new emotion—a thirst for revenge—parched his heart.

He splashed more water and snatched a towel from the floor, realizing too late that he was disturbing a crime scene. Now his fingerprints were all over the house, but trace evidence was not his first priority. Soon Diana would follow him into her bedroom to put the damned parrot in its cage, and he didn't want her to see this. Not yet.

He returned to the bedroom and retrieved the birdcage, which had been toppled off its ornate stand. He carried it from the room, quickly closing the door behind him, and barred Diana from entering.

"What's wrong?" she whimpered. "Is someone in there?"

"No, the intruder's gone." He steered her back into the living room, shaking his head, and then opened the wire door to Perry's cage. "Let's sit here a spell, and your bird can stay with us."

Her eyes widened. She was surely imagining unspeakable destruction behind that closed door, but she asked no questions. Instead, she eased the parrot into its cage and covered it with an afghan. She walked unsteadily to Matthew, and then sank into his open arms. "What now?"

He pulled her head against his chest and stroked her hair. The hatred coiled in his belly would have to wait, because now was the time to comfort Diana. He buried his lips in her hair. "I reckon we should call the police."

TWENTY-SEVEN

The Keystone cops…

They sat side by side on the stoop, waiting for the police to arrive. The evening was clear and balmy, with stars in the sky and the scent of flowers in the air, but the beauty was wasted on Diana. She slumped forward, elbows propped on her knees, aching head cradled in her hands as she tried not to think about the disaster inside.

"Is Sheriff Bearfoot coming?" she asked.

Matthew shook his head. "This isn't his jurisdiction. He's in Iredell County, this is Mecklenburg. The Davidson cops will respond."

She should have known this, but couldn't think clearly. Nothing made sense except Matthew's warm arm against her shoulder.

He nudged her as a silver Crown Victoria, with the blue and white letters of the Davidson police, sped through the manicured entrance and headed towards them.

"They made good time," Matthew said. He stood and flagged them down, guiding the patrol car to a screeching halt at her porch. Two men jumped out.

"Mrs. Rittenhouse?" a wiry young officer barked. She figured he was in his mid-thirties. He wore pressed jeans and a colorful, untucked Hawaiian shirt "This is your place?"

She nodded.

Matthew abruptly lifted her to her feet, saving her from being trampled as both officers rushed up the steps, weapons drawn.

"Take it easy, boys…" Matthew pulled her close. "It's all clear. I already checked."

"We'll be the judge of that…" the wiry one snapped. He shoved the door open with his Brooks running shoe, then stood cautiously to one side.

"Just routine, ma'am." The other officer, an enormous African American, had a voice that was deep and reassuring. He wore a traditional blue uniform. "You folks hang back while we take a look, okay?"

The men charged into the house, zigzagging from room to room.

"The Keystone Cops," Matthew mumbled.

She'd always loved the old black and white films featuring the Keystone Cops, but never would have pegged Matthew as a classic movies buff. "Those two do have a great comedy routine," she agreed as they listened from the entranceway.

The officers were slamming closet doors and opening drapes. Every light in the house blinked on, illuminating the rubble of what had once been her orderly life. Suddenly she felt sick to her stomach. "Will this take long?"

Before he could answer, the white cop signaled them.

"The perpetrator is no longer on the premises," he smugly announced as he holstered his gun. "It's safe to come in now."

The big officer joined them. He had put his gun away long ago. He smiled and extended his hand. "I'm Rodney Woods," he drawled. "Rambo over there is Detective Peter Sokolsky, my boss."

Wood's hand was warm and calloused. Diana liked him instantly. He looked more like a Carolina Panther who had wandered off the football field than a police officer.

When Sokolsky stepped forward, he did not offer his hand. "Sorry about the dramatics, Mrs. Rittenhouse. It's procedure, understand?" He jerked his thumb at Matthew. "Who's he?"

"Matthew Troutman. Pleased to meet you."

She heard the tension in Matthew's voice as he stepped forward to shake hands with both officers.

"Mr. Troutman is my friend," she told them. "Thank God he was with me."

Sokolsky eyed Matthew. "Are you a *close* friend, Mr. Troutman? Do you live here?"

"No, sir, I do not." Matthew bristled.

Woods stepped between them, easing the tension. "Hey, it's Trout! Yeah, I've been to your store lots of times…" He turned to his partner. "C'mon, Pete, you remember. Trout owns that place up on River Highway?"

Sokolsky snorted in the affirmative, but refused to lighten up. "Woody, why don't you do your thing, while I have a chat with Mrs. Rittenhouse?"

"Sure thing, boss." Woods winked at her. "In case you're wondering, *my thing* is photographs and fingerprints. It's kinda messy. By the looks of it, the intruder touched about everything in the house, so I'll be dusting lots of black powder around. And I'll be flashing my camera, recording it all. Just ignore me."

"Don't you have a crime tech to do that work?" Matthew wondered.

"We're a small department, Mr. Troutman. Woody handles it just fine. By the way, we'll need your prints, too."

Sokolsky turned to Matthew and Diana. "Sit on that sofa over there. It'll only take a minute."

They obeyed in silence. Woody retreated to their patrol car and returned with a small red plastic case. He arranged his paraphernalia, then pressed black impressions of each of their fingers onto thin white sheets.

"Process of elimination?" Matthew asked.

Ignoring his question, Sokolsky paced the room. "The suspect entered and exited through the front door, but I see no sign of forced entry. Either the guy had a key, or he's mighty good with a credit card. Who else has a key, Mrs. Rittenhouse?"

"No one."

"Not even Mr. Troutman?" Sokolsky queried suggestively.

"You heard the lady," Matthew grumbled.

Sokolsky snickered. "Do you entertain a lot, Mrs. Rittenhouse? How many sets of fingerprints should I expect to find here?"

This line of questioning was getting on her nerves. "I've only lived here six months, Detective, and I don't have many friends. My mother, my friend Liz, and Matthew—they're the only ones. Won't that make your job easier, to isolate the intruder's prints?"

"I'm afraid it doesn't work that way." Sokolsky glanced at Woods, who had finished dusting around the door and was kneeling over the broken African sculpture.

Woods looked up, flexed his fingers, and shook his head. "So far it looks like the creep was wearing gloves. He was in and out fast, like a pro."

Matthew shifted restlessly and pulled her up from the sofa. "Look, why don't we take a break? Let's move into the kitchen, and I'll make a pot of coffee."

Diana sniggered. "Hey, what makes you think I have a coffee pot, and who said you could use it?

"You don't have a coffee pot, Diana?"

He seemed so surprised and embarrassed, she had to laugh. "Of course I have one, but *I'll* make the coffee, thank you very much."

"All right…" Sokolsky agreed at last. "You two go on into the kitchen, and I'll be there directly."

"He's a real sweetheart," Matthew said as she measured coffee into her machine and switched it to brew.

She sank into her favorite chair at the kitchen table. She was grateful for a moment of peace and privacy, though it was only a reprieve. The refrigerator door hung open, so she pushed it closed with her shoe. "Peter Sokolsky's from New Jersey. That's why he's so rude."

He blinked. "How do you know?" He opened the refrigerator again, sniffed the milk carton, and then poured some into her creamer pitcher.

"I grew up outside Philly, right across the river from Sokolsky. I recognized his accent and attitude. Up north, we all act like him. It's a way of life."

"You're not like him, Diana."

She could have kissed him, but he didn't know the half of it. When she first moved to North Carolina, she'd hated all the *yes ma'ams* and the exaggerated good manners. She'd despised how long it took the natives to spin a tale and never get to the point. But meeting Peter Sokolsky just now had been a culture shock, convincing her how very wrong she'd been.

"You take cream?" he asked.

"Just black," she answered quietly, savoring every moment of his attentiveness.

And then she considered Sokolsky—young, brusque, and intense. His short black hair was sheared in an urban style seldom seen on southern men, and his gray eyes darted in a pale face with sharp, wolf-like features. Not once had his eyes met hers.

The clincher, of course, had been his nasal accent, the distinct New Jersey twang she'd heard all her life. Yes, she recognized Sokolsky from the public schools, the clubs, and the streets of her youth, but felt not one twinge of nostalgia.

"What?" Matthew asked.

She realized she'd been staring at him as he clumsily tried to sweep sugar back into a bowl, which the intruder had upset on the counter. "Oh, nothing, but thank you, Matthew—for everything."

He actually blushed, and then they sat quietly, smiling at one another and sipping coffee. Like all good things, it ended too soon.

Sokolsky burst in. "Come with me now, Mrs. Rittenhouse. I need you to tell me if anything's missing. You wait here, Troutman."

"No sir, I can't do that." Matthew smiled. "I'll tag along for moral support."

The men glared at one another.

"What part of New Jersey?" Diana intervened.

Finally the detective looked her in the eye. "Camden. How did you know?"

"Takes one to know one. I'm from Philly," She captured Matthew's arm and led him into the living room, leaving a surprised Sokolsky following in their wake.

The spectacle of her beloved treasures trashed and broken brought a painful lump to her throat. As they moved around the room, Matthew helped her straighten the paintings one by one.

"At first I assumed kids broke in looking for drug money," Sokolsky said. "But it doesn't add up. Kids would've taken this expensive sound system. Electronics bring fast money on the streets. Why'd they leave that stuff behind? Whoever did this was looking for something specific, and they tore the place apart to find it. What were they looking for, Mrs. Rittenhouse? Obviously they wanted it real bad."

She glanced at Matthew. She'd never told him about the stolen plot plan, and now wasn't the time to confess. She swallowed the lump in her throat. "I don't know what you're talking about, detective."

Sokolsky seemed skeptical, but resumed his pacing. He slid a Mozart CD across the floor with his toe, as Diana considered her next move. If someone broke in for the plot plan, then only two suspects came to mind. Dennis and Brantley weren't her favorite people, but were they capable of a vicious break in? Without proof, implicating them bought her a one-way ticket to the unemployment line.

"Anything missing?" Sokolsky pressed.

"Who knows?" she moaned. "Everything's a total wreck!"

"All right, then..." He frowned. "We'll check out the bedroom. Are you ready?"

Matthew squeezed her arm and nodded encouragement, and she recalled how he'd prevented her from entering earlier. Dread churned her stomach, and she braced herself for the worst. As they pushed through the door, a flashbulb exploded, blinding her, and then Officer Woods apologized as she regained focus.

"Oh, dear God!" Every drawer had been emptied. Her private things—panties and bras—were strung up everywhere in obscene positions. Her new comforter and pillow covers had been slashed, and goose down feathers floated across the carpet. Her jewelry box was upside down, with all the pins, necklaces and bracelets tangled in a heap.

"You all right, ma'am?" Woods lowered his camera.

She wilted onto the bed and saw the imprint of the monster's body where he'd lain on her sheets. When she ran her hand along their silken surface, she touched something wet. A disgusting red liquid had soaked through to the mattress. "Is it *blood*?"

She felt Matthew's solid presence right beside her.

"No, ma'am…" Woods said. "It's not blood. It's nothin' but tomato juice. I already checked. The intruder took it from your refrigerator."

The churning in her stomach bubbled up into her throat, and she knew she'd throw up. Pushing past the men, she rushed towards the bathroom door.

"Don't go in there!" Matthew pleaded.

But she slammed the door, locking it behind her. When she finished heaving and lifted her eyes up from the toilet, her body was clammy with sweat. She was dizzy. Toilet paper was festooned everywhere. The shower curtain was shredded, its rod bent and broken. The medicine cabinet had been emptied. Bottles of pills rolled across the floor, and a box of tampons had been scattered into the tub filled with water. They floated like bloated white dead fish.

Tears rolled down her cheeks, and she couldn't stop sobbing. When she stood up and looked in the mirror, she saw words written on the glass with red lipstick: *Fuck you, bitch!*

She felt like she had been raped, violated, and as the blood drained from her brain, she began to sink. The cold tile floor rushed up to meet her.

TWENTY-EIGHT

Somebody lost a bet...

Diana gazed up at Matthew through blurred eyes. She shook her head to clear her vision and sipped at the hot toddy he'd made for her. Instead of simply dropping a teabag in the boiling cup of water, she'd instructed him to add a jigger of whiskey, squirt of lemon and some sugar. It was her mother's cure-all remedy for everything from the common cold to a nervous breakdown.

She couldn't quite put it together, but she recalled hearing the bathroom door shatter. Yes. Then Matthew had lifted her off the floor and carried her to the couch. Soon after that, the two cops left.

"What happened to me?" she asked.

"Just rest, Diana." He freshened a washcloth with cold water, then laid it on her forehead. "You fainted. You'll be okay real soon."

She struggled upright "Sokolsky kept asking me about affairs and jealous lovers. What the hell was that all about?"

Matthew smiled. "Can't blame the man. I'm curious about those lovers, too."

She punched his arm, then swung her feet over the edge of the couch. "None of your Goddamn business."

"That's exactly what you told Sokolsky. Did you see his face?"

Apparently her rebuke of Sokolsky had given Matthew a degree of satisfaction. But in fact, her head felt like the inside of an aquarium, and the floor wobbled under her feet. Best to sit still awhile longer.

"The cops aren't buying the robbery theory," Matthew continued. "The way that bastard trashed your bedroom? Sokolsky called it personal, *sexual terrorism*, or some such thing."

He reached over and patted her knee. At the same time, she noticed a six-pack of beer sitting on the floor near the couch. She'd already guessed that Matthew didn't drink. "Where'd you get that?" she asked.

He chuckled. "Believe it or not, I wandered out onto your patio after those bozos left and found this beer hidden under a drop cloth. Funny, I didn't picture you as a Budweiser gal."

She laughed. "The condo's maintenance guys are painting out there. No wonder it's taking them so long." Matthew's teasing, coupled with the effect of the hot toddy, was working magic. She was ready to stand up. "I need some fresh air. Let's move out to the patio, okay?"

He helped her up, and they went outside. Moonlight rippled across the water, and the young lovers from the restaurant were still enjoying their blanket on the grass. In two short hours, her life had been turned inside-out, while for them, the world was blissfully unchanged.

Matthew leaned his elbows on the railing. "Diana, why didn't you tell the cops about Roger?"

She couldn't see his face, but she sensed anger behind his words. Actually, she'd never considered Roger a suspect. "Why didn't *you* tell them about Roger?"

Silence stretched between them, until finally he spoke. "It wasn't my place to mention him, but you can bet I'll handle Roger in my own way."

His tone chilled her, but she wasn't up to a confrontation. "Sokolsky knew I was holding back. Should I have been more cooperative?"

"But what could you tell them? What could you prove? When they discover you've pressed charges against Roger, they'll put the case together." Matthew nodded towards the parking lot. "Besides, their patrol car's still down there. If you want to change your story, it's not too late."

Sure enough, Woods and Sokolsky had driven to the lower level near the garages. They were leaning on the hood, comparing notes. How could she change her story when even Matthew didn't know she suspected Dennis and Brantley? Was she ready to admit that she'd stolen the plot plan?

"If they're done with me, why don't they leave? What are they waiting for?" She turned to him. "They won't be coming back, will they?"

"Nope, I think they're done for the night. They're just wasting time, that's all." His eyes were dark, unfathomable pools. "Diana, I'm so sorry about all this. I don't know how to comfort you, and I don't have much confidence in those cops doing the right thing. But one thing I do know—you shouldn't stay here alone tonight."

Was he suggesting a sleepover? The possibility caused a frisson of excitement in her belly. But it was early in their relationship, they barely knew each other. Plus, she was a big girl and could take care of herself. "If you want to protect me, Matthew, you can sleep on the couch."

He actually blushed and shifted foot to foot. "That's just plain silly, Diana. See those cops down there? Ten to one they're making bets on me staying, but I aim to fool them. Much as I appreciate the offer, you need to go inside and call Liz. Ask her to come over. Right now, you hear?"

She was totally charmed. She also knew this was an argument she could not win, so she went inside and made the call. She dialed Danny's place and caught Liz on the third ring. Without going into detail, she asked her to come spend the night. When she agreed without hesitation, Diana felt both grateful and foolish.

"Well?" Matthew ducked in from the patio.

"She's on her way. Satisfied?"

He smiled, then pulled a car key from his pocket. "Now don't give me an argument about this, Diana. Here's the key to my truck. I plan on taking your old Ruby back to the shop with me tonight. The bumper's hanging off and the door's bashed in. It's not safe for you to be driving that bunged-up old heap."

"No way! You'll do no such thing." She never took it gracefully when people insulted Ruby. Besides, Matthew had done too much already. She tried to push the key away, but he caught her wrist.

"Look, I was planning to do this all along…" He pulled her close.

He smelled of Old Spice. "How can I repay you?"

"Wait until you see my bill!"

He held her against his chest and kissed her. She struggled, but not too hard. His lips were warm, his kiss tender and searching. She melted into it, and for the first time that night, she felt safe. Truth was, it was the first time in years she'd felt loved and protected. As his kiss deepened, she responded. She'd nearly forgotten how, but just as her body began to remember, he pulled away. He took her face gently between his hands.

"Will you be all right until Liz comes?"

She nodded and didn't stop him when he pressed the truck key into her hand.

"You're a brave lady." His voice was thick with emotion. "Now, where is Ruby parked?"

"In the garage down there, number seventeen." She trembled when he moved away. Then she followed him to the door and handed him her keys.

"Is the garage locked?"

"No. You said it yourself: Ruby's an *old heap.* Who'd want to steal her?"

He gave her a stern look. At the same time, he touched her cheek and smiled. "When Liz gets here, don't you girls start cleaning house. Get some sleep, you hear?"

She snatched his hand and kissed his fingers. "You worry too much, *you hear?*"

He sighed, gave her one last hug, and then pulled away. He walked rapidly down the sidewalk."

"Be careful!" she called at his back.

The moment she closed the door, she felt utterly alone. Her body was cold without him. She ran out to the patio and watched his long legs striding across the lot. Woods and Sokolsky watched too. They waved at Matthew and jabbed one another with their elbows. Somebody had lost a bet.

The night air took on a sudden chill, and she hugged herself. Then the garage door swung up, creaking on its hinges, and Ruby's backup lights glowed like bloodshot eyes in the dark. The engine sparked to life, and her car drifted backwards out of the garage. Then stopped.

Matthew struggled to open the driver's door, but of course, it was jammed shut. He slid out the passenger side and glanced up in her direction. Did he know she was watching? Then he walked around to open the hood.

Her heart skipped when he bent over and fumbled with the latch, and she remembered being stalled on the country road near his house, how she'd shown him up by flaunting the secret to opening Ruby's hood. Did he remember how to do it?

The explosion shattered her ears and rocked the walls. Her scream was lost in the roar of fire as hunks of burning metal flew into the night sky and smoke billowed across the stars. She was still screaming when Woods and Sokolsky lifted themselves off the concrete and staggered to where Matthew lay burning, face down in the wreckage.

TWENTY-NINE

Ambulance chasing...

Liz cuddled against Danny as his truck rolled through the entrance to Lakeside Condominiums. She was mellow on wine and Norah Jones' *Come Away With Me*, which cried from the radio, adding to the sweetness.

"You didn't have to come," she murmured into his shoulder.

"C'mon, would I miss this?" He yawned. "Any excuse to see Diana..."

She rolled her eyes and wondered if she had time to tug out his shirt and tickle some skin, but then she heard an ambulance. It was rushing straight towards them, its red cherry flashing.

"Pull over!" She grabbed Danny's arm.

"Jesus Christ!" he yelled. "There's another one coming at us from behind!"

She hung on as he spun the wheel and jumped the curb, coming to a stop in a freshly seeded plot of grass. She focused on the vehicle careening out of the complex. "I hate ambulances, they give me the willies."

But Danny was watching the speeding white truck heading into the condos. Its spinning blue light and screaming siren shattered the night. "Forget the ambulance. That white truck almost ran us down! Who the hell are those guys?"

He eased his pickup off the lawn and cautiously proceeded towards Diana's. As they rounded the bend, they saw billowing smoke and smelled the acrid odor of burning rubber.

"It's a fire!" Liz gasped. "Wonder what happened?"

Her heart pounded as they neared the parking lot, where a Davidson fire engine pumped steaming gallons onto the charred remains of an old burgundy station wagon. The glowing wreckage was nestled in the concrete hollow between the condos and the garages. A team of men in blue uniforms began jumping from the white truck to cordon off the area.

"Man, this is awesome!" Danny said. "Those guys are from A.T.F.!"

Liz was more concerned with the burning station wagon, but she glanced at the big white truck. Large blue letters on its side said *Explosives and Bomb Investigative Vehicle*, and at least eighteen men had climbed out.

"It's the Alcohol, Tobacco, and Firearms Response Team," Danny continued. "I saw a special about them on TV."

He dragged her over to the sidewalk, where a crowd of bystanders were gaping and whispering at the perimeter of the crime tape.

"Stand back, people…" An agent pushed back the crowd.

Liz glimpsed a shoulder holster and gun under the man's loose jacket, and a lump tightened in her throat. "Where is Diana?"

But Danny was like a little boy in a toy store as he steered her to the very edge of the tape. "They carry all kinds of equipment in that truck—computers, Jaws of Life machine—you name it."

The smoke and shoving crowd made her sick, and as she fixed on the ruined station wagon, suddenly she knew! A long, keening wail escaped her throat, and she clung to Danny with all her strength.

"What's wrong, Corkie?" He held her tight and stroked her hair.

She tried to speak, but words wouldn't come. Struggling free of Danny's grip, she broke through the tape and was halfway to the smoldering wreck, when strong arms tackled her. The agent folded one arm across her chest, holding her against his body. He braced the other arm across her throat and dragged her backwards, cutting off her windpipe.

"Let her go!" Danny wrestled with a second agent, who pinned his arms behind his back and pulled him to the sidelines.

"It's Diana's car!" Liz screamed. "Diana is dead!"

All at once, they were both hemmed into a circle of blue arms. Liz felt faint when the agent finally released her, and Danny was pale and agitated.

"Are you sure?" Danny choked.

"Of course, I'm sure. That's Diana's Ruby. She's dead, I just know it!"

"Take it easy, lady…" Her captor backed away and smiled. "Don't go jumping to conclusions. No one died here, I promise." He led them to where a group of officers were gathered beside the garage. "We can't have you two running loose, it's not safe. My men are sweeping for another bomb—its standard procedure."

"Did you say *bomb*?" Danny found her hand, then pulled her trembling into his arms.

"You said you recognized the vehicle, Miss?"

"It belongs to my friend, Diana Rittenhouse." She sobbed. "Don't tell me she isn't dead. How could anyone survive that blast?"

The agent cleared his throat. "Well, to begin with, the person injured was a man—no woman involved. For all we know, the victim was the bomber, and he screwed up."

"No, sir, you're wrong." A tall black officer approached wearing the uniform of the Davidson police. "My partner, Detective Peter Sokolsky and me, we saw the whole thing..." The cop held out his hand. "I'm Officer Rodney Woods."

Suddenly Danny brightened. "Woody? Is that really you, man?"

Liz was numb as Danny moved away and pounded Rodney Woods on the back. In her opinion, this was no time for a reunion. When the two old buddies finished greeting one another, Officer Woods turned back to the A.T.F. agent.

"Sokolsky's reporting to your agent in charge." Woods cocked his bald head towards a skinny guy in a Hawaiian shirt pacing near the truck. "We'd responded to a break-in at Mrs. Rittenhouse's place, and we were standing right over there when the wagon blew up..." He paused and mopped his head. "Knocked us clean off our feet. I still can't hear worth spit. We called you A.T.F. guys. No way could we handle this mess."

"Yeah, I know all that," the agent grumbled. "But what do you know about the victim? Who was the man?"

Officer Woods glanced at Danny and Liz, then looked sadly at his boots. "He was a friend of Mrs. Rittenhouse. Good friend, if I read it right. I know him too, a fine man..."

"Well?" the agent snapped.

"His name's Matthew Troutman, but everyone calls him Trout. He runs that store up on River Highway...?"

Liz groaned as she wilted into Danny's arms.

Danny swallowed hard. "Is Trout okay?"

Woods shook his head. "I thought he was dead for sure. If the explosion didn't kill him, the fire should have. He was flaming like a bonfire, when that young couple over there tossed a blanket on him."

They all looked to where a gang of agents was questioning the couple. The pair were huddled together for comfort, gesturing and pointing.

"Those two lovebirds were lying in the grass doing their thing when it exploded," Woods continued. "If they hadn't had that blanket handy, Trout would have burned up. Those kids are heroes."

"So Trout's alive? That ambulance was moving like it meant business," Danny said.

Woods shrugged. "He was still breathing when he left."

"But where's Diana?" Liz's throat hurt as she spoke.

Woods chuckled. "Man, you should have seen her. Mrs. Rittenhouse is one determined lady. The medic kept pushing her out of the ambulance, but she kept on climbing in, again and again. Last I saw, she was on her way to the hospital, along with Trout."

As Liz absorbed this last piece of information, it seemed the world she once knew had gone mad. The men in blue were whistling and working, treating this disaster like a routine occurrence.

One agent was down on his haunches with a measuring tape, laughing and calling out distances to another guy who was making a sketch. A photographer inched around snapping flashbulbs at everything from the demolished car, to the buildings, to the shrubbery, while another team carried tin canisters to collect bits of metal, shards of fabric, and gravel samples.

"All in a day's work for those guys." Rodney Woods mused as he watched a man with cotton balls daubing liquid from the pavement. "If poor Trout dies, they'll haul that car into a bonded warehouse for a secure, sterile investigation. This mess could take weeks to sort out."

"Don't say that! Trout *will not* die." Liz was still reeling from the horror of Brantley's attack, and she knew Diana was still shaken by the incident with Roger's truck.... and now a break-in and car bomb! Enough was enough. She and Diana were tough, but they couldn't take much more.

Rodney Woods scowled as he took Liz and Danny aside. "The damn Feds think they know it all." They coaxed her to sit on a stone wall bordering the drive. "But there's more than meets the eye here. Mrs. Rittenhouse is holding something back. Her apartment was trashed by a deranged psycho, who obviously hates her, and then this bomb. The lady's scared to death, but she's not talking."

Liz knew the deranged psycho: Brantley Craven. An obscene break-in was exactly his style. In fact, she had new information about Brantley, evidence so damning it seemed conclusive, but she had wanted Diana's opinion. Now that would have to wait, because all she could hope for at the moment was to hang onto her sanity.

"What kind of bomb was it?" Danny asked.

"Pipe bomb," Woods answered. "Any fool can go on the Internet and make a shopping list. Then he visits K-Mart and Radio Shack to get all the stuff he needs to blow anything sky-high. He'd buy some leg wires and a battery, hook it to the car's ignition system with a blasting cap, then when some poor sucker turns the key...*kaboom!*"

Danny groaned. "Jesus, how come Trout wasn't blown to Kingdom Come?"

"Beats me." Woods sighed. "Maybe something tipped him off? Maybe he heard a little pop, or smelled something burning...who knows? Anyhow, I saw him get out of the car to check under the hood, and...*kaboom!*"

"Then I guess Trout was lucky," Danny said.

"Not hardly." Woods rubbed his eyes. "You didn't see the poor bastard. If he lives, it'll be God's own miracle."

Suddenly Woods seemed exhausted. He nodded goodbye and walked to where a cluster of bystanders were having a party. They'd set up a boom box and broken open a keg of beer.

Their music and laughter drifted up through the smoke, enraging Liz. She glared at a teenaged girl, who was dancing in a pool of light from the A.T.F. floods. "They're insane! Can't they show a little respect?" she hissed.

Danny said softly, "They're just kids. They don't mean any harm."

But Liz was not in a charitable mood. When she stood upright, all the fear, tension, and horror stabbed like a red-hot poker in her brain. It wasn't fair. She snatched Danny's arm. "C'mon, let's go ambulance chasing," she said. "Take me to the hospital."

THIRTY

The twilight zone...

Diana stumbled over a paint bucket carelessly left in the dim hallway and grabbed onto a wooden crate to steady herself. The crate said *Framed Pictures-Handle with Care.* Other boxes rose from the ghostly darkness, canting at odd angles like debris from a bombed- out city. Carts loaded with potted plants lifted randomly, like misplaced forests in the deathly silence.

Why, in God's name, had they brought Matthew here? Lake Norman Regional Medical Center would someday be a state-of-the-art hospital, designed to serve the growing population. Yes, and it was only minutes from Diana's condo. Problem was, the hospital was still under construction, with only the emergency room up and running. They claimed the Grand Opening was only one week away, but by the looks of things, that was a pipe dream, unless visitors were provided with hard hats.

She tiptoed across a canvas drop cloth and sank onto a roll of carpeting. The bright lights and harsh sounds of the emergency room had driven her into this hinterland seeking sanctuary, but the paint fumes and acrid odor of solvents made her nauseous.

Lowering her head onto her arms, she longed to fall into a blissful, anesthetized sleep and think of nothing at all. Her romantic dinner with Matthew seemed like a lifetime ago. Her new floral jacket was smeared with blood—Matthew's blood—and she couldn't escape this nightmare.

She closed her eyes and gulped air. At the last minute, the medics had relented and allowed her to ride along, jerking her up through the closing doors as the ambulance sped away. She had wrapped her arms around Matthew's broken body, only to be torn away.

"Stay clear, lady, let us do our job," the male medic shouted. His female counterpart forced her to sit in the back of the van.

She'd clung to the handrail and hung on for dear life as the ambulance raced through curves. The screaming siren split her ears, and she'd watched in horror as one medic cut the trousers away from Matthew's skin. The woman hooked up an I.V. drip while a third person covered his face with an oxygen mask. Diana had strained to see his eyes, but they were unseeing slits above the mask.

"Will he be all right?" she had wailed.

No one would tell her anything then, or now. They'd transferred him to a stretcher and whisked him away towards the chaos and blinding light, pushing her aside

"Will someone please talk to me?" She had rushed to the admitting nurse and pounded her fist on the counter. Finally, a matronly woman with blue hair took charge. She got a firm grip on Diana's elbow and steered her to one of the few chairs in the waiting room. The woman removed the plastic shrink- wrap and the cardboard sleeves from the armrests, and then she patted the seat.

"The furniture's brand new, so have a seat and give it a try. I know it doesn't look like it, but we have things under control."

Her tone did not inspire confidence. "Where is everybody? Do you actually have a staff here?"

The older nurse eyed her steadily. "To be honest, Trout's our first patient. Normally they'd have taken him to the old Med Center in downtown Mooresville, because most of the doctors are still there. But as it happened, the emergency unit moved in today, so here we are. Dr. Cook is with him now, and he's one of our best."

"Do you have equipment? Are you really prepared to deal with this?"

The nurse chuckled. "Last I heard, the doctors were tearing open cardboard boxes filled with brand new instruments. Hope they can figure out how to use them…"

Diana was not amused. Had a small young man with a stethoscope not intervened, she might have decked the nurse.

The young man, who looked to be fresh out of high school, proved to be Dr. Cook, Matthew's physician. He came right to the point. "We were able to deal with the burns on his legs. The damage was painful, but minor. I understand the explosion threw Mr. Troutman against a stone retaining wall. That explains his broken arm and cracked ribs. We set the bone and taped his chest…" The boy doctor averted his eyes.

"But…?" Diana demanded.

"He hasn't regained consciousness, and we can't tell what trauma the brain may have suffered. There could be bleeding, damage to the soft tissue…it's hard to know."

"So what are you doing about it?" she snapped.

"Charlotte's top neurosurgeon is on his way. In the meantime, we're taking X-rays and watching his vital signs. We don't have our ultrasound yet, or an MRI on location, I'm afraid."

Not good. "When will this expert get here?" She was behaving like a bitch, but couldn't help it.

Little Dr. Cook grinned. "Any minute now. We're air lifting him by helicopter. He'll be the first to land on our new pad."

Alone in the hallway, on the off chance it might work, she chanted a prayer, pleading for Matthew's life. She wished she believed in Divine Intervention, because lately it seemed everything she touched turned evil. Jed was dead, her dear friend Liz had been brutally attacked by Brantley Craven, Diana had been chased down by a truck, her condo ruined, and now Matthew lay fighting for his life. If he didn't recover, she sensed from the depths of her soul that she'd never be whole again.

As she chanted the prayer, an odd ringing began in her ears. It grew louder and became a steady thumping, like the beating of giant wings. She shook her head and opened her eyes as whirling lights dropped through the night sky and flashed through the plate glass window. The helicopter!

She tripped over another paint can in her rush down the littered hallway, but made it to the emergency room in time to see a tall man with a medical bag peel off his overcoat and disappear through the door to surgery.

At the same moment, a familiar young couple charged across the room, headed in her direction. Liz gathered her into her arms. Her red hair was tousled, her face was pale, and her green eyes were wild with shock.

"Thank God we found you, Diana! Are you okay? We just came from your place, it's a zoo!"

"Where's Trout?" The young man's white face and wide brown eyes were framed by curly brown hair. The tail of a Hard Rock T-shirt hung crookedly from the belt of his faded jeans, which were torn at the knees.

Diana racked her tortured brain. Of course, he was Liz's Danny. "Matthew's in with the doctors," she told him.

"Will he be okay?" Liz said. "What did they tell you?"

Diana could no longer control her tears. They welled up and spilled onto Liz's shoulder, communicating the fear she could not utter aloud. They huddled together. Danny joined them, wrapping his arm around Diana's waist. They all stared out at the black sky, where a lone ladder leaned against the window. Behind the ladder, the helicopter's lights cast eerie shadows on the construction site.

"This is radical," Danny whispered. "Doesn't this place give you the creeps? It's like the twilight zone."

Just then, the tall physician hurried out from the surgery, pulled on his overcoat, and escaped to the helicopter before Diana could stop him.

"Well, that's that…" Dr. Cook approached. "You folks might as well go home. Nothing's going to change tonight."

"What did the neurosurgeon say?" Diana demanded hotly.

"Not much. He looked at the X-rays, examined Mr. Troutman, did a few tests, and then decided it was best to watch and wait."

"Yeah, but how is he?" Danny pressed.

"That's just it, we don't know. He hasn't lapsed into a coma, and that's a good sign. But his responses are very weak. With a little luck, it's only a concussion."

Dr. Cook eyed Diana sadly. "I won't try to gloss this over, ma'am. We might lose Mr. Troutman. If he survives twenty-four hours, we'll have a better idea what's happening…"

She clung to Liz. Danny stepped into the circle, and rested his hand on the small of her back.

220

"How can we help?" Danny asked.

"Go on home. We have your phone number, Mrs. Rittenhouse, so if there's any change...." Dr. Cook turned to face her. "Should anyone else be notified? Does Mr. Troutman have any children?"

His question made her realize how very little she knew about Matthew. "I think so, but I have no idea how to locate them."

"Don't worry, we'll find them," the doctor said. "Now get going. I'll call you tomorrow."

Assisted from both sides, she allowed herself to be led away. As they reached the door, the blue haired nurse bustled up and pressed something into her hand: a sample-sized bottle of Tylenol PM.

"I couldn't help but notice, ma'am, you're pretty upset. You also seem to be coming down with a cold. Trout's a good friend of mine, and I know he'd want me to help."

With that, the nurse left, leaving her stunned by the absurdity of it all—like a couple Tylenol would fix all this? But she appreciated the gesture.

Then, as they neared the parking lot, she was greeted by Detective Peter Sokolsky. He stepped from the shadows, blocking their progress. He folded his arms across his chest and shifted a toothpick back and forth between his teeth.

"Hello again, Mrs. Rittenhouse. I know this isn't the best time for a chat, and I'm sorry for your trouble, but..."

Danny broke in. "Back off, pal. Can't you see she's dead on her feet?"

"Yeah, I'm sure she's beat, but..." The officer from New Jersey eyed her with something close to sympathy. "I need to caution you... don't go home tonight."

Before Diana could respond, Liz said, "She's not going home alone."

"That's right..." Danny towered above the detective. "We're *both* going with her."

"What a relief." Sokolsky smirked. "I'm suppose you're *both* trained to prevent another attempt?"

"Will everybody please shut up?" Diana was perfectly able to speak for herself. "If you have something to say, Detective, spit it out."

Sokolsky took the toothpick from his mouth and used it to clean his fingernails. His eyes were steel slits in his wolf face. "Okay, Mrs. Rittenhouse, I know you weren't entirely forthcoming with me before, but you Philly gals are sharp. I'm sure you know the explosion wasn't an accident. The bomb was a crude, homemade device intended to kill its victim."

Why belabor the obvious? She snagged Liz and Danny and began dragging them away, but Sokolsky called after them:

"Remember, Mrs. Rittenhouse..." His tone was ominous. "That bomb wasn't intended for Troutman. It had your name written all over it."

THIRTY-ONE

Up in smoke…

Liz climbed stiffly from the strange bed and massaged her temples. It felt like a hangover, but lack of sleep and extreme anxiety were the real culprits. Last night Danny had deserted her. He'd gotten all shy and proper when Diana offered them the guest bedroom. He'd actually blushed and slept on the couch, leaving her alone with her nightmares.

She found an old terrycloth robe in Diana's closet, and then padded barefoot into the living room. She planned to ambush Danny-the-traitor in his sleep, but when she sneaked up, a pillow raised high above her head, all set to bash him, the couch was empty.

At the same time, the front door creaked open and a man stumbled in from the rain. Two paper grocery bags concealed his face, and when she screamed out in fear, he dropped the bags.

"Christ, Corkie!" Danny gasped. "You near scared me to death! What's wrong with you?"

They gaped at one another. Then, like clockwork, they turned towards Diana's closed door.

"She still asleep?" he whispered as he gathered packages of bacon, muffins, and a dented orange juice carton off the floor.

Liz sighed. "I don't think she slept a wink. She coughed and sneezed. I think she's coming down with a cold. Even so, she spent the whole night cleaning her room. Didn't you hear the vacuum?"

He peeked into the eggs, only one broken. "What's she doing now?"

She crept close to Diana's door and listened. "Calling the hospital again. She's been on that phone every fifteen minutes since she locked herself inside. I gather there's no news. I'm really worried. What should we do?"

He wandered into the kitchen, she followed. He began searching the cabinets, looking for a frying pan. "We should feed her," he said. "You should see the junk in her fridge—wilted lettuce, wrinkled tomatoes, and a bowl of moldy beans. Hell, Cork, a bird wouldn't eat that crap!"

"I've got news for you, pal. Her bird *does* eat that crap. It's for Perry. I told you about him, remember?"

"Yeah, the parrot with Tourette's syndrome. Little bugger woke me up at the crack of dawn, cussing a blue streak." He finally located a pan on the floor where the intruder had thrown it, and soon the comforting aroma of frying bacon filled the condo.

Normally Danny's culinary efforts stirred her senses to a feeding frenzy, but this morning her stomach was doing flip-flops. The alarming news that Brantley had no alibi was still bottled up inside. She was waiting for the perfect moment to tell Diana. It festered like an ulcer. If she didn't blurt it out soon, it would eat her alive.

"I'll check on her," she said. "Maybe I can lure her out for breakfast."

She tiptoed to Diana's door and knocked softly. She heard her sneeze, cough, and then blow her nose. Finally, her shuffling slippers crossed the room, the lock clicked, and they were face to face.

When she looked into Diana's eyes, she saw vacant blue saucers in the face of a zombie. She was leaning on an upright vacuum cleaner like a crutch, and Liz reached out to touch her tear-stained cheek.

"Hey, can I come in? We need to talk…"

THIRTY-TWO

Waiting for the phone to ring...

Diana settled into her wingback chair, with both her princess phone and her cell cradled on her lap, and watched Liz pace. Finally, Liz perched on the edge of her bed.

"I don't know where to begin, Diana..."

Liz was wearing a rumpled pink shorts outfit under Diana's tattered blue robe. Her hair was mussed and she was clearly nervous. Who wasn't? Her own nerves were shot to hell, so sleep had never been an option. Obviously the girl had something on her mind, and she was grateful that Liz and Danny had stayed the night, but now all she wanted was to be left alone—with her phones.

"I need to tell you something, Diana..."

Whatever she had to say was surely of little consequence compared to Matthew lying unconscious in a hospital bed. Nothing else mattered. A heavy curtain of rain hung outside her patio doors. It seemed a fitting backdrop as she closed her eyes and waited for the phone to ring.

"It's about the break-in and the car bomb," Liz said. "I know who did it."

As Liz's words slowly penetrated, Diana's eyes blinked open. She struggled to separate what she was hearing from the incessant drizzle of the rain.

"Pay attention, Diana! I never really bought Brantley's alibi, but when I left his office with Sheila last week, I was too upset to question it..."

What was she talking about? "Spit it out, will you?"

"Once I cooled off, I got to thinking..." She lowered her voice. "I wanted to hurt him bad, Diana. Like crush his balls and cut off his dick, you know?"

It sounded like a good plan to Diana. After what happened to Matthew, she was ready to buy an assault weapon and go on a shooting spree. Problem was, she wasn't sure where to aim.

"Anyway..." she continued. "I decided to check out his alibi for the night of Jed's murder. That bit about him being in an Atlanta hotel seemed too perfect to be true."

"Didn't his secretary say she dropped him at the airport?"

"Yeah, but Brantley's a snake, remember? It would be easy for him to slink and slither off in a different direction."

Liz bristled with excitement. "I was determined to get the truth. You'd have been proud of me, Diana. I just picked up the phone and called the Peachtree Hotel. I pretended to be Sheila, and told them my boss had left his briefcase in his room by mistake. I told them he'd stayed the night of April ninth, and asked them to check the *Lost and Found...*"

She paused for effect. "Guess what? He never showed! They held his room until late, but he never even bothered to cancel. They charged his credit card anyway, so his receipt *appeared* to be the perfect alibi."

Diana shuddered. Matthew had assumed Roger Keene was responsible. Theoretically even Bobby Porter could have done it, since Matthew had bailed him out of jail. But Craven had always been Diana's top suspect, but for his alibi. She had cleaned away every trace of the brutal intruder from her bedroom, but the obscene message on the bathroom mirror was indelibly etched in her mind.

"I *am* proud of you Liz. But is Brantley really capable of murder?"

Liz ran agitated fingers through her hair. "Hell, yes. He's capable of murder, and much worse..." Her sweeping gesture encompassed the room. "I sneaked in here last night, before you locked the door. I saw all that sick sexual stuff, and believe me, it was Brantley."

Aside from two brief meetings, she'd had no personal contact with the man. The desecration of her apartment spoke of a hatred so intimate it bordered on insanity. "But why?"

Liz flushed with anger. "Think about it, Diana. You've blocked all his moves. He and Dennis were counting on the Porter listing, and when you failed to get it, Brantley took matters into his own hands and killed Jed. Adding insult to injury, you stole the plot plan incriminating Brantley, and that's what he was looking for last night. The car bomb was sheer malice. If he couldn't bury the evidence, he'd bury you—six feet under."

The word *bomb* plummeted her back to the depths of despair. She eyed the phones and prayed for Matthew. "Why don't they call?"

A sudden loud rapping at the door startled them both, and when it opened a crack, she saw Danny wearing her apron.

"Hot buttered biscuits, bacon, and scrambled eggs. Don't let 'em get cold!"

"I'm not hungry!" Liz and she said in unison.

Danny frowned. "C'mon, you gotta eat..."

Liz shook her head and waved him away, while Diana clung to the princess phone, willing it to ring.

"Your loss," Danny said. "I'll eat it all myself."

Once he left, closing the door behind him, Liz turned to her.

"Where did you hide the plot plan, anyway?"

She closed her eyes and pictured the plan folded in Ruby's glove compartment. Like everything else in her life, it had gone up in smoke.

And when the landline finally rang, she lifted the phone to her ear, but found she had no voice.

THIRTY-THREE

To catch a killer…

But it wasn't the hospital calling. It was only Mama, and she seemed determined to give Diana a hard time. She and Clara had learned about the break-in and the car bomb on the morning news, where pictures of the charred Subaru appeared on every local TV channel. She assumed Mama was worried about her, but in fact, she was mainly angry to have received the news second-hand.

"An unidentified *man* was hurt?" Mama said. "What man?"

"He's a friend, Mama. He was doing me a favor."

She covered the mouthpiece, but Diana heard her whispering to Clara, who was undoubtedly camped out in Mother's room. "*Claims* he's just a friend."

Diana begged her to get off the phone, but Mama had her own agenda.

"Clara and I think this mess is connected to Jedidiah's murder, and for your information, I have some important news of my own…"

If Diana ignored her, maybe she'd go away. No such luck.

"Guess who came to see us? Young Amy Keene, Jed's daughter. Remember when I couldn't meet you at the thrift shop? Well, Amy was in the neighborhood, so she came to Shady Oaks. Wasn't that nice? Amy already knew Clara, of course, but she also took quite a shine to me…."

Who cared? Ever since the encounter with Roger's truck, she'd been reluctant to call Amy. She had no idea how she'd feel about Diana, since she'd pressed charges against her husband, and was afraid to find out.

Mama read her mind. "Oh, don't worry, Amy's not mad at you. In fact, she hopes Roger gets locked up for life, after what he did to you."

Curious as she was about Mama's news, she held her tongue and hoped she'd get off the line. She already knew Roger had abused Amy for years, but judging by how Amy had protected him that day at the restaurant, something new must have happened.

"Did you know he was cheating on her?" Mama was relishing every minute. "He was having an affair with some tart he met at the Furniture Mart. Amy found a receipt from an antique shop in Roger's jeans. Seems he bought his girlfriend an expensive piece of jewelry with money from their son's college fund."

"Maybe now she'll have the good sense to divorce the bastard," Diana said.

"Amy moved out," Mama said. "Took her son and went to stay with her married daughter. Soon as Roger packs up and leaves, they'll go back home."

"That's good news, Mama, but will you please get off the phone?"

"Don't get snippy with me, young lady. I'm calling for your own good. Roger's not the reason Amy came to see me. She's discovered something vital concerning the sale of her father's land. Still not interested?"

"Please tell me quickly, Mother."

"No."

231

"What do you mean *no*?"

"Amy came to *me* because she couldn't get in touch with *you*. And since this is so important, I won't tell you over the phone. Come see me in person."

It was blackmail, pure and simple. "C'mon, Mama. I don't even have a car. You want me to spend money on a taxi, or Uber?"

"Smartest money you ever spent."

With that, Mama hung up.

"What was that all about?" Liz, still perched on the corner of Diana's bed, wanted the latest gossip, so Diana filled her in.

"So why don't you call Amy?" Liz said. "Don't let your mama jerk you around."

"Great idea, but I don't have her number. She's staying with her daughter, and I don't even know her daughter's married name." Even if Amy had something truly vital concerning Jed's land, it would just have to wait.

"Doesn't Amy have a cell phone?"

"Nope. Said she couldn't afford one."

"Okay, so what kind of antique jewelry did Roger buy his girlfriend?" Liz asked. "Was it a *sweetheart locket*? Are the slut's initials *CRA*?"

Liz's theory was a long shot. Diana said, "I thought Brantley Craven was your number one suspect? Are you having second thoughts?"

All of a sudden, Liz's face bleached white and her green eyes darted back and forth. "That's it, Diana! How come I didn't think of it before? *CRA* stands for *Craven*! Of course, Brantley did it. I knew it all along."

They stared at one another as Liz's observation sunk in. Outside the window, a bank of fog rolled in from the lake and curled up on Diana's patio. The shadowy hull of a boat floated along the horizon. The determined Sunday fisherman in the boat switched on his red and green running lights.

And then the doorbell rang, startling her back to reality and tolling a message of doom. Her mind closed in on itself. They had undoubtedly sent someone from the hospital to deliver the bad news in person. She could not move.

"Aren't you gonna answer it?" Liz demanded.

But Diana was frozen to the chair.

Moments later, someone knocked on her bedroom door. "Diana...?" Danny eased his head through the crack. "Can you come out here, please?"

They led Diana into the living room. Danny had rolled up his sleeves. Fluffs of soapsuds clung to his forearms, and he wore Diana's ruffled apron tied around his waist. As she followed them into the kitchen, looking for the bearer of bad tidings, the lingering odor of fried bacon made her sick.

Liz ran to the table, where a massive bouquet of spring flowers overflowed from an expensive basket. "Awesome! Look, Diana, the card is for you!"

Diana blinked and tried to process. It had only been the florist at the door. Her hands were trembling too much to open the card, so Liz did it for her.

"Golly, it's from Dennis." Liz seemed startled. "*Best wishes from the gang at Crawford Realty.*"

Danny shrugged. "Now that's a surprise. He doesn't seem like a guy who sends flowers. What's Dennis the Menace up to now?"

"Trying to score Brownie points," Liz said.

Danny buried his forearms in the sink, washing the dishes. "Or maybe he's a jerk most of the time, but managed to do one nice thing?"

"No way…" Liz rolled her eyes. "He knows you got the Porter listing, right, Diana?"

"No, I haven't had a chance to tell him."

"Well, that's weird." Liz frowned. "So the flowers are a genuine gesture of good will?"

In Diana's opinion, a leopard like Dennis rarely changed his spots. She fixed on Liz. "Hey, I'm really tired. You help Danny with the dishes, while I go back to my room to rest…"

She escaped before they could stop her and settled into her chair, with both phones nearby. When her cell phone finally rang, shrill as a scream, she snatched it up before her morbid misgivings got the better of her. "Hello?"

"How you feeling, kiddo?" the cheery male voice said. "Did you get my flowers?"

Dennis' voice filled her with sudden, unreasonable rage. Damn it, why couldn't everyone just stay off her bloody lines? She took a deep breath, allowing her ingrained good manners to take over. "Yes, I got them. Thank you very much." She could almost see her boss patting himself on the back. "But Dennis, I really can't talk right now. I'm expecting an important phone call."

"From Amy Keene, right?" He sounded positively thrilled. "Gotta tell you, Diana, I'm really impressed. Didn't think you could pull it off, but hey, but you scored a touchdown in the final inning. Good job!"

Football metaphors aside, something didn't add up. "How'd you know I got the listing, Dennis?" She listened to the ominous silence.

"Oh, I heard it through the grapevine," he said at last. "Amy told her husband, then Roger told Brantley, and then Brantley told me. You know the drill, good news travels fast."

So did bad news, and this chain of events didn't make sense. Why would Amy tell Roger? She'd taken great pains to keep their transaction secret. Plus, if Mama was right, Amy was furious with Roger for his infidelities.

"Tell the truth, Dennis. How'd you find out I got the listing?"

"Who cares? Brantley's hooked, and that's all that matters. He's wanted the Porter land forever, and we'll make a great team. That's real good news for you, too, Diana."

A vision of the stolen plot plan swam across her eyes, the acres and acres of solid gold investment. "Yes, I know Craven wants to develop the land, but what's that got to do with me?"

"Whew, lady..." He whistled through his teeth. "That explosion must have scrambled your brain. Do the math, Diana. As the listing agent, you stand to make a fortune when the land sells."

"But it could be months, even years, before a qualified buyer comes along," she countered.

"But we already have a qualified buyer. Aren't you listening? Brantley Craven is bringing his offer at noon on Wednesday. If all goes according to schedule, you'll be a very rich woman this time next month."

The small hairs at the nape of her neck prickled. Dennis' implication that she would accept Craven's offer was far from kosher. As Amy's agent, it was her duty to offer the property on the open market and stimulate competitive bidding. Even if she hadn't known Craven was famous for low-ball bids, she'd never lock Amy into a first offer.

"Sorry, Dennis, that's not how I do business. I intend to put Amy's property into the Multiple Listings and fight for the best possible price. That way everyone wins."

"That's crazy. A bird in hand's better than a hundred in the bush." His tenor voice was rapidly moving towards soprano.

She pictured him rubbing his injured football knee in frustration. But no matter how much he begged, or how many clichés he spouted, she wouldn't sell Amy down the river for a quick buck.

"Listen up, Diana. Brantley's bringing in his bid at noon sharp, and I expect you to be there. Missing the meeting is not an option. We'll all shake hands, he'll sign on the dotted line, and you *will* take his offer to Amy. You *will* tell her it's the best offer out there."

The hair prickling at the back of her neck was joined by the familiar twitching of her left eye. "No," she said firmly.

He snorted derisively. "Brantley said you'd give me a hard time. Bad move."

"Are you threatening me, Dennis?"

"Just be there, Diana. You don't wanna screw with Brantley Craven."

Amen to that. She abruptly hung up, shaking with fear and anger. At the same time, she was hungry. Yes, hungry. She stomped through the house to the kitchen, where Danny was building fat sandwiches for himself and Liz.

"Load mine up with mayonnaise," she said.

When the blasted phone rang again, she expected it was Dennis calling back, so she turned to Danny. "Answer that, will you? Tell the little prick to stay off the line."

He seemed startled by her outburst, yet he picked up the receiver and walked the phone into the far corner. Finally, he held it out to Diana. "I really think you should take this one…"

One look at his somber expression, and she sank onto a kitchen chair. It had to be the hospital calling with bad news about Matthew. She held out a shaky hand and took the receiver, as Danny led Liz discreetly out of earshot.

"Hello?" she whispered.

When the male voice began speaking, her blood started pumping double-time. She sneezed, she coughed, and tried to find enough breath to answer. In the end, she choked on her own laughter.

By the time Liz and Danny returned to the room, the call was over, and she was wheezing and hiccupping at the kitchen table. Tears of joy streamed down her face, and she howled like a banshee.

"Diana, are you all right?" Liz's eyes were enormous. "Calm down. What did they say about Matthew?"

"That *was* Matthew! I was talking to *Matthew!*"

"She's kidding, right?" Liz looked to Danny for confirmation.

He shook his head. "No, it's true. I spoke with Trout, too."

He looked like the cat who'd swallowed the canary. Liz shoved at him and turned to Diana. "God, what did he say?"

Diana giggled. "Well, first he told me he has a hard head, and then he asked me to go to his house and feed Ursie.

"What else?" Liz demanded.

"None of your damn business." She blushed.

Liz and Danny watched in awed silence as she tore into not one, but two ham and cheese sandwiches. When she finished,

237

she felt nourished with new strength and purpose. "I have a plan…" She licked her lips. "And I need your help…" She pulled a stray crumb into her mouth with the tip of her tongue.

They looked at one another, and then nodded.

"Since you agree…" She wiped each finger with a paper napkin. "We're in this together, and we're going to catch a killer."

THIRTY-FOUR

Queen Vic...

Danny looked up at the sky. It was good to see the sun again. Now he and Liz could surprise Diana outside by the shimmering water, where bobbing masts made for an ideal photo opportunity. Plus, Diana wouldn't see her present till she rounded the garage. He couldn't wait to see her face.

He tied the bundle of party-colored helium balloons to the antenna and slid the gifts Liz had wrapped onto the dashboard. Savoring the new car aroma, he decided this was a hell of a lot more fun than house painting and didn't regret playing hooky, not one little bit.

If Diana's plan went according to schedule, he'd take Wednesday off as well. He was sorry Liz and he couldn't play a bigger role in the drama, but Diana was determined. Timing was crucial, and Diana was the only one who could bring it all together. Unfortunately, her plan for baiting the trap put her alone, dead center with the killer, leaving Danny and Liz on the sidelines for backup and damage control.

But her plan made sense, in a weird kind of way, and he had to admit the lady had cunning and guts. Especially since the bait was nothing more than an elaborate bluff. It was insane to imagine she could pull it off, but the knot of fear in the pit of his stomach told him she'd do just that. Diana's trap was deadly.

He glanced at his watch just as Liz led a bewildered Diana around the corner, right on time. Her mouth dropped open as Liz dragged her towards the sparkling white Ford.

"What's all this?" she gasped, her eyes flicking wildly from one to the other.

"Well, ma'am..." he drawled. "Every detective needs her ride, and this baby's hot! Got a souped-up V8 engine, state-of-the-art sound system with CB radio, an overhead cam for ultra-fast acceleration—she's fucking loaded!"

He opened the door and pushed Diana in behind the wheel, while Liz scrambled around and climbed into the passenger seat. "Sweet, right?" Danny continued proudly. "Check out the blue leather. One shade darker than your eyes."

Those very eyes registered shock as she stared up at Danny, who was leaning in the window. "What have you done? I can't afford this!"

"Sure you can." Liz piped up. "It's a leased car, fully deductible in our line of work. Once you start chauffeuring your buyers around in this beauty, you'll close every deal."

"I've never seen anything like it..." Her fingers traveled trance-like across the elegantly contoured instrument panel. "It looks like a space ship."

"It's a Crown Victoria, same model the cops use," Danny crowed. "Matter of fact, it's an overstock police vehicle. The dealer had an extra from the fleet he purchased for North Mecklenburg, so now you can take on the bad guys in style, Diana."

"But I don't need all these gadgets."

"Why not?" Liz beamed. "Danny got you a good deal—all this for the same price as the stripped-down version. Besides, just imagine yourself out on the Interstate. You'll leave everything on wheels in your dust. Next time a nasty old truck decides to play games, guess who wins?"

"Now give her the *big* present," Danny said. "Go on and open it, Diana."

Her fingers fumbled with the gift-wrap until she lifted out a little black thing, flat as a playing card. "What's this?"

"Your brand new cell phone," Danny said. "Liz said the one you have is shaped like a brick and weighs a ton. Welcome to the twenty-first century, Diana. Time to get with the program."

She stared at the thing and tapped the screen. She'd watched the other agents thumbing these, of course, but how would her fingers ever work the tiny keyboard? Just as she'd clung to her dear Ruby, she felt defensive about her old cell, which was a flip-phone, not a brick.

"You'll get used to it, I promise." Liz smiled. "And look, you can mount it on the dash, like this…. No more excuses for leaving it behind."

She had to admit, both the astonishing new auto and the sleek little phone had some snazzy appeal. What would Matthew think? She looked from one to the other. "You two are the best!"

"Give her the last present." Danny's voice was hoarse with emotion.

"Not here," Liz insisted. "Let's do it down on the dock."

He smiled. They had planned this ceremony in advance, and so far it had gone smooth as a baby's bottom. Liz hooked Diana's arm and guided her towards the marina, while he untied the balloons and followed.

They all sat side by side on a bench and watched a flock of Canada geese bobbing just beyond the end of the pier.

"Go on, rip it open!" Liz pressed another colorful package into her hands.

241

The world was silent, except for the gentle lapping of waves, as she unwrapped a framed photograph. "Oh, my God…" She breathed. "It's a picture of Ruby!" Tears welled up as she beheld her beloved station wagon parked with Lake Norman in the background. "This is beautiful! Where'd you get it?"

Liz cleared her throat. "No biggie. I was photographing one of our listings, and got Ruby by mistake. I messed around with my computer and came up with this. Never saw the old gal look so good."

Danny captured Diana's hand and led her to the end of the pier, where Liz took over and gave her the balloons.

"What now?" she asked.

"Let 'em fly!" Danny grinned.

"Yeah, it's an old custom, a way to let go of grief…" Liz explained. "Remember Ruby as they sail away, and once they're out of sight, you can go on with your life."

She sensed a weak smile curving the corners of her mouth as a dozen bright balloons floated into the sky. The flock of geese was entranced. They splashed and honked. They flew up and joined the balloons, playing together in the clouds.

"Feel better?" Danny gently inquired.

She nodded.

"Now pick a name for your new car," Liz said.

She wiped her eyes and looked to where the birds and balloons were mere dots in the sky. "Well, you claim this new car is formidable. She'll reign supreme and wield her power, right?"

Both agreed, puzzled.

"In that case, there is only one name for my new Crown Victoria. I shall call her *Queen Vic*."

THIRTY-FIVE

Bait the first hook…

The time had come to bait the first hook, and it was bound to be a tricky maneuver. Diana's timing had to be perfect, but every approach to contacting Roger had its flaws. For one thing, she didn't know his work schedule. Did truck drivers keep regular hours? She was well aware of his eavesdropping habit. He had listened in on her conversation with Amy the day they planned their outing to the thrift shop, and that little faux pas had nearly cost Diana her life.

She did have one advantage: she knew that Amy had moved out, leaving Roger alone in the house. But could she bluff him? Could she call and ask to speak to Amy, or would he know, through some evil osmosis, that she already knew Amy was gone? It was all too complicated and uncertain. In the end, she'd have to take her chances.

She steered Queen Vic into the parking lot at Lake Norman Regional Medical Center and switched off the ignition. Unlike Ruby's after-rattle, the Queen was as silent in repose as she was on the highway. On the open road, Diana had quickly learned to tread lightly on the accelerator. Much as she missed Ruby, the pent-up power and high tech luxuries in her new car really charged Diana's battery.

How silly! But Queen Vic did boost her self-confidence. She fancied people noticed her when she was sitting in the driver's seat. They smiled when they pulled up beside her at stoplights, and—oh, what nonsense!

Even more exciting than her new car, was the fact that she was about to see Matthew for the first time since the accident. She had taken special care dressing for the occasion, choosing a pastel blue angora sweater dress, killer high heels, and her grandmother's pearl necklace. Normally this getup made her feel foolishly feminine, like she was in disguise, but today it was okay.

Was her cold was to blame for these uncharacteristic lapses? The antihistamine she was taking made her fuzzy-brained, so maybe she shouldn't call Roger until her head cleared. Calling him should be her main concern, but instead she found herself worrying about whether her makeup disguised the red edges of her nose. Did she smell like Vicks instead of jasmine? Would Matthew notice? Well, she shouldn't get that close to him anyway. She certainly didn't want him to catch the damned thing.

But back to business. It was now, or never. She blew her nose, took a deep breath, and lifted her new cell phone from its cradle. She consulted her watch and saw it was almost noon. She had memorized Amy's old number, so she touched it onto the keypad and waited, hoping against hope that no one would answer. She panicked after one ring, and almost hung up, but then he answered.

"Yeah?" Roger seemed to be talking through a mouthful of food.

Hearing his voice totally unnerved her, but somehow she got her words out. "Hello. May I speak with Amy?"

"She ain't here. Who's asking?"

She knew he'd recognize her voice. "When will she be home?"

Roger chewed, swallowed, and then cleared his throat. "Oh yeah, you're the real estate lady," he growled, then laughed. "You've got some nerve, bitch."

All the terror came flooding back. She saw the message in red lipstick on her bathroom mirror. Her throat constricted and she feared she couldn't go on.

"Heard you had some car trouble…" The weasel sucked wind through the gap between his two front teeth. "One of them homemade bombs, like you hook up to the ignition? Sucker who connected it must've fucked up. Should've used a heavier gauge wire, don't you reckon?"

The lump in her throat was choking her. Roger had all but confessed his guilt. She knew for a fact that no technical information about the bomb had been released to the media.

"Seems you have bad luck with your automobiles, bitch. Fool who set that bomb had bad luck too—right trap, wrong rat."

She couldn't breathe. The phone was a live, malevolent creature clawing at her hand. She lifted a trembling finger and punched *end call*, killing it. She threw it onto the passenger seat and gasped for air. Sitting very still, she practiced inhaling, then exhaling, until her breathing returned to normal.

The phone lay on its back, its keypad radiating a demonic aura. She was afraid to touch it, to absorb its poison through her fingertips, and worst of all, she had failed her mission. Now that she knew the truth about Roger, how could she catch him? She didn't even get her bait on the hook.

She didn't have the guts to try again.

As she stared at the phone, it began to vibrate, and then played a hyped-up electronic rendition of *Happy Days Are Here*

Again. She was stunned. Danny had told her he'd programmed it with a special ringtone, but this was ridiculous. It played a full chorus before she realized she was supposed to answer.

"Hello?" she croaked.

A man cleared his throat. "Sorry, lady. I didn't mean what I said before…"

Roger. He must have redialed her number

"You gotta understand, I was pissed. You told the sheriff about our little *accident* out on the highway, and now I'm in a shitload of trouble."

Did the asshole expect an apology?

"You hear me, lady? I'm trying to play nice. You wanted to talk to Amy, but she's at work now. I'll give her your message soon as she gets home."

He was lying. She knew Amy wouldn't be going home anytime soon, but Fate had granted her a second chance to bait her hook. From his tone, smooth as greased treacle, he seemed to want to reconcile their differences. More likely, he wanted something else entirely, and so did she.

"Roger, you know Amy hired me to sell her father's land."

"Yeah, I know. Amy and me don't keep secrets."

Another lie. "Did you tell Brantley Craven that I was the listing agent?"

"Who the hell is Brantley Craven?"

He sounded confused. He was too dumb to fake it, so she believed him—Roger did not know Craven. This contradicted Dennis' claim that Roger told Brantley, then Brantley told him. So how the hell had her boss found out? She'd have to sort it out later, because right now, she had to stay on target.

She returned her attention to Roger. "I called with some good news. Just by chance, I've stumbled across some evidence that will lead the police straight to Jedidiah's murderer."

In the pause that followed, she heard the flick of a lighter, a minute crackle, and the intake of breath as Roger lit a cigarette.

"It was just dumb luck…" she bumbled on. "The police had scoured every inch of Jed's farm, but after Amy gave me the listing, I went back up there and did a little snooping of my own…"

"Bullshit!" he barked. "My guess is you found dick."

So much for the niceties. "Well, Sheriff Bearfoot thinks otherwise," she told him. "I'm handing the evidence over to him tomorrow afternoon."

He coughed. "What bullshit evidence?"

She massaged the bridge of her stuffy nose and tried to think. How much should she reveal? A moron like Roger was unlikely to carry a locket around, but then Liz had that theory about Roger's receipt for antique jewelry, a gift for his mistress. She decided to take a chance.

"I found a locket, Roger. It was wedged between the boards of the dock where Jed was killed. Bearfoot thinks the locket will lead directly to the killer."

She tried to read his next silence. His cigarette sizzled as he stubbed it out.

"You're carrying that stupid locket around with you?" he said at last.

"Of course not. It's locked in a safe place until tomorrow, when I give it to Bearfoot."

"You're meeting the sheriff tomorrow."

"Yes, I'm taking the locket to the Hall of Justice, in Statesville. I'll give it to him there, after I stop by the Porter farm to pick up that vase Amy wants…"

"What vase?"

She didn't have the locket, the vase was a figment of her imagination, so she was creating fiction on the fly. But hallelujah, she seemed to be leading Roger by the nose.

"Didn't Amy tell you about the vase?" she continued. "It's an old Willow Ware pattern that belonged to her mama. I promised to get it for her before I started showing buyers through the house. Lucky I know where to find it. It's sitting in plain view on her daddy's dinner table."

"Oh, *that* vase," he said. "Sure, I know how much it means to her."

Roger was very talented to remember an imaginary vase. She was truly impressed. She was even more impressed by her own lies. She was learning to spin yarns with the best of them.

"I'll be at the Porter farm at two in the afternoon," she said. "Tell Amy I'll drop the vase at your house after I finish with the sheriff."

"You goin' to the farm alone?"

How obvious could one man be? "Sure, why not?"

She could almost picture him loading his gun, sharpening his knife, preparing his weapon of choice. Or maybe he'd simply conk her over the head and drop her in the lake. It had worked with poor old Jed.

"I'll tell Amy to expect you, then," he said before hanging up.

THIRTY-SIX

Sharks in the pond...

Even flat on his back, Matthew was charming. Sick as he was, he made Diana feel brand new. Although they were allotted only a few precious minutes together, she forgot her cold, her trashed condo, and even her impending showdown with a killer.

The hard part was the *hands off* policy she'd imposed on herself. She longed to take his face into her hands. His poor head was bandaged mummy-style, but this only emphasized his kind brown eyes and wide sensual mouth. His dark eyes burned warm in a pale face glittering with fever, yet they radiated the same good humor as his crooked grin. She wanted to kiss his lips and run cool fingers along his strong jaw, but she kept her distance.

"How are you feeling?" she whispered.

"Like I told you, I've got a hard old head." He winked. "Seems like you went to great lengths to get yourself a new car, Diana."

"How did you know?" By the glint in his eye, she realized he knew the whole story. "Danny told you, didn't he?"

"Matter of fact, Danny called me for advice. He figured I might offer some mechanical expertise, and I was happy to oblige."

"So Queen Vic is all your fault?"

"Nope. I just told Danny to buy American. The rest is all his fault."

Matthew captured her hand and held on tight. How could she tell him how sorry she was, how responsible she felt for this disaster, when each time she opened her mouth to apologize, he cut her off? They wasted their precious time chatting about V8 engines and Ursie's preferred brand of dog food. Of course, she revealed not one word about her plan, because Matthew would be furious.

From the beginning, he'd warned her to steer clear of danger, and as she watched him lying there, she wished to God she'd taken his advice. But there was no turning back. Matthew would be avenged, but only after the mission was accomplished would he be told the details. Liz, Danny, and she had made a sacred pact not to tell him. They'd agreed to shield him from worry and keep their big mouths shut.

But then, towards the end of their visit, Matthew pulled her down against his chest. He stroked her hair and brushed a kiss across her forehead.

"Stay out of trouble, you hear?" His breath was warm against her ear. "Go home, lock the doors, and stay put till I'm out of here. Promise?"

She nodded, but the evasion was painful. She longed to burrow into his safety and scrap the whole project, but fortunately the nurse kicked her out before she weakened.

She composed herself as the elevator dropped to the lobby, and rather than dwell on her deception, she studied the details of her physical world. The hospital corridors were less terrifying by the light of day. Gangs of workmen hustled in preparation for the Grand Opening. Paint cans still littered the floor, but the plants had been set in place and the art had been uncrated. Even the blue-haired nurse was more perky and efficient.

"Our boy's looking good!" she called from her post behind the reception desk. "Who'd have guessed it? I thought Trout was a goner when they first brought him in."

"Yes, he looks great!" Diana agreed. "But you're spoiling him. He thinks he's a celebrity with all the attention he's getting."

"He is a celebrity, don't you know? Our very first patient, a success story. But you look awful, ma'am. Have you seen a doctor? Colds like yours can turn to pneumonia."

She thanked the nurse for the Tylenol PM she'd given her the other night, and then made a rapid retreat before she got a health lecture. The euphoria of being with Matthew was fading fast, and when the nurse said the word *cold*, her clogged head started to throb and her body ached from her hair to the soles of her feet.

The conversation with Roger had woven a thread of fear into her other unpleasant symptoms, and soon the fear dominated. Her mind reeled with images of violence as she rushed down the corridor and bumped headlong into a ghost.

She shrank away in terror, because she was gazing into the fathomless blue eyes of Jedidiah Porter. The evil stared back at her, as it did in her nightmares, and as the apparition closed in, she tried not to faint.

"Hey, I remember you..." the ghost said. "You're the lady who come with Trout. I seen you at the jail, remember?"

Blood flowed back into her brain and restored her reason. This man was much younger than Jed. He seemed more nervous than evil.

"Bobby Porter?"

"Figured you'd remember me."

She remembered him all too well, but he looked far less menacing today in his threadbare blue suit than he had in black and white stripes. The collar of his white shirt hung too loose around his scrawny neck, and a loud floral tie seemed absurdly out of place on the man.

"I reckon you already been to see Trout." He blushed.

She nodded, mesmerized by the lovely bouquet of spring flowers—daffodils, tulips and lily of the valley—gripped in Bobby's bony hand. She spotted dirt under his fingernails, but otherwise he was scrubbed clean, his old shoes polished to a high sheen.

He followed her gaze. "Oh, I picked the flowers just before I come. I grow 'em out in front of my trailer at Sylvan Acres. Do you think Trout'll like 'em?"

"I'm sure he will." She knew Matthew was absolutely convinced of Bobby's innocence, but her doubts were as strong as ever. She decided to bait the second hook.

"Bobby, I have good news. Someone wants to pay a lot of money for your father's land, and I've also found new evidence that will lead Sheriff Bearfoot to the real killer."

His eyes narrowed and he scratched his jaw. Were two bits of information too much for him to process? She didn't know where her lies would lead this time, but why not fish for all the sharks in the pond?

"What evidence?" he said at last.

The locket story wouldn't work on Bobby. He knew Juanita had the locket he'd given her around her neck, so she'd need to keep her fabrications vague. "Since you signed that consent form that allows me sell the place, I've spent some time out at the farm, cleaning up and so forth. Just by chance, I found something that didn't belong there. I'm sure the killer left it, something *personal*. The sheriff thinks this important evidence will lead directly to the person who murdered your father. I'm giving it to Bearfoot tomorrow."

Bobby's mouth twisted. "That sheriff's an idiot. Even if the killer gave him an engraved calling card, Bearfoot couldn't catch him. Look what happened to me."

Maybe she was the idiot. Clearly Bobby thought so, yet she pressed on with the story. "Anyway, I plan to give Bearfoot this evidence, but first I'll be visiting the farm tomorrow at two in the afternoon…to pick up a vase for Amy…" She delivered the whole spiel, the same lies she'd spun for Roger, and when she finished, Bobby seemed to think she was nuts.

"Beggin' your pardon, ma'am, but that idea's just plain foolish. Dangerous, too. Who else did you tell?"

"No one."

"Not even Trout?"

"Especially not Trout! Matthew's sick, Bobby. He shouldn't be troubled by all this."

She couldn't read his reaction, but his knuckles blanched white around the flower stems and his face turned the same angry red she'd witnessed in the jail. "Promise not to tell Matthew, okay, Bobby?"

As he stared at her, his eyes were dead and calculating. "Trout won't hear it from my lips, ma'am."

And then he walked away, leaving her more uncertain than ever. If Bobby was the killer, he was cool. But then he'd have to be cold as dry ice to murder his own father.

She continued to organize her thoughts as she waited at the electronic glass door leading to the parking lot. When the door sighed open, she spotted another familiar face. *Dear God!* She panicked and ducked behind a concrete pillar just as the man rounded the corner and strode in her direction.

Sheriff Wayne Bearfoot's chiseled features angled into the afternoon sun, like a hound following a suspicious scent. Or maybe he was sniffing the store-bought bouquet in his powerful hand. His raven black hair was combed flat above his darting hunter's eyes and his tall frame moved easily in civilian clothes.

Her life was getting way too complicated. She flattened against the pillar, hoping to blend with the lengthening shadows. She covered her face to stifle the sneeze building in the back of her nose.

Oh what a tangled web we weave, when first we practice to deceive. The demonic litany rolled round and round in her head. The last thing she needed was a confrontation with the High Sheriff. She suspected he'd come to visit Matthew, so he was destined to bump headlong into Bobby. No love lost between those two men. If one said *heads*, the other said *tails*, and Diana would be the lying dog caught in the middle. She prayed Bobby would keep his big mouth shut.

The Great White Spirit must have heard her prayers, because the sneeze didn't explode until the Great Red Hunter disappeared beyond the electronic door. To celebrate, she sneezed a dozen times and felt downright victorious heading into the parking lot.

But then she wasted five minutes looking for Ruby instead of Queen Vic. She lost more time learning she couldn't shift out of *park* until she stepped on the brake. Her mind was a useless fuzz ball, a fact quite helpful to any killer intent on putting out the few lights she had left

THIRTY-SEVEN

Without a parachute…

So far, two potential killers were set to meet Diana at two o'clock tomorrow. At noon tomorrow, she'd add the third suspect to her list, and with a little luck, she'd lose the head cold and regain her wits before it was too late.

She considered her predicament as she lay stretched out on the sofa, watching the sun set on Lake Norman through the V of her feet. She'd enjoyed a little wine before supper, but had no appetite for the tuna salad, even though it was her favorite. Eating alone night after night was a drag, and once upon a time, a million years ago, she'd actually had a family who pampered her when she was sick.

Past history. She closed her eyes and listened to WDAV, the local classical radio station. She should drag herself to the bedroom for a proper sleep, but lacking energy for such an effort, the couch would do just fine. Like her father used to say: *I'll sleep when I'm dead.*

That very afternoon she'd held Ursie's warm face in her hands.

"How you doing, girl?" She'd cooed into the dog's soft ear. "Do you miss your daddy? Don't worry, he'll be home soon."

Ursie had been waiting, just like Matthew said, curled up on a big fluffy quilt under his back steps. The dog smiled when she arrived and held up her knotted, bullet-shot paw. When she hugged the giant creature and felt Ursie's hard body lean against her, she couldn't believe how terrified she'd once been of the gentle Doberman.

Afterwards, she'd stopped by Matthew's store and asked the young man behind the counter to feed Ursie tomorrow, and the next day. Just in case…

She was dreaming about Ursie when the princess phone rang. Her reflex was to answer, but her brain urged her to let the answering machine screen the call.

"*Hello?*" Matthew's deep voice filled the room. "*If you're home, Diana, I sure as heck wish you'd pick up…*"

She chuckled. Obviously talking to an answering machine was not his idea of fun.

"*Well, I guess you're sleeping, but I heard you stopped in at the store. How's Ursie doing? I bet she was mighty glad to see you…*"

She pulled up the blanket and cuddled it, delighted to hear the concern in his voice.

"*The boy said you asked him to take over feeding Ursie. What's up, Diana? Are you still sick with that cold?*" He cleared his throat. "*Listen, now, I know you're up to something. When Bobby came to visit this morning, he told me a yarn that didn't make any sense…*"

She hoisted herself upright and paid attention. So Bobby was a blabbermouth, after all.

"*Call as soon as you get this message, you hear? I'm not fooling, Diana. I got a bad feeling you're poking your nose in where it doesn't belong. I'm of a mind to call Bearfoot. So call me, darn it!*"

He hung up without saying goodbye, and she flopped back down into the cushion. For once she was glad Matthew was confined to a hospital bed. She could ignore his call like it never happened. Besides, he was bluffing. He'd never contact Bearfoot based on some cock and bull story from Bobby Porter, so for the moment, she was safe.

As she drifted into sleep, she smiled and thought about Matthew. Unlike her, he was a practical person. *He* would never jump off a cliff without a parachute.

Roller coaster…

"It belongs to my mother," Danny explained as he pulled a tiny revolver from the pocket of his jeans. "You take it, Diana."

Danny and Liz had arrived at her condo at the crack of dawn.

"Is that a cap gun?" Diana snorted.

His face fell. "Hell no! It's a Derringer, a classic. I'll show you how to load it."

She pushed the gun away. "No thanks. I'll have plenty to worry about without shooting myself in the foot. You keep it, Danny."

"I have my own weapons racked up in the truck," he said.

"*I'll* take it…" Liz snatched the little revolver, along with its ammo clip, and dropped them into her handbag as though such things were routine.

Diana gaped in disbelief. Who were these people? Bonnie and Clyde? She'd heard that every citizen in North Carolina possessed his own arsenal, and now she was tempted to believe it.

"When Brantley comes after you, you'll be sorry you don't have the gun." Liz was dead serious. "I intend to be ready no matter what goes down."

"She's right," Danny added. "Maybe Liz should go to the office with you? How long is Brantley's fuse? What if he explodes prematurely?"

Taking Liz along was tempting, but when she glanced at her stricken face, she knew it was a bad idea. Liz hadn't seen Craven since he tried to rape her, and the prospect clearly terrified her.

"I'll be fine on my own," she reassured them. "Besides, you two have your work cut out for you. It's crucial that you be in place before I arrive."

"You can count on us," were Liz's parting words.

So now it was Diana's turn.

She parked between Dennis' silver Lexus and Brantley's Mercedes SUV. Both cars wore blotchy patches of gray primer as they awaited final repairs. Normally this would have tickled her sense of irony, but today it made her remember the rainy night when she stole the plot plan. She thought about Matthew in his hospital bed and wondered if any of these tragic events would have occurred if she'd minded her own business.

Too late now. She peered through the window and saw the two men were already seated at the conference table. She could almost smell the coffee steaming from their cups. The Offer to Purchase papers were laid out on the table as they simultaneously checked their watches, and then looked at one another in disgust.

Easy, boys. She was ten minutes late and enjoying every minute she kept them waiting. As the crucial showdown approached, she was oddly calm and ready. She welcomed the inevitability of this meeting and the chaos that would follow in its aftermath. It was much like a roller coaster lifting to its highest crest, poised for its final, steepest plunge.

Both men stood when she entered the room, an unexpected courtesy under the circumstances. Were they as nervous as she was? She hoped Craven's nerves would be downright frazzled by the time this meeting was done. It was essential to their plan.

"We started without you, Diana." Her boss wore his Cheshire cat grin, the one reserved for his least important clients. "The Offer is straight forward. No big surprises, right, Brantley?"

"No big surprises." Craven yawned. He had flopped into his seat and planted the elbows of his expensive silk suit firmly on the table. He balanced a pen laterally between the balls of his two index fingers and stared at her from above the pen.

"Offers to Purchase are pretty mundane," she agreed as Dennis, always the gentleman, pulled out her chair before taking his seat. "I'm glad you did the boring paperwork for me."

Craven snickered and began tapping the table with his pen. "C'mon, let's get this sucker signed. I have another appointment uptown."

He rudely tossed the papers towards Diana's end of the table, and she studiously ignored them. She winked at her boss. "Get me a cup of coffee, will you, Dennis?"

Like a little boy called to task by his mommy, Dennis instantly rose and walked to the coffee machine. Seeing the pot was empty, he blushed and looked to Craven for guidance.

She smiled. "Why don't you brew us a fresh pot, Dennis?" She needed to get him out of the room while she hooked Craven. She figured Dennis would go to the restroom to get water, and that would give her all the time she needed. He was on his way out the door, when Craven called him back:

"Get back in here, Crawford!" he growled. "Weren't you listening? I don't have all day."

Dennis was conflicted. A sheen of perspiration spread across his brow as he looked from one to the other. In the end, he fixed on Craven. Not a good sign.

"Sorry, Diana." Dennis blushed. "I'm not much good at making coffee anyway."

All right, if this was how Craven wanted to play, she'd proceed with both men in the room, but first she needed time to formulate her thoughts. She picked up the Offer.

"I'll look this over. Mr. Craven is a savvy businessman, so I should read the fine print."

At a glance, she saw his offer was ridiculously low. No surprise there, but if she recommended this bid to Amy, the Real Estate Board should revoke her license.

"Oh dear, Mr. Craven, surely you can do better than *this*?" She lifted her eyebrows in mock horror.

Craven tossed his pen at her and rolled his eyes. "You're giving me a headache, Diana. Just check the damned thing and take it to your client. I'd do it myself, but it'll carry more weight if Amy sees you."

She lifted her half-frame reading glasses from her purse and bent over the document, ignoring Craven's heavy sighs. As she moved her index finger along the fine print like a dotty schoolmarm, she slowly began telling the story about the evidence she had found.

Without glancing up from her task, she noted an increased restlessness around the table. She heard excessive shuffling of feet and clearing of throats. Craven retrieved his pen, and began tapping it ever more rapidly on the table. When she finished her recitation, including the bit about how she was going to turn the locket over to Bearfoot after her two o'clock visit to the farm, she finally dared to peek. She had a captive audience indeed.

Dennis' sheen had escalated to a profuse sweat. He loosened his tie and massaged his football knee. "That's quite a story, Diana," he said.

"Sounds like a load of crap to me." Craven's crudeness knew no bounds. His black eyes glittered above his twisted lip. The little scar on his jaw glowed red. "Haven't you bought yourself enough trouble lately?"

His inflection put her on guard. Exactly how much did he know about her troubles?

"Are you really carrying the locket around with you?" Dennis blinked. "Isn't that kind of dangerous?"

Ignoring them both, she finished reading the Offer to Purchase and stuffed it into her briefcase. "I'll present this to Amy, but she'll laugh in my face."

"She won't laugh if you do your job, Diana…" Craven followed her to the door. "I'm sure Dennis has cautioned you to do the right thing."

He pushed past, pinning her momentarily against the doorjamb. She felt his heat and heard the racing of his heart. After he allowed her to pass, he trailed her to the parking lot. He was so close, she felt his hot breath on the back of her neck.

"I read about the break-in at your condo." He smiled. "What a pity. And what about that guy who wrote an obscene message on your mirror? Jesus, what a fucked up psycho." Brantley Craven dropped his voice to a ragged whisper. "Haven't you learned your lesson, Diana? You could get yourself killed!"

He slipped into his Mercedes before she could respond. As the implication of his words sunk in, all the courage she possessed drained away like blood from a mortal wound. He slammed his car door and drove off the lot, just before her knees turned to jelly.

Diana leaned against Queen Vic. Eventually she eased the door open, and as she melted into the blue upholstery, she finally knew the truth. Not one newspaper had published anything about the message on her mirror. So, besides the police and her close circle of friends, only the intruder knew that tidbit.

And good old Liz had been right all along.

THIRTY-NINE

Turn back the clock...

The early afternoon sun blazed across the sky, glittering off the dizzy whitecaps and blinding Diana. She pulled over at the Perth Road Bridge to clear her vision and collect her thoughts. This was déjà vu, and not lost upon her that it was the one- month anniversary of the day she'd met Jedidiah Porter. That evening she'd pulled over in this exact same spot as the sun was setting, without one clue about what life held in store. If she'd known what the next thirty days would bring, would she have turned old Ruby around and avoided it all?

This time Diana knew the way. She twisted the key and Queen Vic purred into the traffic with all the power of a mountain cat. The sky was so clear it hurt her eyes, the lake so blue it ached somewhere deep in her soul. What more could a girl want in a farewell party?

She thought about the things she loved, like Chessie, her beloved mare and Ursie, the new dog in her life. Did she prefer animals to humans? What about her children, Robby and Amanda? She missed them so much it hurt, but they had their own lives now. Of course, she still had Mama, and now Matthew. He was new in the last thirty days, so would she turn back the clock?

No way!

The gravel washboard euphemistically called Porter Farm Road brought back vivid memories as she stopped at the foot of the dirt path leading to the homestead. Where the hell were Liz and Danny? She peered deep into the forest, but saw no sign of her backup team.

She checked her watch. It was almost two. Her mysterious visitor would arrive any minute, or worse still, what if he was already up at the house? She panicked and grabbed her cell phone. Danny had programmed his number to speed-dial. At the time, it had seemed foolish, but he'd insisted. And now, as she dialed, she feared she'd been silly not to accept the gun as well.

"Diana?" His voice was a crackly whisper.

"Where are you, Danny? You promised you'd be here!"

"Take it easy, Diana. See that mess of bushes at the end of the path? Watch carefully..."

She stared into the green tangle and saw a set of white lights flash on and off—Danny's headlights.

"See? Told you." Danny crowed.

"You're invisible!"

"That's the whole idea, am I right?"

"Hi, Diana..." Liz came on speaker. "How'd it go at the office? Anybody follow you?"

"I didn't see anyone, but Dennis wanted to come along, can you believe it? He chased me through the parking lot and insisted it was too dangerous for me to go alone. All of a sudden he's my big brother. He almost blew the whole thing."

"Bummer. How'd you stop him?"

"I said *no* about fifty times, and then finally, I just left."

"What about Brantley?"

A shiver of fear shot up the back of Diana's neck, and she glanced over her shoulder. "I agree with you, Liz, Brantley's the one, but I see no sign of him yet. I'm driving up to the farm now, but remember, don't call unless it's an emergency. Give me enough time to get a confession. We don't want to scare him off too soon."

"We understand, Diana." Liz's voice was somber. Much to her credit, she did not say *I told you so* regarding Craven. Instead, her subdued reaction reflected Diana's own fear. Of all the suspects, Brantley Craven inspired true terror.

"Take your phone with you everywhere, Diana," Danny said. "Remember how I taught you to set it to record? Then keep it close, in your shirt pocket, so you can catch everything the fucker says. Most of all, call at the first sign of trouble. Promise?"

"Yeah, yeah, I promise." Contrary to what they seemed to believe, she didn't have a death wish. But she loved them for caring. They were two more precious gifts from her new life. So no, she would not turn back the clock.

Forward was the only option.

They said their goodbyes, and she started walking up the path. Unlike the night she'd first encountered Jed, today the driveway was dry, hard, and navigable. As she eased along the lane, she saw that the trees now bore full young leaves. She let herself to be hypnotized by their dancing patterns on the ground. That evening one month ago, she'd heard the song of a mockingbird, and then the terrifying echo of the creature's footfalls stalking her through the woods. Today's adventure promised to be far more lethal. And yet, it was better to be the hunter, than the hunted.

But was she the hunter? Her name, Diana, in ancient mythology certainly equated her with the hunt. Sure enough, all her senses were heightened as she came out of the forested valley and into the dazzling sunlight. The Porter farmland was silent, deserted, and seemingly as benign as a graveyard. And when she lifted her eyes to the ridge, to the grove of pecan trees, she remembered how afraid she'd been when the fearsome creature howled.

The view from this meadow was still stupendous, with Lake Norman glistening on three sides of a magnificent promontory. And perhaps it was the haunting beauty of the moment, or the way the sun bleached the roof of Jed's sleeping bungalow, but Diana was at peace.

FORTY

Watching and waiting…

Danny grumbled, "No one's coming. The guy should be here by now."

Liz squinted through the underbrush for a better look up the road. "Give him time. It's only ten after two. Brantley will show."

He sighed and rolled down the windows. Birds chirped and darted in the overgrown meadow behind them. Otherwise, the silence was profound.

The earthy smell of new growth filled her nostrils as Liz strained to listen. Then, from far away, she heard the whine of an engine and saw dust lifting off the gravel.

"He's coming!" Danny stiffened on the seat beside her. "Yeah, check it out. He's really moving."

Sure enough, a silver Lexus spun around the corner, barely slowing as it curved into Jed's driveway.

"Oh, shit, it's only *Dennis,*" she moaned. "Why didn't that asshole listen for once in his life, and stay the hell away?" She snatched the phone and dialed Diana. "He'll ruin everything!"

Danny looked on as Liz ranted to Diana. "What did she say?" he asked when she hung up.

"She's pissed, but what can we do? She figures it'll still work if we keep our cool, but she'll have to stall Dennis at the house until Brantley arrives."

"Yeah, but once Brantley sees Dennis' car, won't he freak?"

She sighed. "Who knows? Diana thinks it would be worse if he saw Dennis' car *leaving* the farm. In that case, he'd just turn around and leave, too, figuring he'd been made. Diana says just *showing up* is an indication of Brantley's guilt."

"Try selling that theory to the cops."

Danny was clearly disappointed, and so was she. "There's not one damn thing we can do about it." She sighed deeply. "Diana wants us to wait thirty minutes and not call her under any circumstances. So if Brantley hasn't arrived by then, we'll all go home."

They joined hands and slid closer together on the truck seat, watching and waiting.

FORTY-ONE

That crazy dog...

"Damn it, Dennis, I told you not to come!"

She tucked the phone into the pocket of her blazer and climbed out of the car. No point recording yet. She crossed her arms and scowled as her boss limped up the stony grade. At least he'd parked at the bottom of the drive, where his Lexus was well concealed behind a bank of bushes. If Craven did show up, he wouldn't see Dennis' car right away.

"Sorry, Diana." He grinned sheepishly. "I was worried about you. What's the big deal?"

She growled under her breath. The man was behaving like a naughty little boy, and she wanted to spank his bottom raw. Besides, since when had he been concerned about her safety?

"Why are you really here, Dennis?"

"Hey, I've never even seen this place, and we've already sold it. It's my duty as a broker to eyeball a major listing."

She could barely contain her irritation as he followed her to Jedidiah's front porch. Maybe he'd never actually seen the property, but he was sure as hell intimately acquainted with the lay of the land, as his secret plot plan proved.

The strange inner peace she'd enjoyed before he arrived quickly vanished at Jed's door. The floorboards creaked under their feet. She could almost see the old man leaning against the doorjamb, appraising her from behind thick glasses. As they entered the silent house, she saw the same clutter of dusty antique furniture, smelled the musty dampness, and noticed something she'd almost forgotten—the scent of cinnamon.

"Man, what a dump!" Dennis said as he followed her inside.

An uneasy sadness lingered in the unnaturally cold air, and a lone fly buzzed over the sink of unwashed supper dishes.

"Yes, it's not much, but the old man seemed happy here," she murmured.

Dennis grunted derisively and began poking around, exploring the few rooms and peeking into closets. "Hey, Diana," he said. "Weren't you supposed to fetch something for Amy?"

Her mind balked, but then she remembered. She'd fed the same line to Craven that she used on Roger, and, of course, Dennis had overheard, too.

"Yes, the Willow Ware vase." She gulped. "Thanks for reminding me."

He crossed the room and ran his fingers nervously through his short blond hair. "You said it was sitting in plain view on Jed's table. I don't see it, Diana."

Something in his tone unnerved her. It was edgy, accusatory. "Maybe I was mistaken? Maybe Mr. Porter moved it…?"

"Stupid old coot!" he snapped.

Now she was truly alarmed. Dennis' color was all wrong, and his forehead was damp with sweat. "Why'd you call him *an old coot*, Dennis?"

He sighed and looked at the ceiling. "No reason. It's just so stupid and sad. The old man could've been rich, but instead he lived alone in this dump with that crazy dog."

An alarm bell sounded. Dennis was talking about Ursie. She leaned against the old oak table for support. She knew for a fact that Bobby Porter had taken Ursie away to live with Matthew the night of the murder. If anyone else had seen the dog at the farm, it was before Jed's death.

"How did you know about the dog, Dennis?"

FORTY-TWO

The wrong man…

When Liz's phone rang, she and Danny nearly jumped out of their skins.

"It must be Diana!" She answered the call. "Hope she's okay." As she listened, her stomach clenched into a thousand knots and she tried not to panic.

"Well?" he demanded the moment she disconnected.

"That was Sheila, Brantley Craven's secretary," she gasped. "We've got a problem, Danny. Sheila claims Brantley now has a verified alibi for the night of the murder."

He seemed totally confused. "What the hell? You checked out his alibi yourself. You told me he never stayed in that Atlanta hotel, right?"

"Yeah, but he didn't kill Jed, either."

"How would Sheila know? I thought she quit."

"She quit all right, but she stayed in touch with Brantley's latest lover…" Liz swallowed hard. "It seems the snake's been fucking the wife of his biggest investor. The night Jed was murdered, Brantley spent the whole time in that woman's bed."

She couldn't hold back her tears. "I can't believe it. Brantley fooled us all. We bet on the wrong man." She picked up her phone. "I'm calling Diana…"

Danny snatched it from her hand. "Hold on, Corkie, we promised we'd give her thirty minutes. Brantley didn't do it, and that's a bummer, but *somebody* killed Jedidiah. Diana baited more than one hook. Let's give him time to make his move."

It seemed like a longshot, but she sighed and leaned out her window. Birds still chirped in the meadow, and in the distance, a cloud of dust lifted off the road. She squinted to get a better look and heard the churning of an engine—someone driving in their direction, moving fast. She scrolled through the short list of suspects and came up with one name.

"God, it must be Roger! Diana was right all along."

They were well-concealed, their camouflage impenetrable, but they slumped lower in their seats and strained to identify the vehicle speeding ever closer. Every panel on the bizarre white van was hand-painted with colorful flowers. They tried to see the driver through the filthy windows as the van careened onto the dirt lane.

"Was that Roger?" Danny said.

She'd only seen Roger Keene briefly at Jedidiah's funeral. "Who the hell knows?"

FORTY-THREE

The presence of a madman…

Dennis stared at Diana. His eyes were glazed and oddly unfocused.

"How did you know Jedidiah had a dog?" she repeated.

He seemed to snap out of the stupor. "Oh yeah, now I remember. Amy told me about the dog. She said her father loved the animal."

A heavy sorrow descended as she recalled Amy's exact words: *Daddy never had no dog. He hated all animals.* Amy didn't even know her father owned Ursie, so Dennis had lied. All the pieces were falling into place, and the fit made her very sad.

"What are you waiting for, Diana? Go find the dumb vase."

She slowly shook her head and looked him squarely in the eye. "You came to get the locket, didn't you, Dennis?" Finally it all made sense. *CRA* stood for *Crawford.* Why hadn't she seen it sooner?

But Dennis looked blank.

"Did it belong to your mother?" It was a wild theory, but ever since his father died, he'd been extremely close to his mother. Several agents called him *mama's boy* behind his back.

"Are you nuts?" he said.

Either he was an excellent liar, or he actually knew nothing about the locket. Something was very wrong, though, because he was sweating profusely and his complexion was alarmingly red.

"Truth is, I came here to ask you a question, Diana…" He moved across the room and stood too close. She could smell his panic. "The night you came here, Jed gave you something…" He lifted his hand and touched her face. "I need you give it to me, Diana."

His eyes blinked incessantly as his fingers dropped to her throat. Suddenly she understood she was in the presence of a madman, and she had no idea what he wanted from her.

"Why did you do it, Dennis?" She gently pushed his hand away. "Why did you kill Jedidiah Porter?"

His mouth began opening and closing, like a beached fish gasping for air. She reached into her pocket and brought out her phone, but he knocked it across the room. He twisted her wrists in a vise-like grip.

"I'm sorry, Diana…" he whimpered with tears in his eyes. "Why'd you have to accuse me? Why couldn't you leave it alone?"

She fought for balance and winced from the pain in her wrists. He was unhinged, out of control. "Please let go, you're hurting me." She struggled to keep her voice calm.

He loosened his hold, ever so slightly. "It was an accident, swear to God. I never meant to hurt him." His voice became a child's falsetto. "I came out here to talk to him, that's all. When you didn't get the listing, I thought he might listen to me."

She realized with chilling certainly that Dennis had slipped beyond all reason. Her only hope was to contact Liz and Danny, but the phone had fallen out of reach.

"The old man was loony," he whined. "Acted like I wasn't even there, like I was invisible. He walked right past me and headed down to the dock.

"When I followed and tried to talk some sense into him, he took the oar and started swinging. Hit me real hard on the shoulder, then chopped at my knees. He was set on killing me, Diana, and that's God's own truth!"

He paused, panting, and loosened his grip on her ever so slightly.

"We struggled," he continued, "I twisted the oar out of his hands and swung at him. God, his head split open like a ripe melon! He kind of melted backwards, this look of surprise in his eyes, and then he fell in the lake…"

"Didn't you try to help him?"

"He was dead before he hit the water. I threw the oar away and ran. That fool dog kept howling and barking, like it wanted to tear me apart."

He caught her shoulders and shook her. "You believe me, don't you, Diana?"

From the little she knew about Jed Porter, she was inclined to believe Dennis had acted in self-defense. But she was terrified, and all she could say was, "You broke into my condo, didn't you, Dennis?"

He abruptly released her, vigorously shaking his head. "That was Brantley's idea," he answered in a little boy's voice.

Who the hell cared? Dennis had killed Porter. She recalled the obscene devastation inflicted upon her home, and Matthew lying in flames on the concrete. Both were guilty as sin. Her fear turned to rage. She balled her fist and hit Dennis in the chest, punched him hard.

His eyes registered surprise as he staggered backwards.

At the same moment, she dived for the phone. Her knees hit the floor, but as she reached out, Dennis' shoe came down on her arm. When she looked up, he was holding the barrel of a gun. *Dear God in heaven!* She extended her free hand palms up, in a wordless appeal, just before the gun smashed into the side of her head.

By the time Dennis hauled her to her feet, she'd lost all track of time. Hammers pounded behind her eyes. She tasted metal in her mouth, where she'd bitten her tongue. She couldn't bring the sequence of events into context as he walked her to the door and out onto the porch.

His voice was a muffled ringing in her ears, and her legs wouldn't carry her. Yet, she stumbled ahead of him, down a hill and towards the dock. Through her pain, she felt his gun wedged in the small of her back. And through her agony, a raging fury boiled to overflowing.

"You won't get away with this," she choked. "I'm not alone. People with guns are waiting at the end of the road."

His crazed laugh echoed through the valley. He wasn't buying it. By the look in his eyes, the entire U.S. Marine force could come to her defense, and it wouldn't make a difference.

She knew she was going to die.

With her last remaining strength, she broke away and ran towards the lake. She heard an explosion, and the searing bullet entered her body, just as the water closed over her head.

FORTY-FOUR

Almost forgotten dream…

Matthew could not keep up. The wounds on his legs burned inside his jeans. Every muscle screamed in protest as he stumbled up the hillside. He should have stayed in the van, like they told him, but once he got free of the wheelchair, it was like asking the ball to crawl back in the cannon, after the powder was lit.

He hugged his broken arm against his cracked ribs. Using his good hand for balance, he picked up speed. But the blasted bandage kept slipping down over his eyes, so he tore the damned thing off and threw it away.

By the time he reached the crest of the ridge, he was delirious, his lungs imploding with the sheer effort of drawing breath. He hadn't been here for years, not since the lake rose up, and as he looked around, the lay of the land and the forest was familiar, yet utterly changed.

Like an almost forgotten dream, he looked to the crest of the next ridge and was transported back to his childhood. He saw his friend, Bobby, scrawny as when they were boys. He was running with his daddy's old squirrel rifle gripped in both hands. Matthew never liked hunting, but he often tagged along when Bobby went out to shoot rabbits.

Matthew dropped to his knees, wiped the sweat from his brow, and tried to focus. He remembered why he was here when he saw her run onto the dock. The man chasing her raised his arm, fired the handgun, and his beloved Diana went into the water.

At the same desperate moment, before blackness engulfed him, he lifted his eyes to where Bobby stood with his feet wide apart. Bobby hefted the rifle to his shoulder and took aim. A second gunshot sent smoke drifting into the still air. And in slow motion, the man on the dock collapsed, felled by Bobby's bullet.

FORTY-FIVE

In mysterious ways…

Bobby

The walls of the tiny hospital room closed in on him, and Bobby Porter was glad they allowed only four to visit at one time. He squeezed Juanita's hand and looked at Trout for moral support.

Trout didn't look half bad, considering. The doctors had given Bobby holy hell when they brought Trout back to the hospital. His clothes were all muddy, and maybe he'd knocked a screw loose, because he wouldn't stop screaming till they'd loaded Diana into the ambulance. Like as not, Trout would be stuck in that wheelchair for a couple more weeks.

Diana was a different story. Bad as she looked now, lying in the hospital bed, the docs said she'd be up and running in no time. He peeked into her deep blue eyes. They looked so big in her pale white face. White face, white hair, white pillows…and with her shoulder all trussed up like a broken wing, she put him in mind of an angel. He felt shy around her, but he smiled anyhow.

"I see they got an empty bed in this room," he said to her. "Since Trout's been hangin' around all the time anyway, maybe they'll let him move in? You want a roommate, Miss Diana?"

She laughed, but it got her coughing. Seemed like she was more troubled by her cold than by the bullet hole in her shoulder.

Juanita jabbed him in the ribs. She was telling their story all over again, and kept on calling Bobby a *hero*. He wished she'd shut up. He wished she hadn't spent all the cookie jar money to get his van out of hock—but it sure came in handy yesterday.

Most of all, he wished Juanita would marry him.

He loosened his tie. The sheriff was leaning against the far wall, like a big ole turkey buzzard.

"Yeah, Bobby may be a hero…" Bearfoot never cracked a smile. "But don't forget, he shot a man. There'll be an inquiry. You understand that, don't you, Bobby?"

Bobby frowned at his shoes. No way was he going back to jail. He dropped Juanita's hand and inched towards the door. "I'll wait out in the hall, darlin'. A man can't breathe in here."

"Hold on, Bobby…" The sheriff crossed the room in three long strides. "You did a good thing yesterday, and I hate to admit it, but I was all wrong about you." He reached out and shook his hand. "Don't you worry now. In my opinion, they should give you a medal."

His fingers burned where the sheriff touched them, and he couldn't believe his ears. Maybe Bearfoot wasn't an asshole, after all. He nodded to Trout and Diana, and then fled the room. If his dear departed daddy taught him anything useful, it was *you best get goin', whilst the gettin's good*.

Juanita

Juanita Cruz felt shy around Bearfoot. She still felt guilty about the slutty way she'd acted when he came to the trailer—prancing around half-naked in a bath towel, like a border town whore. "They'll give Bobby a medal?"

282

He frowned and took up his old position against the wall. "Don't go getting your hopes up. There's still that problem about the money Bobby stole."

"That was his inheritance. He deserved every penny!" She thrust out her jaw and went back to her story.

"Anyhow, Diana, Bobby came to the hospital and helped Trout pull on his jeans. We got him into a wheelchair, laid a blanket across his lap, and wheeled him right out the front door."

"But how'd you sneak him past the front desk?" Diana's voice was barely audible.

"That nurse with the blue hair? She's Trout's friend. I told her I was taking him out for a cigarette break."

Matthew laughed. "By the time the nurse remembered I don't smoke, we were long gone."

Juanita paused and studied Diana. She looked so pathetic lying there, all hooked up to tubes and monitors. Juanita was ashamed about that day at the beauty salon, when she'd threatened her and her redheaded friend with a pair of scissors.

"It's good thing you told Bobby about your stupid plan, Diana…about going to the farm all by yourself. I still don't know *why* you told him, but I'm glad he broke his promise and told Trout, otherwise…"

Matthew said, "No matter how you slice it, it was wrong-headed, Diana. After Bobby told me, I guessed what you were up to…" He frowned at Bearfoot. "I even told Wayne about it, but the good sheriff wasn't inclined to get off his duff and do anything about it."

"Sounded like a cock n' bull story to me," the sheriff grumbled.

"So, I called Bobby, and he and Juanita agreed to help," Matthew said, giving Juanita a *thumbs up*. "You should've seen this little gal pushing me through the hospital corridors. She was racing like a NASCAR pro."

"Bobby was waiting right outside in his van," Juanita said. "We pushed Trout up the ramp and split."

Juanita's heart filled with pride. Maybe Bobby wasn't such a loser, after all? A few hours ago, when Trout called and asked him to stop by the nursing home, Bobby had agreed and didn't even fuss. They'd picked up the two old ladies, who were waiting in the hall.

Juanita said, "Would you mind stepping outside, Sheriff? There's two more waiting to see Diana, but they won't let so many in at once."

Bearfoot grumbled, but then loped out the door without an argument.

"Be right back…" Juanita winked.

Clara

Clara Gable was amazed to see Bobby in the hall when she steered her electric scooter into Diana's room. She hadn't seen him since he was a scrawny little boy, hiding from his daddy and sleeping in their barn. Seemed like he turned out pretty good, though. He was still skinny, his Mexican girlfriend wore her skirt too high and her blouse too low, but all in all, they seemed like nice kids.

Vivian shoved past Clara and hobbled to Diana's bed. Like any mother, Viv was worried sick, and who could blame her? She pulled up a chair and burst into tears. Clara figured her important mission of the day was to keep Viv from smothering Diana with affection, or abusing her for putting herself in danger.

She smiled at the handsome man in the wheelchair when Juanita introduced them. She figured Matthew was the *friend*

Diana had been telling them about, so now Clara had another mission: keeping Viv from giving Matthew the third degree. Whenever the subject of Diana and men came up, Vivian was hell on wheels and likely to embarrass them all.

When Clara smiled at Juanita, who'd just finished telling the story of Diana's rescue, something caught her eye. The girl was fingering a unique piece of jewelry that hung on a chain in her cleavage.

"That's an interesting locket..." Clara softly noted. "Mind if I take a closer look?"

Juanita glanced at Diana, who had scooted upright in her pillows, and then said, "Bobby gave it to me." She warily unclasped the chain and placed the locket in Clara's upturned palm. "He found it on his daddy's dock. Isn't it pretty?"

"Very pretty..." Clara felt light-headed. She fell back through time to an old fashioned picnic on the grass. When she looked closely at the inscription on the locket, her beloved Charlie's face appeared. It was the day he asked her to marry him.

Her eyes filled with tears. "My husband, Charles, wore this locket almost fifty years ago. I wore its mate."

Four pairs of eyes gaped at her. Vivian blinked in surprise, Matthew let out a deep sigh, Diana fell back into her pillows, and Juanita blushed crimson.

Juanita sputtered. "I don't understand..."

Clara held the locket up to the light. "*CRA* were my initials before I got married. They stand for *Clara Rose Anderson*. The other sweetheart heart had his initials, *CRG* for *Charles Robert Gable*. I still wear mine. He lost his a long time ago." She reached under her blouse and pulled out a shinier duplicate bearing her husband's initials.

Diana dragged the covers up over her head.

Juanita was crestfallen. "Then you should keep it, ma'am." She folded Clara's fingers around the locket.

Clara made a quick decision. "Nope..." She lifted her arms and looped the chain over Juanita's long black hair. "You keep it, Juanita. Your Bobby meant a lot to Charlie and me, but now I'm an old woman. I got no use for such trinkets, and Charlie would want it this way."

"Many thanks, Senora." Juanita lowered her eyes. She tucked the locket between her breasts, and then buttoned her blouse almost to the collar. "But how did your husband's locket ended up on Mr. Porter's dock?"

Clara knew how it had happened. She recalled the day Charlie lost it. He'd been heartbroken, figured he'd dropped it in the garden. Years passed and the waters kept on rising: *If you was to stand at the end of Jed's dock and look out across the water, you'd be looking' at our front yard...the row of tall willow oaks, the pump and wishing' well, and the big old wooden house itself.*

But the locket found its way back to the land of the living. God worked in mysterious ways.

Vivian

Vivian Whitaker didn't know what ailed her daughter. She rapped on the covers till Diana came out. Her reaction to Clara's tale was ridiculous. Even Diana's *friend*, Matthew, seemed shaken by the story.

She took a long look at Matthew and liked what she saw. Below the head bandage, he was strikingly handsome, with warm, gentle eyes, strong jaw, and a wide, generous mouth. He was a big man, but he seemed steady and slow to anger. Yes, Matthew, with his quiet strength, was just what Diana needed.

"Don't stare at him, Vivian!" Clara smacked her knee. "Pay attention to Diana!"

Vivian dragged her eyes back to the bed. It broke her heart to see her little girl hurt.

"Like I said, Mama, the bullet went clean through. No permanent damage. I'll be up and around in no time."

Her child hated to be fussed with, but she laid her hand on Diana's forehead. "You're burning up with fever. You best be careful, or that cold will go to your chest."

Juanita interrupted. "Did you know Diana swam to shore herself? It's true, Bobby told me! She did the sidestroke with her good arm, like she never even got shot. She came up on shore right into Bobby's arms."

"She's a strong woman," Clara said.

"I don't remember a thing," Diana admitted.

"Neither do I," Matthew muttered.

Vivian smiled. Her daughter was stubborn as a Mississippi mule, but she was courageous. "*I* taught her how to swim."

"No, *Daddy* taught me." Diana yawned, closed her eyes, and rubbed her nose with the back of her hand. She'd done that ever since she was a baby. It meant sleep was only seconds away.

"My daughter needs to rest," Vivian announced. "Everybody should leave now."

"Yes, ma'am." Juanita followed Clara's scooter out the door.

But Matthew didn't move. He looked Vivian squarely in the eye. "I reckon I'll be staying. It was nice to meet you, Vivian."

Another Mississippi mule, but she liked that quality—*in a man.* "Take good care of her, Matthew." Her heart swelled with love, and she knew it was time to go.

FORTY-SIX

Everyone was guilty…

Bearfoot

Diana was sound asleep when Wayne Bearfoot slipped back into the room. But that was okay, since his business was mainly with Trout.

"You lucky old son of a gun," he growled in a whisper. "It's a miracle you're alive."

Trout's brown eyes sparked in his pale face. "No thanks to you."

Wayne swallowed hard. "Maybe I was a little slow on the draw, but who in his right mind would believe she'd actually follow through with that fool plan?"

"I believed her. So did Bobby, and it was a good thing, too."

Wayne pulled up a chair and crossed his long legs. "Even if I'd believed her, I was dead wrong about the likely suspect. I'd convinced Detective Sokolsky to bring in Brantley Craven for questioning. They picked him up when he left Crawford Realty. Once he was in custody, I figured Diana was safe."

"You figured wrong," Trout grumbled. "What made you think Craven was the killer?"

"Sokolsky's a self-important prick, but he nailed Craven for the break-in at Diana's condo…" He paused to gaze fondly at Diana, who was still fast asleep. "They found one clear set of prints on the birdcage. Brantley took off his gloves to open the tiny latch and get at the damned bird. He wanted to wring its neck, can you believe it?"

Trout laughed. "Knowing Diana's parrot? Yeah, I believe it, but what was the bastard looking for?"

Wayne rubbed his tired eyes. "Fact is, I still don't know what they were after."

"They?"

"Craven wasn't alone that night. Dennis Crawford was with him at the condo, but according to Craven, he just sat there like a useless lump. Sokolsky found a set of Dennis' prints on Diana's briefcase."

"He opened my briefcase?" Diana's voice lifted from her pillow. "So that's how he found out!"

Both men turned to her as she opened her sleepy eyes.

Her words were slurred as she spoke. "Somehow Dennis knew Amy had given me the listing contract. He congratulated me the morning he sent the flowers. It didn't make sense…"

Diana didn't make sense. Bearfoot figured the painkillers had muddled her thinking.

"Don't you see?" She yawned. "The *listing contract* was in my briefcase, but they were looking for the *plot plan*."

"What's she talking about?" Trout leaned forward in his wheelchair as Diana drifted away again.

"Sokolsky found a plot plan locked in Dennis' desk at the office. It proved that they'd planned to develop Jed's land three months *before* his death."

"That would be incriminating." Trout frowned. "But if the plan was locked in Dennis' desk, why'd they trash Diana's place looking for it?"

"Beats me…" From what Wayne had heard about Brantley Craven, the guy was a sexual predator who'd trash a woman's apartment for the sheer thrill of it. "Craven says they expected Jed to sell once the price was right. When the old man refused, Dennis asked Amy to have her father committed to a nursing home, but Amy wouldn't do it…

"Then when Diana failed to get the listing, they were desperate. They'd already invested big bucks. They forged Amy's signature on the plan to convince the Loftus Company, a reputable firm, to do the design work. Loftus would never have proceeded without the Porter family's blessing."

Trout held up his hand, and Wayne lowered his voice. Obviously Trout didn't want Diana disturbed, but Wayne sensed that his old friend had something else on his mind.

"So Craven and Crawford planted the bomb in Diana's car?" Trout demanded.

Wayne shifted his haunches on the hard chair. He'd hoped to save this revelation for later, because Trout, propped up in his wheelchair and bandaged like a mummy, appeared to have heard enough.

"Well?" Trout's knuckles were white as he gripped the arms of his chair.

Wayne cleared his throat. "When it comes to Diana's suspect list, it seems *everyone* was guilty. Roger Keene planted the bomb. Craven and Crawford weren't involved."

"I knew it!" Trout hissed.

"But Roger's not the brightest bulb in the box. The A.T.F. agents found prints on a pair of pliers left in Diana's garage. When they ran the prints through the database, Roger's criminal record provided an abundance of positive matches."

"But why? Just because she pressed charges after he tried to run her off the road?"

"Yeah, that was one reason…" Wayne took a deep breath. "But it seems Roger has a girlfriend who also happens to be a real estate agent. When she heard about Jed's land, she saw the potential and began counting her million dollar commission."

"Nice little nest egg for her and Roger to make a new start."

"Exactly. They'd been planning it for months. If Roger could prevent Amy from giving the listing to Diana, and then steer the business to his girlfriend, Roger figured he'd share in the wealth and file for divorce. But Diana kept getting in the way. When she pressed charges, Roger believed Diana had ruined his life."

"Does Amy know?" Trout asked.

"Not yet, but she'll find out when we catch him." Wayne peeked at Trout, who seemed sad. "Roger gave us the slip, but we have a nationwide APB out for his rig. We'll catch him, I promise, but in the meantime, we've posted two officers out in the hallway."

"Two cops?" Diana's eyes popped open.

Wayne suspected she'd been listening all along. "Yes, one to keep *you* safe, the other to make sure *Dennis* stays put. Believe it, or not, he's lying in a hospital room four doors down the hall."

"Thank God, he's not dead!" She motioned Wayne to her bedside and captured his hand with her warm fingers. "How is he?"

"He'll survive. Bobby shot low, aimed for his legs, but young Crawford won't be playing football up at the Big House, that's for damned sure."

"He'll go to prison, then," she said. "It's all so sad. Dennis is sick, but I really believe he killed Jed in self-defense. He needs professional help."

He and Trout frowned at one another. Wayne sensed that neither shared Diana's inclination towards leniency.

Trout said, "If you'd been in my shoes, Diana, and seen Crawford pumping bullets at your back, maybe you'd be less forgiving. Far as I'm concerned, they should throw away the key."

Wayne said, "Let the jury decide."

At that moment, a timid knocking sounded on Diana's door, and when Wayne opened it, he found Liz and Danny waiting outside.

"Well, look what the cat drug in, it's Bonnie and Clyde." he grabbed the pair by the scruffs of their necks and pulled them into the room. "What have you two vigilantes been up to today? Hanging out in the truck, gunning for another showdown? Lucky you weren't killed."

Danny stared at his shoes, but Liz's green eyes snapped. "Eat crow, Sheriff. Where were you when the shooting began?"

Wayne's neck burned. He held up his hand in a parody of the old Indian peace gesture. He aimed a long finger at Liz, then Danny, and then Diana. "Have you three ever considered a career in law enforcement?"

The trio smiled at one another.

"Well, if you ever consider such a career..." Wayne grinned. "For God's sake don't apply to my department!"

FORTY-SEVEN

A great team...

Danny

When Bearfoot left, Liz rushed Danny to the edge of Diana's bed. "Danny blames himself that you got shot."

He said. "Yeah, when we saw Bobby's van, we figured it was Roger, but they moved so fast, I never even got my rifle off the rack."

"He feels guilty, Diana," Liz said. "He's *in love* with you, I swear. If he sneaked into this room without me, he'd ask you to marry him."

He felt heat rushing to the roots of his hair. "She's right, Diana, but it's her own fault. I ask Liz to marry me every day, but all I hear is no, no, no."

It did his heart good to see Diana roar with laughter.

"Please stop, both of you!" She grasped her wounded shoulder.

"Yeah, get lost, Danny." Liz shoved him towards the door. "Diana and I have girl talk."

But he brushed Liz aside, bent over Diana's bed, and kissed her full on the lips.

"Hey, should I be jealous?" Trout spoke up from his wheelchair.

"Seriously, can you both please give us some privacy?" Liz said.

Trout grumbled, but then wheeled himself to the door and turned to Danny. "C'mon, son, we know when we're not wanted."

Danny grabbed the kiss Liz threw from across the room, and by the tender look on her face, he began to hope all over again--- *maybe she loves me, after all?*

Liz

Once the men were gone, she perched on the edge of Diana's bed, her eyes swimming with tears. "Jesus, you scared me half to death! When I heard those gunshots, I thought you were dead for sure. When the ambulance came and took you away…"

Diana reached up with her good arm and pulled her close. "Hey, I'm fine, see? You and Danny were great. Where would I be without you?"

Diana smelled of gauze, alcohol, and warm soap. Liz hugged her so hard, she squealed in pain. "I screwed up, Diana. When Bearfoot questioned me about Dennis, I told him Dennis couldn't have done it because he was at a zoning meeting."

"Yes, that's what you told me, too. What happened?"

"The cops checked it out. Dennis showed up at the meeting, all right, but he arrived at the tail end. He told the zoning folks he was too sick to give his speech."

"It's all so sad."

"Yes, but some good's come of it…" She touched Diana's forehead, hot as a biscuit fresh from the oven. "You gave me courage, Diana. I'm bringing charges against Brantley, for attempted rape that day at the office. Sheila will back me up."

"You go, girl!" Diana high-fived her. "That, along with his trashing of my condo, should put the snake away for a very long time."

Liz smiled. "We make a great team."

"Maybe so, but we missed the bulls eye." Diana told her about the locket.

"No way! So the locket had nothing to do with the killer?"

"Nope, we were just lucky that our bluff paid off."

"Lucky we aren't dead," Liz amended. "And we are unemployed. Crawford Realty's gone out of business. They say Dennis was barely treading water. No wonder he freaked."

Diana closed her eyes. "I'll stand right beside you in the unemployment line."

"Hey, partner, I've got a better idea." Liz winked. "We have our broker's licenses. We can open an office together, and…."

But her friend was sound asleep.

FORTY-EIGHT

From Daddy...

Amy

Amy had been waiting alone in the hall, so she was thrilled to see a familiar face. Trout rolled out of the room and took her down to the cafeteria for lunch. At first the grouchy nurse wouldn't let him leave the floor, but in the end, he got his way.

"I've been around wheels all my life," he argued. "I reckon I can wheel myself and this young lady down for a bite to eat. I can wheel myself back again, too."

While they ate, he brought her up to date and explained that Diana needed to rest. By the way he spoke her name, she could tell he really liked Diana, and her heart was glad for him. He didn't talk about Roger, and she was glad about that, too. Everyone was trying to spare her feelings, but she'd already guessed her husband's role in the miseries.

Most of all, she was bursting with news of her own, but her lips were sealed. Even Trout, who was a very persuasive man, couldn't pry her secret loose. Her words were for Diana alone, who'd given her the strength to leave Roger and to stand on her own.

Diana was still drowsy when she and Trout returned to her room, but she reached out to them. She gave her strong right hand to Amy, and the one on her hurt side to Trout.

"Did the others leave?" Diana asked.

"They've flown the coop," Amy answered. "Nobody here now but us chickens." She was squeezing Diana's hand too hard, but it hurt so bad to see her this way.

"I visited your mama the other day..." she began. "Told her I had real important news, and she promised she'd get you to call me. Don't you remember?"

Diana didn't have a clue.

"I gave her my new phone number," Amy said as all her frustrations boiled to the surface. "Darn it, Diana, if you'd a called me, none of this would've happened."

Diana seemed to focus. "Now I remember. Mama did call. She said you'd confided in her, but she wouldn't tell me anything unless I met her in person. But I never got a chance..."

"Never mind." Amy cut her off and started from the beginning. "You gave me a book at Daddy's funeral, remember?"

Diana's eyes sparkled like blue flames. "Yes, it was *The Yearling*. Jedidiah wanted you to have it."

"But then I misplaced it, don't you know, and I didn't find it till that day I saw your mama..." She pulled her hand free from Diana's and dug into her purse. She brought out the book. "I was lookin' at all the pretty pictures, when this envelope fell out. It said on the front: *To Amy, from Daddy when I die.*"

She unfolded the big page and passed it to Diana, then leaned over the bed while Diana and Trout read in silence.

"Good Lord, it's Jed's Last Will and Testament!" Trout said.

"Incredible!" Diana exclaimed. "Look, Matthew, Jedidiah left his entire estate to North Carolina. The provision says it must be preserved as a state park. It can never be sold for any other purpose."

"Is it legal?" Trout gasped.

"Absolutely." Diana smiled. "It's drawn by a lawyer and properly notarized."

"And look at this part..." Amy ran her fingers down the text. "It's to be called *Porter Park*, where folks can go to have picnics and enjoy nature."

"The foxy old buzzard." Trout laughed. "Read this part about Bobby..."

Diana's lips formed the sentences: "*The house goes to my son, Robert Porter, to live in for the rest of his natural life. He shall be paid a yearly salary as grounds keeper.*"

There was also a provision for Amy to work as the salaried hostess of a nature center, to be established in the name of her mother, Ida. Both children's salaries, as established by Jed, were generous indeed. The state was required to pay these salaries in order to receive the land.

Diana reared up on the pillow. "Now I understand! Just before he shot me, Dennis said: *what did Jed give you*? He wanted me to give *it* to *him*, but I had no idea what he was talking about. I'm sure Dennis and Brantley were looking for the will, not the plot plan, when they broke into my condo. But how'd they know Jed had given me the will, when I didn't even know?"

Trout shook his head. "My guess is Jed told Dennis about the will the night Dennis killed him. He likely told Dennis his land could never be sold, that it was legally impossible. Jed must've told him he gave the will to you, Diana, and that you intended to give it to Amy."

"Makes sense," Amy said. "He come up to me at the funeral and asked about Daddy's will. I told him there was no such thing. That's when he figured Diana still had it."

"Sounds about right to me, but we won't know for sure until they question Dennis," Trout said.

"So all this violence was for nothing," Diana said sadly.

Trout gave Amy a bear hug. "But Amy's a rich lady!"

"Yeah, and I'll be single, too." She winked at Diana. "I already gave Roger his walkin' papers, and now I'll get me a divorce."

"Is that a fact?" Trout grinned. "How'd you feel about marrying a sorry old school pal like *me*?"

"You best not ask me twice, Matthew Troutman. Right now I feel obliged to Diana, but if you keep on sweet talkin', I'm liable to forget her altogether."

FORTY-NINE

Diana...

Silence descended like a blessing as she slipped in and out of sleep. Bars of light filtered through the blinds in flickering patterns across her bed, and the late afternoon sun dropped in the sky. Far away, from the hallway, she heard the muffled sounds of nurses pushing carts of medications and dinner trays.

She squeezed his hand. "Thank you, Matthew."

He was her constant and her warmth. His low voice murmured through her consciousness, and his gentle brown eyes drifted in her dreams. All the images of violence and fear washed away down a summer river as he held her hand.

She saw rolling meadows, forests, and the glistening waters of a beautiful park—a place where people would one day find peace, but the vision made her sad.

"None of this should have happened," she whispered. "It was all for nothing."

"Oh, I don't know..." Matthew's words drifted down the stream. "You deserved a better boss than Dennis, Bobby needed a job, Amy's rid of a bad husband, and I ..."

She smiled as his kiss brushed her lips. "What did you get, Matthew?"

He stirred in his chair and cleared his throat. "I got me a good dog."

ABOUT the AUTHOR

Kate Merrill is an art gallery owner and real estate broker with a lifelong passion for writing. She lives with her family on a lake in North Carolina. When she is not writing, working with the art community, or selling real estate, she enjoys swimming, boating, and allowing her two strong-headed Golden Retrievers to take her for a walk.

Diana Rittenhouse Mystery Series
A Lethal Listing
Blood Brothers
Crimes of Commission
Dooley is Dead
Buyer Beware
Amanda Rittenhouse Mystery Series

Murder at Metrolina
Homicide in Hatteras
Assault in Asheville
The Mayberry Murders

Mainstream Romance
Northern Lights (as Christie Cole)
Flames of Summer

www.katemerrillbooks.com
merrilljennings@aol.com

www.ingramcontent.com/pod-product-compliance
Lightning Source LLC
Chambersburg PA
CBHW070305260626
47160CB00003B/723